ESTHER P. GOODWIN

the BODY AMONG *the* PINES

Content Warning

This story includes elements that might not be suitable for some readers. Themes such as racism and suicide are mentioned. There are other themes that some may find triggering. Readers who may be sensitive to these elements, please take note.

To Ashley:

A friend, a coworker, and gym buddy.
I wish you many years of sobriety.
I'm rooting for you.

· **Prologue**

Monday, July 9th, 1986

James Edlin leaped over a shrub, landing on a massive ant hill. He scrambled to his feet and sprinted deeper into the woods. Adrenaline coursed through his veins as he weaved in and out of the trees, his breaths coming in short gasps. He didn't dare turn back for fear of being caught by his pursuers. Their footsteps grew louder, drawing nearer with every passing moment. They were close, hastening, as were his heavy breaths.

"Stop it!" James yelled, his eyes not breaking from the trees ahead. "I was just being nice!"

Muffled voices trailed James, demanding he stop running. But he kept at it, darting past every evergreen he encountered. He dashed past a large tree and hid behind it, leaving the bustling footsteps to rush by. But then the chase ceased, and a voice called out, causing James to tense up.

"James? Come out wherever you are."

A heavy silence descended, broken only by the soft hum of crickets and the croak of nearby frogs. It was the darkest of nights, with the new moon casting everything in pitch blackness. James noticed a handful of fireflies dancing overhead, their flickering lights resembling stars in the sky. He struggled to catch his breath, his chest heaving as he gasped for air. Suddenly, he began coughing. The harsh sound echoed through the quiet woods.

It was game over.

They were back on him.

Without hesitation, James sprinted into the darkness, his heart pounding in his chest. But he stumbled over an above-ground root just as he got into a good stride.

Crash!

James let out a pained cry as his face cracked against the hard ground. The impact reverberated through his skull. Dazed, he dug his fingers into the dirt and tried to steady himself. However, before he could even breathe, a hand slammed down on the back of his head, driving his face back into the ground.

"I told you to stay away from her, and you didn't listen," the person striking him said.

"I was just being nice," James managed to get out through panicked breaths, bits and pieces of dirt and grass getting in his mouth.

"I don't care." The person struck him again, causing James to shrink into a huddled state.

"Why?" James cried, shielding his head from the constant blows he received.

However, nobody answered. They just kept kicking him repeatedly until he was rendered unconscious. Then, long after James stopped moving, someone slipped a rope around his neck. With each passing moment, he was dragged through the dirt until his torturer tossed the rope over a large limb and slowly hoisted him in the air. Amid the climb, James regained consciousness, his mind in disarray and his body in excruciating pain. He gasped for air once he realized what was happening.

Desperate to save himself, James reached out into the darkness, searching for anything that might help him escape the rope's merciless hold. But there was nothing to grab onto, nothing to save him from his fate. His body ascended higher and higher until he was suspended among the branches of a great maple tree, his breaths coming in ragged gasps as his life slowly slipped away. And there, amid the fluttering of fireflies and the rustle of leaves, James took his last breath, his lifeless body forever lost in the wilderness.

Thirty Years Later

1 · Kacy

KARMA IS A BITCH—OR at least, that's what they say.

There I was, holding on for dear life. I was leaving an abandoned building I'd been exploring when the rotted wooden planks beneath me gave way, dropping me between the floor joists. And now I was stuck, my body left to dangle between two floors.

I winced in pain as my chest tightened and my breathing slowed. Though my backpack kept me from slipping further, the floor's rough edges dug into my flesh, causing me to writhe in pain. Sweat dripped down my face as I strained to break free, but for some reason, I couldn't. I'd always prided myself on my physical fitness, but now it seemed like all my efforts had been for nothing. The pain in my chest intensified, and I gritted my teeth, refusing to give up.

Dammit, Kacy. You're better than this.

I gritted my teeth, cursing myself for my foolishness.

The heat and the pain only made me more angry. If only I had answered when my father had called, then maybe this wouldn't have happened. Perhaps this was the universe's doing, disciplining me for ignoring him. Maybe I'd be sitting in my car, parked just outside the residence—beyond the rusty gate and cobblestone fence I'd climbed over as I trespassed—relaxing in the air conditioning instead of sweating my ass off in this rotting place. A feeling of regret loomed, knowing I probably wouldn't be in this predicament if I'd just answered his call.

Regardless, my father and I weren't on speaking terms. So, like many times before when he'd call, I tapped decline and slipped the phone back into my pocket. I preferred it that way because he had torn our family apart. And because of that reason, we hadn't spoken to each other in years. I never planned to talk to him again once I left Oklahoma because no amount of time apart would help me forgive him for what he'd done.

The floor creaked, bringing my focus back to the situation at hand. I scanned the darkness in search of my equipment. My camera and portable light had been thrown across the room, disappearing into the shadows of the night, its quaking sounds interrupting the pleasant lullaby of mother nature's evening tunes. Even with the help of the full moon shining through the half-collapsed upper floor, sending streaks of light to where I was in the foyer below, it still didn't help. I couldn't find my stuff. And I needed to get to it so I could finish the job.

I was lucky I hadn't fallen through when the floor gave way. However, at this point, I felt there was no other way to go but down. I feared what creatures might be lurking in the abyss below—snakes, spiders, Pennywise from Stephen King's *It*. I immediately pushed the thought away, not wanting to picture that scary clown in my midst.

I only wanted to shoot another video, not for me, but for my subscribers. That was what they enjoyed most—seeing me explore abandoned places. I would show them the unseen and how beautiful it could be, how unique the world is when left untouched and unbothered, how the dust settles, and vines grow, encapsulating what was once ruled by man, now left to be reclaimed by nature. I found a calm in it, and clearly, so did they.

It was truly a blessing to be a successful YouTuber.

Straining to lift myself once more, the creaking of the planks echoed through the desolate space. Without warning, the wood splintered and broke apart beneath my weight, causing me to fall into the black abyss of the basement.

Splash!

My descent was sudden and abrupt as I smashed into the murky substance below. The liquid swallowed me whole, leaving no part of my body untouched. The water was shallow and thick, like a mucky swamp. So shallow I had cracked my back against the uneven floor beneath the waterline. I thrashed about wildly, causing the thick liquid to churn and swirl in a chaotic dance.

Which way is up?

My lungs screamed for air as I fought my way to the surface. After realizing how shallow the water was, my frantic thrashing subsided, and I calmed my frayed nerves. After standing, I found the liquid only came up to my waist. And now my clothes were thoroughly drenched. I was pissed, my blood boiling like a cauldron over a flame. I had every right to be angry, though. My once-pristine hair was now dirty and tangled, and the water made it curl in an unappealing fashion. But that was nothing compared to the honey-like substance that clung to my skin.

I smacked at the rippling water in a rage. *There's no need to overreact, Kacy. Toughen up. This isn't the first time something like this has happened.*

And it was true. I'd fallen many times before, from many heights, on many excursions into the depths of places deemed unsafe. I was lucky water had cushioned my fall this time.

With nothing but darkness to guide me, I trudged forward, dreading the thought of encountering another dangerous obstacle. Knowing I was in the basement, my sole focus was finding the staircase. With my arms outstretched, I groped blindly for anything that could lead me to safety. Eventually, I brushed against a railing, leading me to let out a sigh of relief.

Carefully pulling myself toward it, I climbed the rotting steps—half swimming and half walking—until I emerged onto the main floor of the New England home. Dripping and shivering in the night air, I thoroughly searched for the rest of my things until I managed to find them. After collecting my equipment, I cautiously crossed the foyer, watching for any holes or obstacles in my path as I made my way out the front door and back to my car.

————

Light seeped through the closed blinds of my small apartment, beaming a scattered ray across my face. I groaned and rolled over, attempting to drift back off to sleep. Some might suggest I desperately wanted a partner to join me, considering how I spooned my pillow, but I disagreed. I was happily single, unlike a few friends of mine who were trapped in unhappy marriages. They would often brag about their cheating exploits, sharing details of their girls' trips to Vegas and secret rendezvous while their husbands were away on business.

Despite what others might have thought, I liked living alone, even if loneliness often stopped by to pay me a visit. I believed that feeling came with the territory of following your dreams, of climbing the never-ending mountain that led to bright stage lights, award shows, and TED Talks—all from being a YouTube sensation.

Lost in thought, I imagined myself standing on a stage, commanding an auditorium full of people with my words. Suddenly, a buzzing sound snapped me back to reality, and my eyes shot open in annoyance. I rolled over to find my cell phone, which I'd left in a container of rice overnight to dry out, buzzing. I yawned, raked it out, and answered it, hoping the unknown number was a new sponsor with an exciting business proposal.

"Hello? Who's this?" I asked, pressing the phone to my face.

"Hello? Is this Kacy Roe?" a woman's voice asked.

Wiping the sleep from my eyes, I glanced at the clock on my nightstand, wondering why someone was calling me so early. But once I discovered it was noon, I realized it was rather late in the day. I had slept in later than I intended. A pang of guilt hit me for wasting so much of the day. But I knew I needed my rest after the night I had.

"Speaking," I said.

"Sorry to bother you, Ma'am. We tried calling yesterday but didn't get an answer."

"And who's 'we'?"

"My apologies. I'm calling from Saint Francis Hospital in Tulsa, Oklahoma."

I couldn't for the life of me figure out which company would be calling me from Oklahoma. My brain was still half-asleep, which explained why. Shrugging off the cozy comforter, I planted my feet onto the beige Berber carpet and asked, "What's this about?"

"I'm sorry to inform you of the news like this, but your father had a heart attack yesterday."

A sudden tightness gripped my chest, and I thought I might be on the verge of having a heart attack of my very own. "What?!"

I clasped my hand over my mouth in shock as I remembered my father calling the previous night. *Maybe that's why he called three times yesterday? Perhaps they were the ones calling, using his phone...*

"Kacy?"

The woman on the other end interrupted my thoughts.

"Yes? I'm sorry, but is there something you need from me?"

"You're the only person he has listed as his emergency contact."

God, don't tell me he— "You sure? I swear he had a friend or someone else on there. My aunt even."

"Our records show one number for a Kacy Roe..."

My mind wandered once more as the woman trailed off, and I sighed deeply. *Shit. Out of all the people he could have chosen, why me? Does he really think getting sick is what's going to get me to come back home after all these years? Clever move.* I knew his game—get his only daughter to take care of him. However, I most certainly wouldn't. I refused to play the fool. Sure, I'd check on him, but taking care of him was out of the question.

"...As of right now, he's stable. The doctor plans on holding him for at least two weeks. From there..."

I cradled the phone against my shoulder as the nurse rambled on about my father's condition. I made mental notes of all the crucial details, nodding and mhmm'ing occasionally to indicate that I was still listening. And when I finally ended the call, I took a deep breath.

I guess I'm going home.

2 · **Kacy**

TWO WEEKS HAD PASSED before I landed at Tulsa International Airport. As soon as the plane docked, I regretted it. Coming home was a bad idea. The sweltering heat was one thing, but having to see my father again was even worse. The hot and humid air wrapped around me like a thick blanket as I exited the plane. Monday mornings were always comfortable in July—at least, they were back where I lived in Maine. However, the temperature here in Tulsa was a different story.

Jet engines whistled overhead through the connecting cracks of the loading bridge as I approached the gate, the deafening noise rattling my cup of coffee like a subwoofer. Once I got inside the air-conditioned terminal, I sighed in relief and loosened my shirt collar. The cool air felt calm against my damp skin. It would have felt even cooler if I hadn't chosen coffee as my in-flight beverage, but that was all in the past.

Despite the heat flash, I was experiencing, my hopes of being relieved from the scorching heat were short-lived. Amid my short walk through the airport, I found myself outside once again. The sun bore down on me, beating against my skin with its merciless rays. It was then that I knew I should have worn something more appropriate. My sweats were not the best choice for this trip. But I looked at the bright side of the situation. I wouldn't have to stand on the curb, waiting for a taxi like the other hapless travelers outside the airport because I had scheduled a ride to pick me up when I landed. It wasn't just any ride, though, but rather a private car service.

I scanned the crowd of drivers, anxiously looking for my ride. And there it was, a sleek black Suburban with tinted windows, waiting for me.

Being an influencer sure has its perks, I thought as I approached the vehicle. The trunk opened, and the driver stepped out. But I was too quick for him. I muscled my luggage into the back before he could even ask. Then I nestled into the spacious back seat, hoping the driver couldn't smell the eggy stench stemming from my armpits.

After we exchanged pleasantries, I said, "Saint Francis Hospital, please."

———

My father, Daniel, sat in a wheelchair, awaiting my arrival. By the time we reached the hospital, it was raining—storming. And yet, despite the downpour, he and the nurse were still sitting outside under the overhang that stretched the length of the wrap-around circular drive.

The suburban stopped at the entrance.

My father looked unkempt and disheveled, dressed in the same clothes he must have worn the day he was admitted. His half-buttoned flannel was stained with food, and his black jeans were threadbare in some places. And his matching loafers were scuffed as well. From the relieved expression on the nurse's face, I could tell they had been waiting for quite some time. Perhaps an hour or so, not just a few minutes.

After seconds of stepping out of the SUV, I was drenched. The sky was dark gray as thunder crackled overhead, leading me to believe Tulsa was experiencing some strange weather. I dashed for shelter under the overhang and approached my father, whose face lit up like the fourth of July.

"I was wondering when you were going to show," he said. He glanced up at the nurse—her young face and tight cheekbones—then shifted back at me. "She was starting to get worried. Thought she was going to have to call me a taxi," he joked.

I couldn't help but roll my eyes at my father's attempt at humor. His cheesy greeting may have amused others, but it certainly didn't earn a laugh from me. I didn't want to give him the satisfaction of thinking everything was all right between us after being apart for almost a decade. Despite my reluctance, I forced a hug, hoping to at least feign some sense of affection. However, his warm embrace was overwhelming with how he wrapped around me tightly, stealing my breath from my lungs.

It was as if he feared losing me. What also caught my attention was his amount of unrelenting strength. He had lost quite a lot of weight over the years and even looked lighter than me now. Granted, I had gained a few pounds over the past year from the amount of stress I'd been under with my valiant efforts to come up with better YouTube content and stay relevant on social media. But still, he looked more than just a *little* sick, as if it were cancer.

I pushed the thought away and broke free from his grasp to take a second look. His eyes were still the same shade of green but appeared sunken and tired. The wrinkles on his face had deepened, and there were faint lines around his lips. He looked nothing like the strong, robust father I remembered from childhood. Maybe it *was* cancer, or perhaps time hadn't treated him well. Whatever the reason, I smiled and said, "You look good, Dad."

I had lied through my teeth. But it was for a good reason. I felt no need to stir up any extra emotion, especially with the storm progressively worsening with each minute that passed. A strike of thunder roared, drawing our attention to the pouring rain. It was then that the nurse rolled my father closer to the back door of the suburban and helped me get him into the back seat.

"Thank you," I said, turning to face the woman. "Hopefully, this will be the last time you see us."

"Let's hope," she replied. "I wish nothing but the best of health for you both." The nurse smiled before waving good-bye, then returned to her duties.

I closed the passenger door and made my way to the other side of the vehicle, nestling into the seat behind the driver. From there, the suburban eased out from the hospital's pickup zone and headed for the interstate.

For the first half of the ride, we sat in total silence. Only the ongoing hum of the highway filled the void. I tried to ignore my father's glee from out of the corner of my eye, but I couldn't. He was peering out the window and back at me every few seconds as if he were on a stimulant like Cocaine. However, I knew the chances of him acquiring such a substance while under the hospital's care were slim.

"I'm so glad you came," he finally said, breaking the daunting silence.

I didn't even give him a chance to say more. Turning to him, I said, "Look, Dad. Just because I'm here doesn't mean everything is all sunshine and rainbows, okay? I'm just being a good daughter, that's all."

He reached for my hand to calm me. "Dear, I just thought that maybe, if I made you my emergency contact, you'd—"

I yanked my hand away. "*Please*, spare me the sob story."

As we continued down the road, the rain picked up, pelting against the suburban's windows like a million tiny pebbles. I couldn't help but think of how much I missed Maine, where the rain was more like a gentle mist. But now, in Tulsa, I faced extreme weather conditions. Either blistering heat or torrential downpours.

Gazing out the window, I admired the never-ending rolling hills we passed. We were on a steady course set for home. Luckily, traffic wasn't too bad, so I wouldn't have to endure any more of my father's pestering. Hopefully, it would only be about fifteen more minutes of riding in silence before we'd arrive home, and I could lock myself away in my old bedroom.

My father sank his head and exhaled in frustration, his heavy breathing catching my ear. He was about to say something else; I knew it. I just didn't know what.

"Look, Kacy...I know you're angry. Furious even. And I get it. You should be mad. But it's been nine years. Surely, you would've forgiven me by—"

"No, I haven't," I interrupted. "I'll never forgive you."

My gaze met with the driver's as he peered back through the rearview mirror, sending a fleeting wave of insecurity my way. I knew the driver had no intention of listening to our conversation. But my sudden outburst of negativity had drawn his attention.

"There's nothing I could have done, and you know that, Kacy."

My brows furrowed deeply. "You always say that. But the thing is, you had a choice. You just made the *wrong* one."

I couldn't help but shake my head in disappointment. Then I peered out the window as we passed by an old summer camp named Camp Mercy—a dilapidated place that had been long forgotten. It had piqued my curiosity for the longest, but my reluctance to return home had prevented me from exploring it.

My father sighed. "I'm..." He couldn't finish his sentence.

Hopefully, he realized his efforts in doing so were pointless. There was no use in persuading me otherwise, to appeal to my rational side when I had already decided what I thought and how I felt about the matter years ago. Continuing his efforts would only drain his energy and leave him depleted. As I continued watching the pouring rain, I crossed my arms and exhaled a sigh of relief, knowing he'd given up. Now we both were left to dwell in the awkward silence for the rest of the ride home.

3 · Kacy

We arrived home around noon, and God, did the place look exactly how I had left it. The sturdy brick rambler was nestled behind some brush just off the main road. Seeing that the acorn I'd planted near the shed had sprouted and grown nearly ten feet in my absence was heartening. While it was apparent that some of the vines had proliferated considerably over much of the house, giving the impression of a place that had been neglected, the house still retained its beauty. In some spots, the vegetation had even gone under the shingles, lifting them slightly from the roof in places. Despite that, the house still appeared to be structurally sound.

I hurriedly stepped out of the SUV and hustled around to the other side of the vehicle. Feeling eager to shelter my father from the pelting rain, I quickly ushered him inside. Then I made a mad dash to the trunk to retrieve my luggage. Despite my valiant efforts to stay dry, the rain had other plans. I was drenched to the bone by the time I made it back inside. But I knew better than to dwell on such things. With a quick wave to the driver, I bid him farewell and sent him on his way.

As I closed the front door, my father reached for my suitcase. "Let me help you with that."

I pulled away from him. "I got it, Dad. You shouldn't be overexerting yourself just yet." But what I wanted to say was, "Back off. I don't want you having another heart attack on my watch."

I took my bag and headed to my room. Walking down the long L-shaped hallway, I was drawn to the family photos that still adorned the walls in a zig-zag pattern. I wondered why my father still had them up. They may have provided some small measure of comfort to his loneliness. Regardless of his reasons, seeing those snapshots of us together led me to smile. My favorite was the one taken during our family trip to the Grand Canyon after my freshman year of high school. God, was that an experience. I could still hear my mother's voice warning me to be careful near the canyon's edge.

After I entered my room and muscled my suitcase onto my bed, I unpacked.

"How have things been in your life, Kacy?" my father called from the kitchen, the bass in his voice traveling easily.

"Everything's been fine, Dad," I shouted back. *As if you really care.*

With my suitcase unzipped, I turned to the bottom drawer of my dresser to start unpacking my jeans. It was where I'd always kept them back when I lived here. But when I opened the drawer, I stumbled upon something I hadn't seen since the day I left after graduation—my first camera, a gift from my mother on my sixteenth birthday.

A tear bubbled in my eye as I turned the dusty focus ring on the lens, remembering the joy I felt while learning photography from my mother. She was an angel, someone who will forever hold a special place in my heart.

"You need any help unpacking?" my father asked.

I quickly wiped the tear from my eye, set the camera down, and picked another drawer to store my denim in. "No, I'm good," I answered. "Thanks, though."

With my suitcase now unpacked and stowed away under my bed, I strolled down the hallway and into the kitchen, where I found my father sitting at the dinette. I sat across from him, noticing the chair he was in. It was the one I'd made for him in woodworking class back in high school. Even though it was an eye sore from the lime green color I had painted it, it was comforting to see him still using it.

"How have you been, Dad?" I felt I needed to ask.

Based on his appearance, it was evident that my father was not in good shape. His significant weight loss and the puffy bags under his eyes were concerning. Assuming he still had one, it could have been due to job-related stress. Alternatively, it might have resulted from his many years of alcohol abuse. Or perhaps it was simply old age that had caught up with him. Regardless, seeing him looking so exhausted and worn out was difficult because it was a look that was more appropriate for someone who had spent a decade or more in prison.

He whisked his hand through his short, greasy, jet-black

hair and scratched the back of his head as I waited for an answer. "About that...business has been hectic lately."

Well, that answered my question about him having a job. "So, you've finally managed to build a successful business?" I asked.

"Yes. But now I feel I'm getting too old for this." He sighed deeply and leaned forward slightly in his seat, his gaze fixing on something outside.

I followed his line of sight to find the mailman, adding more envelopes to our overflowing mailbox, which had accumulated over the past two weeks due to my father's absence.

"I think it's about time I retire," he finished, leaning back in the chair.

I was unsure of how to react, torn between feelings of calmness and anger. My father had always dreamed of being a pillar in the community, owning a business that could cater to the masses, be it a restaurant, farm, or mechanic's shop. It didn't matter which, as long as it turned a profit. However, he had encountered numerous challenges in pursuing this dream. Nonetheless, I guess he refused to give up, and now I couldn't help but feel proud of his tenacity.

But now, I had to respond with something sensible—something positive and uplifting. It was only right. "Well, if that's what you want to do, then do it."

I stood from the table and went for the fridge, hoping to find something to eat. To my dismay, the fridge was nearly empty, with only a moldy, half-eaten sub alongside a half-gallon of expired 2% milk. Checking the cupboards didn't prove to be much better, either. I had skipped breakfast before my flight into town. Well, mostly. But a bagel with some cream cheese doesn't exactly scream real food. My stomach rumbled with disappointment amid the realization that I needed to go shopping.

"When was the last time you went grocery shopping?" I asked.

"Don't remember. I mostly eat at my restaurant. Don't really have time to shop anymore."

I rolled my eyes and closed the cupboard. "It's fine. I'll just go grab something from one of the restaurants in town and bring it back because you need to eat something."

My father shot me a thumbs up alongside a recommendation. "Go to Navajo Bar & Grill on East Fifteen Street. I want you to experience it for yourself—my restaurant, that is."

So, a restaurant. A bar of all things. Well, I guess it's better than nothing.

"Okay," I said.

After a quick search for the keys to my father's Ford F-150, I spotted them resting idly in a quaint, decorative bowl on the kitchen counter beside the microwave. That was my ticket to finally alleviating my hunger pains, using his dramatic loss in weight as an elaborate excuse. Grabbing the keys, I headed out the door. Within seconds of closing it, he called out to me.

"Before you go, can you bring me the mail, please?"

Despite the dampness of my clothes from the drenching I'd received earlier, I didn't want to seem rude or ungrateful. So I shot him a gentle smile, flashed him a quick thumbs-up, and then fetched the mail.

4 · Kacy

I WAS seventeen years old the last time I had set foot in this town. I hadn't spoken to my father since then, either. I just up and left everything, and everyone, including my boyfriend at the time, Robert. I desperately needed an escape, a change, a getaway of sorts. With nothing but the clothes on my back and the shoes on my feet, I'd headed for Maine to discover who I was and what I wanted out of life. Looking back now, it was the best decision I ever made.

As I made my way through the town, every pothole and red light seemed like an obstacle to overcome. Memories of this place, which I had tried to forget for so long, kept coming back to me in a rush of emotion. Tulsa hadn't changed a bit, and as I drove by Memorial High, memories of my childhood came flooding back. I could hear the sweet sound of the marching band playing, the clarinet notes still ringing. And then there was the football team, dumping the cooler of Gatorade over the coach's head after winning the state championship. It was a moment that was etched into my memory forever.

Many of the businesses I drove passed were still there, chain restaurants and familiar stores lining the streets. The grocer on the corner, where I used to buy snacks after class each day, was still open for business. God, were there so many memories. It was as if I'd gone back in time. I remembered everything like it was yesterday.

Before I knew it, I had arrived at Navajo Bar & Grill. Pulling into the parking lot, I got out of the vehicle and headed for the entrance. Stepping inside, I noticed how beautiful the establishment was. My father had spared no expense in decorating the place. There were many pictures of chiefs standing tall, with their arrowed staffs in hand, as horses stood behind them. There was also a giant wooden carving of a beautiful stallion in the center of the restaurant. Every detail of our heritage was carefully crafted, and the stunning depictions of Native American culture that lined the walls were a sight to behold.

The door closed behind me with a thud, catching the bartender's attention.

The woman gasped. "Well, I'll be damned. If it ain't Kacy Roe in the flesh!"

The voice sounded familiar. *Wait, is that? No, it can't be.*

From within the shadows of the restaurant, I couldn't quite make out who stood behind the bar. It wasn't until I got closer that I recognized her. I sat on a barstool and ran a hand through my jet-black hair, pushing it behind my ear. "Janet? What are you doing here?"

Janet tossed her dishtowel over her shoulder and put

one hand on her hip. "I work here, hon. What's your excuse?"

"Came back to check on my father, that's all. I don't plan on staying long."

"Oh, hon. I said the same thing when I was your age: I'd leave after graduation. And yet, I'm still here. Don't be surprised if you end up staying like me."

I couldn't help but feel a tinge of sadness at Janet's words. But that wasn't what concerned me, but rather the fact she worked for my father, being my mother's sister and all. "I don't want to keep you from the other customers. I just came for some food for me and my dad since he doesn't have anything at the house to eat. What would you recommend?"

"Poyha," she suggested, heading to the computer screen to put in the order. "How's your father, by the way?"

I shrugged and sank my elbows into the heavily stained wooden countertop as I answered. "He's fine. Just getting old is all."

"Good. When it happened, I wasn't sure if he was going to make it or not."

"So you must've brought him to the hospital," I said.

"Sure did!"

"Thank you for that."

I examined my surroundings as Janet tended to the other customers at the bar. The restaurant seemed crowded, considering it was Monday. That possibly could have contributed to my father's heart attack. The constant chaos of hungry customers and the high volume of orders could have been too much for him. I shuddered at the thought of what weekends were like. As I continued admiring the pub's interior, someone tapped me on the shoulder, startling me.

"Excuse me, are you Kacy Roe?" a young voice said from behind.

I turned and beamed. "You know it!"

The nerdy boy's eyes lit up like a lighthouse, his glasses gleaming under the bar lighting. The amount of excitement plastered on his face was of cataclysmic proportions.

"I knew it! I knew it was you," he said. "Are you here to explore Camp Mercy?"

Camp Mercy? Hmm. I remembered seeing parts of it from the interstate earlier that morning. I did need new content for my channel. It had been a week since I'd uploaded anything. Even though I was in Tulsa to care for my father, maybe checking out the camp was a good idea. It could be worth my while. It could possibly go viral. It was worth a shot.

"I might be," I whispered. I pressed my finger to my lips. "Shhh, don't tell anyone."

The young boy beamed, then ran back to a booth in the corner of the restaurant to join what looked like his parents to finish off his plate of food.

"Looks like you've got quite the fanbase," Janet commented.

"Close to two million subscribers," I admitted, turning back to her. "Even though a majority of my viewers are families with young kids. But the numbers aren't what I'm most proud of. I'm just thankful I get to do what I enjoy for a living." Then back on the subject of Camp Mercy, I asked, "Did they ever find out who hung that boy?"

Janet pulled her hand from the beer mug she was

cleaning and placed it on the rack behind her. "What, at Camp Mercy? Don't tell me you're one of those conspiracy theorists."

"The news claimed he had a battered face, Janet. Someone had to have beaten him, which means it's highly unlikely that he died by suicide."

"Well, it could've been a hate crime. But we'll never know. The police deemed it a suicide thirty years ago, Kacy. If someone did lynch that boy, the bastard who did it is probably long gone by now." Janet printed out the tab and slid it over to a customer at the end of the bar.

I braced myself against the counter and stood. "Well, that sounds like a good enough story for me to talk about on YouTube. I guess I'll be exploring that place tonight."

One of the employees burst through the kitchen's double doors with a plastic bag in hand. They placed it on the counter behind the bar, then returned to the kitchen.

"Looks like my food's ready."

"Sure does," Janet said, passing the bag to me.

The food's warmth heated my stomach as I held it tight against my core.

"Do me a favor and tell your father I said hey, okay?"

I smiled and nodded. "Will do."

5 · Kacy

FINALLY, at eight in the evening, I slipped away from my father's watchful eye. He had been dropping hints all day about discussing my mother's death and everything I'd been up to for the past nine years. I was more than ready to focus on the task at hand rather than delving into the past.

With my father passed out on the couch, I grabbed my MacBook from my room. An hour's worth of research on the camp's history had me itching to explore it. Quietly tiptoeing to the kitchen, I snagged my father's truck keys from the decorative bowl and rode into the night. Within twenty minutes, I arrived at the front gate of the summer camp.

Camp Mercy, the one and only place where you can get away with murder. I giggled. *That sounds like the perfect title for this video.*

With my backpack and portable light nestled by my side on the passenger seat, I swung open the truck door and stepped out onto the unfamiliar terrain. Gently, I reached for my trusty Canon camera and meticulously attached the zoom lens and Rode microphone. Caution hung heavy on my mind as I secured the light to my forehead. The property was unfamiliar, and I couldn't predict what lay ahead. Fear of the unknown made my heart race. There was no telling who or what might be out there. My mind conjured up images of rabid animals and vicious hunters lurking around the premises. Despite the eerie ambiance of the place, it was still perfect for the caliber of video I wanted to create.

I discovered a private property sign slung around the lock as I approached the gate. Then something creaked above my head. Looking up, I found an arched sign, one side of it hanging on by a thread as if the bolts holding it up had rusted away. It could have dropped at any moment. I feared a gust of wind would send it tumbling on top of me, crushing my bones beyond repair. However, my only way onto the property was by climbing over the gate, so I needed to be careful. I didn't want to end up in the hospital, forcing my barely fit father to care for me, nor did I want to remain in Tulsa longer than necessary.

I took a deep breath, adjusted the ISO as high as I could without creating noise in the footage, then tapped the red button.

Action! "Hey, guys! Kacy, here with *another* amazing place to explore. Have you heard of Camp Mercy? No? Well, it used to be a summer camp in the state of Oklahoma. Quite the fun place, too, I'd imagine."

I flipped the camera around, showcasing the name on the crooked sign above, then turned it back on myself. "This isn't just an ordinary summer camp, though. What makes this place different from my other explorations is that a kid was murdered here. At least, that's what some people think." *And scene.*

I draped the camera strap over my head and scaled the tall metal gate. Over the years, I'd gotten used to finding clever ways to trespass. Climbing in through broken windows and climbing up downspouts onto the second floors of some buildings were just a few of the many ways.

I didn't expect any difficulty getting onto the camp's grounds since it was practically a barren wasteland. The rain had lowered the temperature considerably, chilling the night air to where I didn't even break a sweat upon climbing. However, despite my easy feat, the weather had left the grounds muddy and foggy. The moon above me lit the way as I trekked down the long dirt path past the desolate two-foot-tall grassy field lining the road. Every snap of a twig and every rustle of leaves set me on edge.

Action! "As for a little history on the place, it opened back in 1947. As a matter of fact, it was the biggest summer camp in Oklahoma at the time, which is what made it so popular." I zoomed in on my face. "But I know you guys want the juicy stuff, so here it is. For decades, business was good. Kids packed the place out every summer. It was the perfect summer escape to drop your kids off for two weeks of freedom," I scoffed. "But one night in 1986, something crazy happened. Some kid was out in the woods, on one of the many trails, when they stumbled upon a boy hanging in a tree." *And scene.*

Continuing down the wretched trail, narrowly avoiding the muddy puddles that threatened to ruin my boots, I scoured the area for any signs of danger. Luckily, I didn't encounter anything life-threatening; no stray dogs, no poisonous snakes, and no people. I was completely alone. And after a few minutes of wandering further down the trail, my perseverance paid off. I stumbled upon a row of wooden cabins hidden behind a cluster of majestic Bur Oak trees. From what I could make out, they seemed large enough to accommodate at least four bunks each.

Score! I've got to get this on camera.

I steadied my breathing and pressed the record button again as I inched closer to the deserted cabins. Though the wooden structures appeared vacant, there was no telling if anyone had sought shelter in one of them. The secluded location was far from the city, making it the perfect hideout for anyone running from the law. So, I remained on high alert.

As I reached the first cabin, my camera still aimed at the buildings, a debilitating stench crept up my nostrils. However, I knew the show had to go on. So, I turned the camera toward myself, drew in a breath, and continued.

Action! "The police investigated but found nothing that led to murder. So, they labeled it a suicide. When they finally reopened the camp, the story of what had happened cursed the place. Rumors spread, prompting many to believe the boy had been murdered. After that, no one wanted their kids at a camp with a possible killer on the loose."

As I went to enter the cabin, I found the steps leading up to it were missing entirely. Without a second thought, I launched myself forward, my body propelling me upward as I managed to clear the three-foot gap and latch onto the door frame. The rotting door groaned in protest to my weight, threatening to collapse in at any moment. It was the only way to prevent myself from falling back into the murky puddle below. Luckily, the door didn't give way, which allowed me to regain my footing and enter.

"Now, this is all that remains of the camp. Nothing but the terrifying story of a dead boy and a possible killer on the loose."

I flashed the camera around the quarters, capturing the depressing sight of the four rusty bedframes, the sunken floor caused by rainfall from part of the roof caving in some time ago, and the heaps of garbage and contraband that other explorers had left behind. I think they probably weren't explorers at all, but junkies looking for a safe place to get high. But I would never know for sure.

I stepped forward, feeling the soggy wooden planks disintegrating beneath my feet. I quickly retreated, latching onto the somewhat sturdy door frame. I wasn't going to risk falling into a dark abyss again. Because of the sunken floor, I couldn't explore the lodge's contents, so I left and headed for the cabin next door, hoping its condition was better.

"Let's see if there's anything exciting in the next one."

But as I approached the other cabin, the lingering odor became unbearable. I could barely breathe; it was that bad. "There's definitely a dead animal in here, guys."

Covering my nose, I climbed up the steps and kicked open the door. It swung wide with ease but stopped upon smacking against a heavy object on the other side. The floor looked questionable, but in my years of exploring, I understood the risks involved. Because nothing great comes without risk. That was the quote I lived by, the words I repeated to myself daily.

I took it one step at a time, cautiously inching across the

bowed planks. One flexed a little too much for my liking, feeling like it would snap. I froze, not wanting to fall through, fearing what lay under the floorboards of this forsaken place. Then, after a second of stillness, I pushed onward.

"As you can see, nothing looks preserved. Dust is covering everything, and cobwebs are in the corners. This is what nearly thirty years of neglect looks like. I'm surprised these cabins are still standing."

As I showed more of the inside to my viewers, something reflected the bright light strapped to my head. I caught a glimpse of it from out the corner of my eye. "I think I just found something, guys. Let's check it out."

I zeroed in on a pile of something in the corner of the cabin. It was hard to determine exactly what it was from where I stood, but I could tell it was light in color. *Is that an animal? Albino skunk, maybe?* That could have certainly explained the smell. Whatever it was, I was adamant about figuring it out.

I took a few steps closer, changing the camera's angle slightly. "It looks like we've found the remains of an animal and a pretty big one at that."

But as I got within a foot of it, aimed the light toward the pile, and zoomed the camera in to capture it on screen, I figured out what it truly was. I gasped, causing the horrid stench to fly down my throat and make me gag.

That's not an animal!

6 · Robert

My coffee tasted bitter. I should have known better than to drink it after noticing the stains on the pot. I should have asked the cashier to brew a fresh cup, but it's best not to waste any more time when you're already late to a crime scene. It was clear the coffee was leftover from earlier in the day. I highly doubted even reheating it in a microwave would have made much of a difference; it was stale dog shit at best. Having expectations of a shitty gas station on the outskirts of town at nine o'clock at night was my mistake. Lesson learned.

When I arrived at the camp, I cruised down the long, winding, muddied path, hitting every God-forsaken pothole and uneven patch of ground imaginable until I reached the roped-off crime scene. My car's suspension had taken a serious beating.

The flashing red and blue lights from the patrol cars were like a knife to my already throbbing headache. Damn, did I hate those lights. It seemed like nothing was going my way, especially after my previous week. I closed my eyes, took a deep breath, and exhaled. *Hopefully, this case is cut and paste.*

Stepping out of my vehicle, I caught many looks from my fellow officers. At that moment, I knew I was the last to arrive on the scene. *So much for showing up fashionably late.*

I slogged through the mud toward the cabin where the body had been found. I really had shown up late by the looks of it. Forensics had already staged the scene, setting up lamps to illuminate every inch of the cabin, tagging items that may have been used in the crime, and meticulously photographing every angle of the body so I could clear it for removal. Everyone was on their A-game, which made my job even easier.

I approached the body, kneeling to inspect it as Rachel, an analyst from my team, searched for prints. The smell was pungent; nothing I wasn't used to, though. Upon examining the body, I couldn't determine whether the corpse was male or female due to the significant amount of decomposition. Perhaps they had been dead a month—three tops. The M.E. report would estimate how long exactly.

As I continued my examination of the corpse, I found both wrists and feet were bound with zip ties, and one shoulder was out of place as if it had been dislocated. Despite the substantial tissue loss, I could still make out the battered face. Considering the factors at play, I assumed the decedent was beaten and tortured before receiving a bullet to the head.

After surveying the site and taking note of the shell casing that had been left behind, I concluded my report, leaving the evidence for Rachel and the rest of the team to collect. Sadly, no weapon was left behind. However, that didn't mean we couldn't find the bastard who had committed the crime.

As I stood, a flash of light went off behind me. I almost crashed into Leonard, another member of my team, on the way up.

"Sorry," I said, moving to the side.

"It's not your fault," Leonard said. "I shouldn't have been right behind you."

"Have you noticed any footprints in or around the cabin?"

"Not besides the footprints from the woman who found the body."

I exhaled. "You guys already checked that?"

He nodded. "I took a picture of the bottom of her shoes and matched them to the prints in the mud. They're hers."

"Thanks. Let me know if anything else comes up, okay?"

"Gotcha."

Rachel and Leonard remained in the cabin as I left, a flicker of the flash going off a few more times. I carefully walked down the spongey steps into the slippery grass and headed toward the group of officers, where I noticed a young Indigenous woman perched on the hood of one of their patrol cars. She must have been the woman who had found the body because Officer Jones was questioning her.

"Officer Jones," I said, grabbing ahold of his shoulder. "I've got it from here. Thank you."

He nodded and showed me his notepad, allowing me to give it the once over before my turn at questioning the woman. As I glossed over his notes, I caught the woman jittering nervously out of the corner of my eye.

"So, I hear you're the one to blame for why I'm not in bed right now," I joked, not bearing a glance.

Her jittering ceased. "My apologies, sir...officer...eh..."

The woman paused for a beat as if she didn't know how to address me. Perhaps she was just shaken from having discovered a body.

"Stone. Detective Stone." I looked up from the notepad and sipped from my paper cup. Somehow, the taste of my coffee had worsened.

"Right. Sorry."

She whisked her hand through her lengthy hair, brushing it out of her face as if to make herself more visible to me in the night air. Then, at a moment's glance, I picked up on something I hadn't seen in years—a tiny J-shaped scar above her eyebrow. Instantly, I remembered the name Officer Jones had written on his notepad. Kacy Roe.

"When did you get back in town?" I asked, suddenly struck by how beautiful the woman before me was. I blamed the time of day for not having noticed sooner. Hell, it could have even been my headache. The most probable reason I failed to recognize her was that we hadn't seen each other in nearly a decade. "What's it been? Seven—wait, no, nine years?"

Kacy's yellow-brown eyes glistened in the moonlight as she tilted her head to the side and shot me an innocent smile. "Took you long enough to remember. I was beginning to think you'd forgotten about me." She placed a hand on my arm. "You look good, Rob."

I chuckled. "I'll never forget the one who broke my

heart. But thanks for the compliment. Beards do wonders, don't they?"

Kacy nodded.

"So, what are you doing back here in Tulsa? I thought you'd never set foot in this city again."

"I could ask you the same thing," she playfully shot back. "I recall you saying you were going to travel the world and whatnot."

I scratched at the scruff on my face. "Well, things change. You see, I'm a detective now. What better place to be one than at home? Now what's your excuse?"

She looked away, trying to hide the shame on her face. "Eh...I'd rather not say."

"Okay. Let me rephrase the question since you don't want to get personal. You mind telling me what you were doing out here at this hour?"

Kacy bit her fingernail. "Well, like I told the other guy... I'm a YouTuber. And I explore abandoned places for a living."

"So that's what you've been up to since you left—trespassing regularly, huh? That's not something you want to admit to an officer of the law."

"It's my job," she admitted. "As long as I don't get caught or hurt, I don't see an issue."

"Okay, then...Why Camp Mercy? Out of all the places you could have explored in this country, why this place?"

Kacy kicked her foot up on the bumper of the patrol car, getting really comfortable in my presence. It wasn't a smart move, in my opinion. She ought to have more respect for law enforcement property. However, I couldn't expect much from a trespasser.

"Someone reminded me about the place. Figured it'd be perfect for a video."

"You think that *someone* could be responsible for the body?"

"No, not at all. It was just some kid…a fan, and they wanted me to do a video on it."

I took another sip of my disgusting coffee, nodded, and poured the last of it into the muddy grass. "Some kid? Does this kid have a name?"

"I'm sure he does, but I don't know it. I just got back in town this morning. I highly doubt that kid had anything to do with what I found. He was like…ten years old."

"Speaking of what you found, *how* exactly did you come across the body?"

Kacy shifted her weight once more. "Well, like I said, I stumbled upon it while exploring. I just walked in and found it."

"That's quite convenient, isn't it?"

"*Convenient?*" she questioned as if I had implied she'd murdered the person. "Hopefully, you don't think I killed that person, do you?"

"I don't make assumptions, Kacy. I just stick to the facts."

If I were to contact the airlines about her claim of just flying, I'm sure her alibi would check out. It didn't make much sense for the killer to report their own crime from such a remote location since they would instantly be labeled the first suspect. She couldn't be the killer.

And as I continued, contemplating how Kacy could have done it, she added, "I'd show you how I found the guy on my camera, but your guys haven't given it back yet."

"And we won't for at least a couple of days."

"Couple of days?" Her voice got louder. "That's my equipment!"

"And this is an active murder investigation," I shot back. "Your camera is evidence now."

I turned and headed for my cruiser.

"Wait, Rob!" she called out.

I doubled back.

"I'm sorry about that outburst. I just need my equipment." Standing on her tip-toes, Kacy leaned into my ear and whispered, "Like...when can I get it back? Because, much like you, I need it to do my job too."

"Well, in situations like this, there are a lot of variables. Hopefully, forensics will be quick on identifying the remains. Once they do, they'll scrub your footage for any possible leads. The department will return your camera to you within a few weeks. However, your footage, on the other hand, will be held indefinitely."

"Few weeks!" she exclaimed. Her tone was dismal.

Why was she in such a rush? Had her patience worn thin? She had returned to Tulsa but seemed to be in a hurry to leave again. I couldn't figure out why. Despite not knowing her reasons, seeing her slump her shoulders and exhale a sigh of frustration made me want to offer my help. After all, we had a shared history.

"How about this? I'll call you when your stuff's been cleared. I'll even bring it to you. We can meet for lunch somewhere around town. My treat."

Her chin shot up, followed by a scrunching expression. "Sounds like you're asking me out."

I scoffed. "No, I'm not. Just being nice is all."

She crossed her arms and shifted her weight onto one hip. "And why's that?"

Standing at a mere five-foot-three, she exuded strength and fitness. I recalled how she used to be shy and fragile when we were kids, but that didn't seem to be the case anymore. As we talked, I took note of her stern demeanor and unyielding attitude. She had clearly changed, and it seemed to be for the better.

She was clearly a woman now, her curves giving more oomph to her petite frame. But her hips weren't the only thing that had grown. Her dimples had become more prominent, accentuating her words like musical notes on a page. I had picked up on it during our conversation.

"Because I have no reason to be mean," I finally answered. "But look, you don't have to if you don't want. I'll just tell the guys in the lab to drag their feet a little. Might stretch this thing out a month or two."

"C'mon, Rob. Don't be that guy."

I was definitely being that guy.

"Be what guy?" I asked, turning to head back to my cruiser with a wide grin that hurt my cheeks. "I'm just being myself."

7 · Robert

AFTER TURNING the bend in the road, I reached Mrs. Carter's petite, yellow vinyl-sided home at the end of a quiet cul-de-sac. The residence exuded a quaint allure, blessing my presence with a colorful array of petunias and tulips that adorned the red-brick walkway leading up to the front door. I pulled into the driveway behind her and her husband's sedans and got out.

It had been five days since the human remains were discovered at Camp Mercy.

When I rang the doorbell, I expected her to answer within a minute, believing she might have been cleaning up in the kitchen since it was still early in the morning. However, as I stood on the front porch, waiting for the door to open, it didn't. I rang the doorbell yet again and still received the same result. Perhaps she was in the shower. That could have possibly explained her lack of a response. The thought of her being asleep also came to mind, but I knew she would have answered the door by now, given the time elapsed.

I stepped off the porch and peered in through the nearest window, hoping to find Mrs. Carter lost amid a recreational activity. But to my surprise, I was met with an abundance of darkness as if she wasn't home.

Hmm. How strange.

My police instincts kicked in, leading me to inspect the premises. Keeping a firm grip on my holster, prepared to draw my service pistol at a moment's notice, I crept along the side of the house until I arrived at another window. I peered inside, but the outcome remained unchanged—she was nowhere to be found.

Suddenly, a sound penetrated my eardrums—a constant munching that resembled digging. I had my Glock-9 within arm's reach, my finger resting on the trigger guard. But as I cautiously peered around the corner of the house, I stumbled upon Mrs. Carter on her knees across the yard, holding what seemed to be a trowel. She was merely pulling weeds.

I re-clipped the strap on my holster, stepped out from around the corner, and called her name. "Mrs. Carter, do you have a minute?"

Upon drawing her attention, she redirected her gaze toward me, her expression dull and mute, as if the soothing act of gardening failed to quell her sentiments regarding the loss of her spouse.

"Sorry to intrude," I said, coming up beside her. "But I rang the doorbell, and no one answered."

"What can I do for you, Detective Stone?"

"If you don't mind, can we go inside?"

She brushed the fresh dirt from her gloves and stood. "Sure. Follow me."

I followed her through the back patio into the kitchen, dreading how I'd break the news to her about the death of her husband. I couldn't comprehend how surgeons and nurses managed to dish out bad news daily. Telling someone their loved one was dead—murdered even—was always difficult for me. I couldn't just rip the bandaid off like many of my co-workers. That just wasn't me. After removing her dirt-covered sandals and rubber gloves, we transitioned to the living area, where I joined her on a burgundy sofa. Now that she was seated, it was time to break the news to her.

I swallowed the lump in my throat. "Mrs. Carter, your husband, Charles..." I noticed tears welling up in her eyes.

Damn, she is really making this difficult for me.

There was no telling how Mrs. Carter would react to the news; whether she'd break down sobbing, clenching onto my shirt, expecting me to hug her, or start screaming and yelling in anger, making a big scene because we hadn't done a good enough job of finding her husband sooner. In my experience, I'd seen enough of both and didn't enjoy either. But if I had to choose, it'd be the former.

Mrs. Carter stared at me, her eyes glistening in the rays of the morning sun coming from the window behind the sofa. She was patiently waiting for me to say something— anything really—that would put an end to the tension that hung in the room.

And finally, I spoke. "I apologize for the suspense, Mrs. Carter. I'm sorry to inform you that your husband's body has been found."

She gasped, sinking her face into her palms. Clearly, she wasn't prepared to hear that he had died following his disappearance three months prior. Then, in a moment of doubt, she drew her head from her lap and asked, "Are you sure it's him?"

I exhaled, somehow mustering up the courage to continue. "We ran the DNA you provided upon his disappearance against a body that was found five days ago. Forensics confirmed it was him. They also found a bullet casing near his remains, which confirmed there was foul play involved. A woman found him in one of the cabins at Camp Mercy."

"Camp Mercy?" she questioned. "Do you think that kid he was helping had something to do with this?"

"Possibly. That might explain why his body was just left there. There was no effort to bury him. It could have been a rush job—purely amateur."

"I understood why Charles wanted to help the kid, but I don't know why one of his students would want to kill him," she said, shuddering. "I don't even know why he'd want to visit that place again anyway. The only time he'd ever been there was when we were kids. But when James was murdered—"

"Suicide—officially," I corrected. "The police labeled it a suicide."

Mrs. Carter scratched at her afro that was neatly tied back on her head. "Yes, I know. But you weren't there. I was. I saw how they treated James. How he could have been murdered, and how it could have been covered up."

At that moment, I remained speechless. I didn't have a response because she was right. I knew nothing of the event that took place in 1986. Just what was in the public record. I hadn't even been born then.

"You know what...Do you have any photos?" she asked.

"I do. They're in my car. Are you sure you want to see them?"

She nodded.

"Okay. Give me a sec?" After retrieving the manila folder from my cruiser, I laid out a collection of photographs on her coffee table. The disturbing images showcased a decomposing body ravaged by clusters of voracious maggots and interior and exterior sections of the cabin. I knew the many vermin of Oklahoma had a field day on his corpse, but I wouldn't dare tell her that.

Mrs. Carter sifted through the photos one by one, indicating she was searching for something specific with the way her eyes darted between them.

"He had two broken ribs, a dislocated shoulder, and a bullet wound to the head," I continued. "From the looks of it, he'd been badly beaten beforehand."

Suddenly, she gasped upon further dissection of a picture with the cabin. "I had a feeling that was the cabin he was in when..." She stopped talking.

"When what?" I urged.

Mrs. Carter pointed at the number two above the cabin's door. "The cabin Charles stayed in the night James was hanged!"

"And how do you know this?"

"Detective Stone, Camp Mercy is where Charles and I met for the first time," she admitted. She began tearing up. "I'd sneak into his bunk after lights out to play board games with him and his bunkmates." She turned to the foyer, eyes watery.

I wasn't the emotional type, so I didn't carry around a wad of tissues in my pocket. If I had, I would have pulled a few to give. I could picture Mrs. Carter grabbing the clump from my hand and patting her face dry.

"So what are you saying?" I asked.

"I'm saying whoever killed Charles might be the same person who hung that boy thirty years ago."

"Mrs. Carter. Please. There wasn't any evidence found that concluded James was murdered. Now if you want us to find the killer who murdered your husband, you can help by—"

"Well, I believe James was!"

What a bold assumption. But I get it. She's dealing with a lot right now.

Mrs. Carter hadn't the slightest clue about how policing worked, but it was clear she was trying to make sense of things. Or perhaps... Could she be covering her tracks, leading us away from the crime *she* might have committed? Anything was possible.

I leaned back into the sofa and fell deep in thought. *She did mention something about him possibly cheating on her back when she first filed the missing person's report. It could be a crime of passion committed by her. Or by whoever he'd been cheating with.*

Then her words broke my train of thought.

"Why did I even think the police could help?" she said, standing abruptly. "What about the person who found him? Could *they* have any information? Why were they even there in the first place?"

There were too many questions and not enough answers to retort. I regretted not being able to provide Mrs. Carter with information on the other possible suspects. I seized her arm and eased her onto the plush surface, hoping to alleviate her anxiety. Our interrogation of Kacy had yielded no results, and her alibi had checked out. Though she was still considered a person of interest, no evidence implicated her.

Mrs. Carter shot up from the sofa again. "He disappeared three months ago! That person could be—"

"Mrs. Carter?" I reached for her hand again, but she snatched it away before I could grab ahold. "That *person* you're referring to hasn't been ruled out yet."

I lied.

Though Kacy lived in another state entirely, we'd still run a background check on her. And after looking into her bank records, we found receipts dating back to the week Mr. Carter had gone missing. As far as I was concerned, Kacy had nothing to do with his disappearance, let alone his murder.

Mrs. Carter huffed. "Good. Anyone could be the killer."

She headed for the front door and opened it. I stood from the sofa and looked down the hall, wondering what she was doing.

"Now, if you don't mind, I've got some flowers that need weeding," she said, gesturing for me to leave.

"Someone will be in touch about the arrangements for your husband's burial," I said, exiting her humble abode. However, nothing but the angry smack of the door closing shut and locking followed me out.

I could tell Mrs. Carter was furious. It was to be

expected, though. Most people cry after the death of a loved one. Others turn irate and yell and scream. People deal with loss in different ways. That's just the way it is. I couldn't hold that against her.

As I headed down the driveway toward my cruiser, I noted how our conversation had abruptly ended. An assumption of a thirty-year-old suicide turned murder, her efforts at pushing said claim as if it were true, and her anger toward my doubts of it being connected to her husband's murder made me think Mrs. Carter could have killed her husband. There was a legitimate motive for doing so. I just needed evidence to prove it. I pulled my cell phone from my pocket and tapped Leonard's contact.

He answered after the first ring.

"You've got Leonard!"

Leonard was my go-to for all things information regarding potential suspect data.

"Hey, Leonard, it's Robert. I need a favor."

"That's what I'm here for," he said with a laugh.

"Do a search for any firearms registered to a Charles E. Carter. Also, run a search for his wife. Eloise M. Carter."

"Got it. If anything comes up, I'll have it on your desk by the time you get back. If not, you know the reason."

The incessant computer keys clacking in the backdrop signified Leonard's sense of urgency. It was all part of the job, given that he spent most of his days locked away in a dimly lit room behind a computer screen. However, that was what I admired about him. He was quick, and to the point, and in this line of work, that was what saved lives.

"Thanks," I said.

Then I ended the call.

To: Professor Carter (tulsauniversity.carter@gmail.com)

From: Jeremy Saunders (jsaunders1994@gmail.com)

Date: Sunday, March 27, 2016 01:24:53 EST

Subject: School Project

Dear Professor,

I want to thank you again for giving me more time to choose a topic for my report on tragic events. I decided to pick Camp Mercy as the focus. I hope that's okay.

To: Jeremy Saunders (jsaunders1994@gmail.com)

From: Professor Carter (tulsauniversity.carter@gmail.com)

Date: Sunday, March 27, 2016 03:47:21 EST

Subject: Re: School Project

Dear Jeremy,

I'm glad you took advantage of the extra time I gave you. Camp Mercy is an excellent choice. There should be plenty of online resources available to draw from. I'm looking forward to reading your report, Jeremy. Don't hesitate to reach back out if you have any other questions regarding the assignment.

8 · Kacy

It was eleven in the morning when I pulled into the police station's parking lot. Robert had promised to call me once the body was identified, but I wanted to beat him to the punch to save myself from having to accept his lunch offer. It wasn't that I didn't want to catch up with him, but thinking about how things had ended between us, with me leaving without even a simple goodbye, made my stomach churn. The mere thought of explaining why I had ended things so abruptly sent shivers down my spine.

I headed inside and approached the front counter, where a man stood. Luckily, he wasn't helping anyone else, allowing me to stroll up and say, "Excuse me. Where can I find Detective Stone?"

"He's not in at the moment. You'll have to wait until he's—"

I slammed the newspaper on the counter and pointed out the headline: MISSING MAN FOUND. "He told me that after this man was identified—which, according to this, has happened—I would get my stuff back. Do you know when he'll be—"

A tap on my shoulder caught me by surprise. I spun around to find Robert standing right behind me.

"Oh, there you are," I said, pulling away from the counter.

"Hey," he said.

"Can I have my equipment back now?" I boldly asked.

"I said I'd call you once your stuff was cleared." He turned and walked down the hall.

I followed him, ignoring the officer at the counter, saying I couldn't go beyond the lobby without a visitor's pass.

"Well, I'm here now, so there's no need."

Robert's sudden stop caught me off guard, and I nearly collided with him. I took a step back, creating some distance between us. I couldn't speak for him, but we were too close for comfort.

"Kacy, there are rules to this. I can't just pull evidence whenever I feel like—"

"I've just got things to do, Rob," I lied, knowing I had nothing to do besides keep tabs on my father and film and edit another video for my channel, which would take an entire day—two tops.

Deep down, I didn't want to give Robert the time of day. Despite how devilishly handsome he'd become with his neatly trimmed beard and the pounds of muscle he'd put on since the last I saw him, I was trying to leave town. I wanted to return home come the end of the week, so I could get back to my life, away from what I'd tried so hard to forget.

Robert sighed at my lie. "Fine. Wait here."

I settled onto a bench in the lobby, patiently awaiting his return. I had no idea how long he would be gone or whether he would even come back with my belongings. Some part of me felt he was toying with me, exacting revenge for what I'd done to him years ago. However, I played a mini-game on my cell phone to distract myself from that gruesome thought.

When he finally returned and handed over my equipment, I said, "Thank you." Then I stood from the bench and left.

As I left the building, I pondered how unexpectedly smooth the interaction with him had gone. I had anticipated more bureaucracy and red tape, yet somehow, Robert had made it painless. I wondered what else I didn't know about law enforcement. Despite the awkwardness of our past, I had to admit that Robert was a man of his word, a kind heart, which led me to reconsider his lunch offer.

———

Armed with my camera gear, I was eager to head home and shoot more footage. However, as fate would have it, a familiar voice beckoned me by name just as I reached my father's truck.

"Kacy, wait!"

I spun, and my heart sank as I caught sight of Robert making his way toward me. I feared what he might say. It could have been anything, ranging from a simple invitation to dinner instead of lunch or pressing me for more information about the night I discovered the body. I couldn't make out his intentions through his stern stride.

And as we met in the middle of the parking lot, he said, "You forgot this."

In his hand, I found the newspaper I'd brought in. I must have left it on the bench when he returned with my belongings. It was trash now, considering I'd retrieved what I'd come for. However, Robert's courtesy had left me bewildered. He could have simply thrown it away. I guess he *was* being nice, first by returning my camera, and now this. I couldn't imagine what he'd do next.

"Thank you," I said, taking the paper from him. "Even though you could've simply thrown it away."

Then suddenly, a car door slammed, and an unfamiliar voice interrupted the kind gesture. "Are you the person who found my husband at Camp Mercy?" a woman asked.

I wasn't prepared to answer any questions, especially not one as serious as that. I didn't know how to respond.

I turned to face the woman who had interrupted us. "Yes...eh...I'm sorry for your loss." I stumbled over my words.

"Mrs. Carter?" Robert interjected. "What are you doing here?"

"I came to apologize for how I acted earlier," the woman said. "It was unacceptable."

Hmm. How she acted earlier? I wonder what she's talking about.

"It's okay, Mrs. Carter," Robert said. "No offense taken. This isn't the first time something like this has happened."

Then the woman turned to me and extended a hand. "I'm Eloise Carter. What's your name?"

I scanned the woman from head to toe, taking into account her black hair that was pulled back, her blemish-free skin a shade darker than mine, and her tiny frame. Her beauty was stunning. We shook hands.

"Kacy Roe. Nice to meet you."

"If you don't mind me asking, why were you out there? That camp's been shut down for years."

Again with the questions. "Eh...it's weird, I know, but—"

Eloise scoffed. "You got that right. Did you happen to see anyone else while you were out there?"

"Now, Mrs. Carter, we already questioned her," Robert cut in. "Please, go home. I'll give you a call when we have more information."

Eloise shot him a menacing glare.

"Go home," he repeated. His tone was stern.

Her attempt at putting her foot down fell flat. At this point, there was nothing Eloise could do besides leave. She stormed off, huffing and puffing as she returned to her sedan parked beside my father's truck.

I turned back to Robert. "That wasn't nice. You know she's just trying to find out what happened to her husband."

"Kacy, there's a lot you don't know about this case. I suggest you do the same as her and go home."

A sigh escaped my lips. My business at the police station was taken care of, so I saw no reason to refuse Robert's request. However, as I returned to my father's truck, I couldn't help but notice Eloise sobbing hysterically in the neighboring vehicle. It was impossible not to make eye contact with her, considering our cars were facing the same direction. I thought to say something to her. It was only right. After returning my camera to my backpack, which lay in the truck's passenger seat, I closed the door and walked over to tap on the driver-side window of Eloise's sedan.

"Are you okay?" I asked.

She nodded as she wiped away the tears on her shirt's sleeve. Then she rolled down the window and poked her head out. "I'm fine. Just upset, that's all."

Her hazel eyes mirrored the anguish she was experiencing, and the sound of mucus gurgling in her throat as she struggled to calm down only added to my sympathy for her. I knew that pain all too well—the agony of losing a loved one without warning. Grief is a heavy burden that weighs down on you, bringing with it the bitter sting of regret. It makes you wish you had spent more time with whoever you lost and reminds you of the little things you take for granted.

I sniffled, remembering my mother and the school lunches she used to pack. I could picture the sticky note she'd put in my lunch box that bore a life lesson. Sometimes, I'd even dream of her. But that was it. That was all I could do now that she was gone. And though I didn't know the specifics of Eloise's husband's death—whether it was murder or suicide—it was clear that she was grieving deeply, much like I had done upon my mother's death.

"I lost my mother a long time ago, so I know what it's like," I admitted. Leaning in, I placed my hand on the window frame and added, "So if there's anything I can do, or if you just want to talk, I can give you my—"

I didn't even get a chance to finish before she said, "Do you mind if we talk now?"

Do I mind if we talk now? Eh...yes.

I scratched the back of my head, a twinge of reluctance creeping up on me. I didn't want to come across as callous or hurtful, but I also didn't want to give up any more of my limited time. But after a second thought, I caved. "Now? Eh...sure, not a problem."

"Follow me back to my house. We can talk there."

I nodded, then returned to my vehicle. As I waited for Eloise to back out of her parking space, I put the key in the ignition and brought the truck to life. Then I backed out after her.

9 · **Kacy**

Twenty minutes later, I parked in Eloise's driveway. Her charming one-story home gawked back at me. When she emerged from her car, she looked at me. And though her expression wasn't necessarily menacing, it left my stomach trembling. The prospect of entering a stranger's home brought an onslaught of fears.

Eloise mouthed the words, "You coming?"

I opened the driver-side door and forced a smile, nodding in her direction. Though what I really wanted to say was, "Something's come up," and bolt. However, that would have been rude and uncalled for. I couldn't just abandon her in her time of need and make myself look like an ass. So, I stepped out of the truck, closed the door, and followed Eloise into her home.

"Do you want any coffee or tea?" she asked, closing the front door.

"No, thank you," I answered.

As soon as I set foot inside Eloise's humble abode, my eyes were met with beauty and grace. At first, I noticed an array of large, colorful paintings that adorned the sunny yellow walls. Then, moving further into the home, my gaze shifted to the mahogany hardwood beneath us. I felt as if I were wandering through a sunflower field, surrounded by the sweet aroma of mandarin, amyris, and vanilla.

"So, what did you want to talk to me about?" I asked, finally snapping myself out of the blissful state.

Eloise motioned me to follow her down the short hallway to the living area, where a long sofa sat before a forty-inch flat-screen TV. A red-brick fireplace was nestled between them.

Eloise sat down first, then I followed suit. My body sank pretty deep into the burgundy sofa as if its cushions were clouds. As I planted my hands on the bottom cushion to prepare myself to dart out of the house in case Eloise attacked me because she thought I had killed her husband, I noticed her twiddling her thumbs in hesitation, like she, too, had grown uncertain about chatting with a woman she'd just met.

Then she finally spoke. "I just want to know if you saw anything out of the ordinary while you were out there."

"Out where? The camp?"

She nodded.

"No. Nothing. No one was around but me." I tucked my hair behind my ear. "At least from what I saw. I didn't get much of a chance to explore the whole site, though."

Eloise drew in a breath. "Well, that's too bad because it leads me to believe *you* killed my husband."

I was at a loss for words. My body tensed so much that I

couldn't even muster the strength to move. It felt like a boa constrictor was squeezing the life out of me. I suddenly wanted to flee the house, fearing that Eloise might stab me or worse. But my limbs refused to cooperate. They were numb, leaving me stranded and helpless.

As I sat there in stunned silence, my mind began to think logically. If I ran out of her house screaming to high heavens, that action alone would incriminate me, giving her even more of a reason to suspect me as her husband's killer. In my moment of contemplation, she rested her hand on mine.

"Oh, who am I kidding?" she muttered. "You couldn't have done it. You have no reason to. You don't even know my husband."

At that moment, my body had broken free from the shackles of my subconscious mind—the artificial restraint that had kept me from becoming the prime suspect in the death of Eloise's husband. With a newfound sense of freedom, I placed my other hand on hers, offering comfort and support.

"I'm sorry," she said.

"There's no need to be sorry, Eloise. I understand why you thought I murdered your husband. You have every right to wonder. So, I'm not upset."

Eloise pulled her hand away in shame. We both remained quiet for a second too long. Then she broke the silence. "Are you familiar with the camp's history?"

I nodded.

"Good. So you're familiar with the theory that James Edlin was murdered." Eloise fidgeted in her spot as if she was unsure of how I might respond to what she was about to say. "Well, since it seems you didn't murder my husband, I'm going to return to my original claim that whoever killed him also murdered James thirty years ago."

I narrowed my eyes in disbelief and sank back into the cushions, crossing my arms instinctively. "I'm sorry, but I must ask—how did you come to that conclusion?"

"Because where you found his body was where he bunked the night that kid was hung."

"What?" I wasn't following. "Were you there when it happened?"

"Yes."

I was taken aback by her answer. I hadn't pegged Eloise as old, but being present during the incident suggested she was at least in her mid-to-late forties. I had to admit, she looked fantastic for her age. *God, I hope I look that good when I'm that old,* I thought. But as for her claim about who murdered her husband, I didn't believe her.

"Eh...it could just be a coincidence," I suggested.

She stood from the sofa and started pacing. "I told Detective Stone this, but he didn't believe me either."

I sat forward, pressing my elbows deep into my knees. "You can't blame him. It's kind of a stretch when you think about it."

"I know, but..." She stopped pacing and turned to face me. "I don't know what else to do. Three months have passed, and all they've done is uncover his body. It's like they're not even trying."

I understood her frustration. Not entirely, but enough to where I could sense how angry she was. "Well, maybe you need to take it into your own hands," I suggested. But what I wanted to say was, "Maybe it's time to let go."

But not everyone can let go of the past. I certainly hadn't with what my father had done to my mother. Perhaps it wasn't that easy. Holding on to pain and resentment is a difficult thing to let go of. Maybe I, too, faced the same troubles as Eloise, the feeling of not wanting to let go, not wanting to forgive in fear that I'd forget, and not wanting to accept what had ultimately torn our family apart.

"I will! We will!" she said.

Eloise's statement broke my trance. I shot her a *what the fuck* look as if I misheard what she'd said. "Say again? We?"

Eloise sat down beside me and placed her hand on my thigh. "Well, I guess…that's *if* you'll help me. Will you?"

At first, I didn't want to, but then I remembered how uncovering Eloise's husband's remains left my video incomplete—a story without an ending. Returning to the scene of the crime was a terrible idea, regardless if police patrolled the area or not. I could simply trespass again and run the risk of getting arrested. But then I thought, *Why does she want my help? Certainly, she doesn't believe I know anything about her husband's murder. Does she think I can help uncover the truth somehow? Maybe help her attain closure?*

I nodded slowly, pondering her words. Perhaps she was onto something. There may have been a bigger story at play. And maybe helping her could help me. It wasn't like I had anything else to do around town anyway.

"Alright," I said, coming to a decision. "I'll help you. Where do we start?"

To: Professor Carter (tulsauniversity.carter@gmail.com)
From: Jeremy Saunders (jsaunders1994@gmail.com)
Date: Sunday, March 27, 2016 7:59:17 EST
Subject: Re: Re: School Project

Well, I actually do have a question…I was thinking of exploring the camp to try to get a better understanding of what took place there. The internet is great and all, but I feel like if I rummage through some of the remains of the camp, I might come up with some cool ideas. Is that something you'd recommend?

To: Jeremy Saunders (jsaunders1994@gmail.com)
From: Professor Carter (tulsauniversity.carter@gmail.com)
Date: Monday, March 28, 2016 6:12:03 EST
Subject: Re: Re: Re: School Project

I like your willingness to try and better understand what went down at Camp Mercy, but as a teacher, I can't recommend that. Not only is it not safe, but it is also illegal. A better alternative would be to question some of the people who might have been there during the time the event took place. For example, I was there that night, along with a few others.

10 · Kacy

ELOISE RUMMAGED through her linen closet, yanking out boxes and tossing them carelessly onto the floor. She was slowly creating a haphazard pile that threatened to topple over. With my back fixed to the opposite wall, I watched her. Her frantic search seemed to border on obsession. I couldn't help but wonder what could be so important that she was willing to make such a mess.

"It's in here somewhere. It has to be!" she said, her voice muffled by the crisp cotton sheets and soft, plush towels. "It wouldn't be anywhere else."

I'd been standing there for about ten minutes, counting away every ticking second. At this point, I believed she'd never find it. "You know, you might've just thrown it—"

"Found it!" she said, pulling an old, tattered book out from the clutter in the closet. She turned to me. "Sorry it took so long. Didn't think it was buried that far back." She laughed.

"It's fine. At least you've found it. That's all that matters." I pulled the book from her hands and vigorously flipped through the pages, unable to hide my curiosity. "So, what is this thing?"

"It's my first journal." She headed toward the kitchen.

"Really?" I flipped through the book, landing on the very last page. I looked at the entry date: Sunday, July 8th, 1986. "Wow, you sure hold onto things."

"Yes, I do." Her voice trailed from a distance.

I strolled down the hallway and into the kitchen, my senses awash with the sweet scent of fresh oranges. Eloise was pouring herself a tall glass of juice.

I sat at the dinette. "So, what's the journal for?"

She returned the carton of juice to the refrigerator and approached the table. "Names."

"Names? Of whom?"

Eloise flipped through the book with a sense of reverence, her fingers tracing the delicate pages until she came upon the one she sought. On it were many tinged photographs, some of which had become unglued with age. I ran my hand across the page, being careful as to not pull up a few more. Further inspecting the images, I discovered it was a collage of teenagers—some playing volleyball, others playing soccer, and some even roasting marshmallows around a campfire while laughing and smiling.

"Back then, I was into photography," she said, sitting opposite me. "Like, really into it." She spun the book around and examined the people in the photos. "I figured if we contact some of them and ask if they remember anything about that day, really *anything* from their camp experience, we might learn a thing or two."

My finger tapped along the tabletop, my uncertainty apparent. "Are you sure that's the right move?"

"It's either this, or we try to find the kid my husband was teaching."

"Kid?" I questioned.

"Yes. My husband taught at the university. He was helping one of his students with a history project that was centered on Camp Mercy."

"Why does it sound like the kid was a dead end?"

"Because the police never found him. I tried emailing the kid and received no response. The police contacted his parents, but they hadn't heard from him either. He'd gone missing too." Eloise's eyes wandered from the page, her expression full of discouragement. "This is why I strongly believe James was murdered, Kacy—why Charles was murdered by the same person. I believe he and his student uncovered the truth of what really happened in eighty-six, and someone silenced him. Silenced them both."

The hairs on the back of my neck shot up. What Eloise had said was similar to something out of a horror story—a chilling nightmare.

She tapped her finger on one of the photos. "I'm not saying we track down every person. Just the ones I knew. The ones involved in James' death."

"I can't believe you've managed to stay in contact with all these people."

"I haven't whatsoever." Leaning back in the wooden chair, Eloise crossed her legs and threw back the last of her juice. "I wasn't necessarily in with the popular crowd and didn't want to be either. Had no reason to. So, finding these people might be a little tricky. But once we do, maybe someone will give us a clue that'll point us in the right direction."

I slid the book back toward myself and examined the photos some more. "Sounds like a plan. Who should we start with first?"

"Him," she said, pointing to a ginger boy in one of the images. "Last I remember, he was the one who found James that night. Think his name was Griffen."

I stood, ready to begin the search for the ginger boy she had pointed out. "Have any clue where we can find him?"

Eloise glanced up at me with another look of discouragement. "Unfortunately not." Nothing but a sigh followed her admission.

"Alrighty, then...I guess I'll see what I can find online. But while I'm here, is there anyone else that comes to mind?"

I braced myself against the wall that separated the kitchen from the hallway, waiting as Eloise struggled to recall a name from her distant past. I couldn't help but wonder whose name she was trying to remember—a family member, a coworker, or perhaps someone from her fellow congregation if she was devoted to the church in any way. It seemed unlikely that she could recall a name from thirty years ago.

"The sheriff!" she suddenly shouted. "I completely forgot."

"The sheriff?"

"Yes. Sheriff Wells. He was one of Charles' bunkmates at the time."

"I guess we're heading back to the police station then."

"Not exactly. He's probably out and about doing something in the community since it's Saturday."

"Eh...you're probably right."

Then suddenly, my cell phone buzzed. Fishing it out of my pocket, I found my father had texted.

DAD:

> Need the truck to go to work. You still at the station?

Of all the times to be interrupted, my father was the one responsible. I sighed inwardly, knowing that I couldn't do anything about it. After all, it wasn't my vehicle I was using. I also had been away for longer than I'd intended. I knew then that it was time for me to leave. I replied.

> On my way home now.

I returned the phone to my pocket. "Look, I've got to go. We'll pick this back up on Monday. In the meantime, I'll hit the library to see if I can dig up anything else on Camp Mercy."

I traveled down the hall toward the front door.

Eloise followed, opening it for me.

"You just relax, okay? If you remember any more names, text me."

Eloise nodded, then closed the door as I stepped off the porch and headed to the truck.

———

The thought of what my father might say when I walked through the front door never dawned on me. But when I set foot inside, he flipped.

"When I said you could use the truck, I didn't mean you could hog it for the entire day," he said as I walked in. He was leaning against the refrigerator, his arms crossed, one foot pressed against the stainless steel. "You know I've got things to do, Kacy."

The creases on his forehead were a roadmap of irritation, etched deep with lines that spoke of his simmering anger. I knew he couldn't afford to get so worked up—after all, he'd already survived one heart attack. If he didn't learn to control his temper, he might not be so lucky a second go around.

I closed the front door. "I know, I know. I'm sorry. I just got wrapped up in something, that's all." I walked past him and set my backpack on the counter beside the microwave.

"Wrapped up in something?" he questioned. "What could you have possibly gotten *wrapped up in* at the police station? You already uncovered a body. Certainly, they don't believe you murdered that man, too, do they?"

"Dad, no! Of course not. It's something completely different." I rubbed my temples, feeling the beginnings of a headache start to form. I had to be careful with my words—after all, the conversation had already taken a heated turn, and I didn't want it to escalate further. If I didn't handle the situation carefully, it could quickly become a full-blown argument. I knew the best course of action was to get him out of the house as soon as possible. "It's nothing you need to worry about, Dad. Here are the keys."

I couldn't wait for him to leave. I held out my hand, the

keys dangling from my fingers. It was a simple exchange. He just had to take them and be on his way. But as I stood there, waiting for him to grab the keys, something inside me stirred. It was a feeling I couldn't ignore, a surge of emotions that felt right in the moment. I didn't even bother to look him in the eyes.

"Dinner will be ready at seven. Don't be late."

It was as if my mother was speaking through me. Or maybe my sense of guilt drove me to speak up. Whatever the reason, his rigid posture relaxed, and his hostile glare softened into one of heartfelt sincerity.

"I'm sorry, dear. I'm just behind on everything at—"

"You don't need to explain, Dad. I understand."

I jiggled the keys once more. Then finally, he plucked them out of my hand and left. The truck's exhaust was quick to gargle as he backed out of the driveway and sped off. I was alone at last. And in an instant, it seemed like all my stresses had disappeared.

I traveled down the hall toward my bedroom as I fell deep in thought. I was relieved that my father had left to attend to more pressing matters, leaving me to deal with my own affairs. And more than that, I was grateful that our disagreement hadn't escalated into a full-blown argument over something so trivial.

I jumped on my bed face-first into a pile of decorative pillows. *Maybe he has changed.*

Thirty minutes had passed before I finally got to work. Rolling over, I reached for my backpack on the floor and retrieved my MacBook. I powered it on, then searched 'unsolved murders in Tulsa' on Google. Thousands of search results appeared.

Shit. There are too many for me to look over.

I needed to narrow down the search. I scrolled up to the search bar and typed 'camp mercy murder.' That yielded fewer than two hundred results. *That's more like it.*

From there, I began my search. What I uncovered in the many different articles shocked me. The hanging of a Black boy was the kind of tragedy that made national news. No wonder the camp went under. With magazines such as Esquire and Time covering the story, its fall was inevitable. Even if it *had* been a suicide.

I continued down a virtual rabbit hole, visiting a plethora of third-party websites, skipping more and more links the further I went until—

Wait a minute!

The second from the last link on the previous page caught my eye. I was moving so fast that I'd skipped to the next page before my eyes finished scrolling. I hit the back button, then clicked on it. The tail end of the URL read: classof86. The link directed me straight to Memorial High's website. It was at that moment an idea arose.

If I can get a copy of that yearbook, I can match the names to their faces!

I pulled out my phone and called Eloise. It rang and rang until, finally, she answered. And before she could even say a word, I blurted out, "*Please,* tell me you still have your yearbook from 1986."

"Eh...I think so. Let me check."

Given the commotion of shuffling boxes and papers in the background, I imagined she'd put me on speakerphone and set it down somewhere. At one point, it even sounded like an avalanche of items tumbling to the ground. Perhaps she was in the closest again—the same one in the hall from when I was there earlier.

But after a minute of silence from her—waiting as she searched for the yearbook—she finally returned to the line. "Sorry, don't have a single one. They were probably all at my mother's house."

"Is there any way we can get 'em?"

"Unfortunately not. Her place burned down last year. Firemen couldn't save a single thing."

"Dammit. I'm sorry to hear that. Well, thanks anyway. I'll talk to you later. Keep thinking about those names, okay?"

"Will do." Eloise ended the call.

Luck wasn't on my side. But that didn't matter because, at least now, I had a plan. I had created a mental list of things to do. Starting tomorrow, I was going to take my father's truck to the public library in search of the yearbook and whatever other information I could find.

Hopefully, they'll have a copy I can examine. Maybe then I can finally make some progress.

11 · Robert

THE END of my shift was drawing near. From the copious amounts of paperwork to the latest break in the Carter case, I was nearly ready to throw in the towel. But as I leaned back in my chair and reflected on Mrs. Carter's earlier comment about her husband's death being connected to James Edlin's alleged suicide at Camp Mercy, I couldn't shake the notion that she might be onto something. It was quite a presumptuous claim. Certainly, one she was entitled to have, considering I didn't provide her with any other evidence. Regardless, I only had the cabin number where her husband had been found. It was nowhere near what I considered a solid lead, but it was worth looking into.

My number of cases gone unsolved was one. During my last three years as a detective, I was lucky to have only one remaining at the bottom of the stack. And this case, having been drawn out for the last three months, made me wonder if it would be my second if I didn't solve it soon.

But I wouldn't allow that to happen. So I thought, *Why not check it out? Why not look into a suicide case from thirty years ago?*

I had nothing to lose.

I shot up from my desk and marched out of my office. Walking down the thinly carpeted hallway, I took a left, then a right, until I reached the elevator. I pushed the button and stepped inside. Ideas began to loom as I traveled down four floors in hushed silence.

The elevator dinged, and the door opened, leading to the basement archives.

"Good afternoon, Rick," I said to the heavyset man sitting at a desk behind the steel-wired fence opposite the elevator.

"Afternoon, Robert," Rick replied. He pulled a donut from his box of a half-dozen and took a hefty bite. "I haven't seen you in a while."

"Yeah, I haven't needed to come here for anything lately. You could say work is good," I joked as I approached the slot in the fence.

Rick laughed, his mouth full of sprinkles and glaze. He rubbed his hands together, brushing them free of the crumbs. "What can I do for you today?"

"Need a case from you. A pretty old one, in fact. The Camp Mercy suicide."

Rick retrieved a form from a compartment beneath the tiny platform, grabbed a pen from the nearby holder, and slid it toward me. Then he turned and strolled down an aisle, disappearing into the labyrinth of towering metal shelves.

I grabbed the pen and jotted down my information,

such as badge number, time and date, and reason for checking out the item. "How's Diane?"

"She's great!" Rick shouted back from somewhere. "Just picked up scrapbooking. Since she retired, she's had a lot of time. More than she knows what to do with."

I chuckled. "I guess it's time for you to retire then too."

Rick came from around a corner and wobbled back down the aisle with a large, lidded cardboard box in hand. "No can do. I plan to wait it out. I'm going to milk every penny I can get from social security." He slid the large box through the slot, taking the document in exchange.

"Well, I wish you the best. It's no easy feat devoting your life to the force." Then I turned and tapped the button for the elevator with the box under my arm.

"You can say that again."

The elevator doors opened. I stepped inside and spun around. "I'll see you around."

He waved goodbye as the doors closed.

As I rode the elevator up to my office, I read the tag on the box.

VICTIM: James Edlin
DEPT: Homicide
DATE: 07/09/1986
CASE #: E12-43618902

A part of me secretly wished that the case was linked to Charles Carter's matter. However, another part of me prayed it wasn't, as it would only complicate things. Nonetheless, delving into the past was the only way to unearth the answers I sought.

It seems time has a peculiar habit of slipping away when one is engrossed in research. I, for one, am no exception to this rule. It was two hours after I'd retrieved the files from the archives. A heavy downpour raged outside my office window, while inside, papers littered the room as if a cyclone had passed through.

I stood before my corkboard, examining the many pictures of James Edlin. Some photos showed him where he was found, hanging from a tree by a noose, and some were of him on the ground after they'd cut him down. Then I read over the M.E. report.

TIME OF INJURY: APPROX—2100
PLACE OF INJURY: Summer Camp (Camp Mercy)
AGE: 15
HEIGHT: 5'7" (67 inches)
EYE COLOR: Hazel
RACE: African American
IMMEDIATE CAUSE: Asphyxia
UNDERLYING CAUSE: Hanging by the neck
DID TOBACCO USE CONTRIBUTE TO DEATH: No

Then I read the most important thing, the Medical Examiner's description of how the injury occurred and the manner of death.

DESCRIPTION: Hanging by rope from tree.
MANNER OF DEATH: Suicide

Hmm. I wonder why they didn't consider it a homicide. Given the time, James' death could have easily been a hate crime. Then I caught a glimpse of who the Criminal Investigator on the case was. *Rick? I wonder why he didn't mention he'd been on the case.*

My gaze shifted back to the corkboard, landing on the written statement I'd pinned under the photos. It was from the boy who had found James. Name was Griffen Houser. His statement was riddled with misspellings and punctuation errors.

> *I was walking in the woods when I found him. The tree wasnt to far from the lake. I ran back to the camp and reported it to the furst counseler I saw.*

Man, that must have been tough for a kid to see. A body just hanging there like that.

My gaze returned to the photographs. James' face was battered. The thought of him being beaten up before his demise made me wonder. Perhaps being bullied had led him to turn to suicide. Then another question emerged. Why would James kill himself at a camp and not at home? Why not do it in the privacy of his bedroom? Perhaps he was afraid his parents would intervene. Or maybe—

I was beginning to question the information in front of me.

I glanced to my right, honing in on the details of the cabin number where James was stationed. Number two. Interesting. My gaze then drifted further down the corkboard to a paper listing the names of James' bunkmates.

Charles Carter's name was the first on the roster to catch my attention.

So, Mrs. Carter was telling the truth. But then my eyes trailed even further, noticing a second name—a name I knew from having worked alongside this man for some time, ever since I'd joined the force. Sheriff Blake Wells. *Hmm. I wonder why he neglected to mention he knew Mr. Carter as far back as high school when Reynolds questioned him about his disappearance three months ago. I guess I'll find out first thing Monday.*

A flash of lightning danced across the sky, drawing my attention away from the corkboard in front of me. I peered out at the dark sky and realized it was late. I glanced at my Rolex. 9:03 p.m.

Dammit. Another day that got away from me.

Despite having grown weary from the day, I sighed and sat at my desk to take a break. Leaning back, I stretched, and my spine cracked. As I leaned forward, my gaze fell upon Kacy's telephone number on the yellow sticky note pasted to the bottom corner of my computer monitor. I mulled over calling her, knowing I'd obtained it without her knowledge, utilizing Officer Jones' notes the night she discovered the body as my source.

Of all the things to happen, she'd fallen back into my life. However, I'd moved on long ago, dating other people over the past nine years. But I'd never really connected with any of them on a deeper level as I had with her. That was what drew me to think about her just now. Kacy coming back into the picture only stirred up old emotions. Instead of reflecting on what could have been, I thought more about what could be. What *we* could be. What was the worst that could happen?

I went ahead and pulled my phone from my pocket and dialed her number. It rang five times. Five times too many, in my opinion, thinking she wasn't going to answer, but then—

"Hello?"

Her voice sounded calm on the other end.

"Hey, Kacy. It's Robert."

I had no idea what she was doing. Perhaps she had just gotten out of the shower and was lying in bed on top of the comforter while skimming through a magazine or something. Perhaps she was doing that in nothing but an oversized T-shirt. Maybe, even her hair was pulled back in a sloppy bun. She could have pulled that look off so easily.

"It's kinda late to be calling, don't you think?" she asked, snapping me back to reality.

"Yes, I know it's late. Just needed a little break from this case, is all."

"Crime never sleeps."

She was right about that.

"But we do. So maybe you should be getting some," she suggested.

Kacy was right again. I needed to sleep, but how else would I solve the Carter case? "I'll sleep when I'm dead," I said, trying to joke.

Some shuffling lingered in the background. Perhaps she had rolled over onto her front and kicked her feet in the air, the tail of her shirt barely covering her ass. That was if she was even wearing a shirt. She might have been in a onesie or in a robe.

"Well, now that you've got me on the line. What did you want to talk about?"

I scratched the back of my head, hesitating. "Eh...well, you could tell me where you'd like to go for dinner tomorrow night." I took a chance, feeling hopeful about her answer. But she didn't respond. The thought of my ask being too bold emerged. But then I pushed the doubt away.

"That's quite bold of you," she said, breaking the daunting silence. "If I didn't know any better, I'd say you *did* ask me out the other night."

"It wasn't on purpose," I admitted. "I really *was* just being nice."

Kacy mhmm'd as if she believed I was lying, then she asked, "Are you familiar with Navajo Bar & Grill?"

"I am. Six o'clock sound good?"

She mhmm'd again.

"Good. Your father still live on Cedar Plank Road?"

"He sure does."

"Good. I'll see you tomorrow then. Goodnight."

"Goodnight."

After I ended the call, I returned the phone to my pocket and continued reading over the files I had spread around my office.

To: Professor Carter (tulsauniversity.carter@gmail.com)

From: Jeremy Saunders (jsaunders1994@gmail.com)

Date: Monday, March 28, 2016 2:22:59 EST

Subject: Re: Re: Re: Re: School Project

You were there that night? I don't believe it. This must be a very touchy subject for you then.

To: Jeremy Saunders (jsaunders1994@gmail.com)

From: Professor Carter (tulsauniversity.carter@gmail.com)

Date: Monday, March 28, 2016 6:21:15 EST

Subject: Re: Re: Re: Re: Re: School Project

Yes, my wife and I both were. And no, it's not a touchy subject, Jeremy. James was a friend of mine, like many others, but it's been thirty years. I've certainly moved on. To get you started, come up with some questions, and I'll be your first interviewee. I'll see if I can reach out to a couple of other people who were there that night and see if we can get you some insight into what happened.

12 · Kacy

WHEN I AWOKE the following morning, I didn't expect to have close to two thousand comments on my YouTube discussion board, wondering where I'd been and why I hadn't posted a new video in nearly two weeks. I was surprised not to have one posted. But between discovering the body at the camp and my father's health scare, it set me back some. Despite my troubles, I needed to put something together fast because I didn't want to start losing subscribers.

It was then that I thought of something crazy—something so outrageous that it might break the Internet. *I'll tell them that I'm going to solve a murder! That'll definitely get them excited. Then they'll be a little more patient for the big reveal. At least, I hope they will be.*

Sliding to the edge of my bed, I fished out my DSLR from my backpack, attached the lens, and turned it on myself—no makeup, bedhead, and all.

Action! "Hey, guys! Kacy here...but sadly not with another amazing place to explore this time." I scratched my head, causing my messy bun to wobble back and forth. "As you can see, I'm still in my PJs, and my hair's a mess, but just ignore how I look right now." I giggled. "I'm recording this because I have a surprise for all of you. An experience like no other. It's about this place in my hometown in Oklahoma. A summer camp." My nose itched, and I scratched at my studded nose ring. "I don't know how to say this, but I'm going to try to solve a murder!" *And scene.*

I jumped from my bed and grabbed my MacBook from the dresser. After powering it on, I pulled the SD card from my camera and put it into the computer's slot. It didn't take but a minute to extract the footage, trim it down in Final Cut and export the clip. Afterward, I made a simple thumb-nail in Photoshop and attached it to the clip, and voilà! The video was ready. All I had to do then was open YouTube and upload it.

Within minutes, the view count skyrocketed. One thou-sand, two thousand, three. As the numbers continued to rise, I couldn't help but fascinate over how many people were actually online at nine a.m. on a Sunday. I expected less. However, that wasn't the case. Regardless, the amount didn't matter as long as my fans knew what I was doing. As I closed the web browser and powered off my computer, my father called out from the kitchen, announcing breakfast was ready.

The aroma of crispy bacon, scrambled eggs, and pancakes wafted down the hall, making its way into my room and up my nostrils. "Coming!" I shouted back, hurriedly tucking the edges of my comforter between the mattress and bed frame, then racing down the hallway into the kitchen to grab a plate.

"Hopefully, you slept well," my father said, placing the last three strips of bacon on a plate and turning off the gas burner.

"I could've used one more hour." I rubbed the dried crust from the corners of my eyes, then sat at the dinette.

With two plates in hand, he joined me. I could sense him watching me with a guilty stare as I drenched my pancakes in syrup, grabbed the utensils, and carved away. I was hungry. What could I say? There was no need to talk; just eat. And that was what I did until he decided to speak on a sensitive subject.

"You know it's been a week already since you've been back, and we still haven't spoken about—"

"Don't," I interrupted, my mouth full of syrupy fluff. "There's nothing else to talk about."

He shot me a worried look. "Kacy, I know you saw the camera in your dresser. I had left it there just for you, in case you ever came back."

I froze; I'd stopped chewing too.

"I didn't get rid of *everything*," he admitted. "I just want you to know that."

"What is it that you want from me?"

"I just want you to forgive me, Kacy, that's all. I'd like things between us to be okay, so we can return to the way things used to be. You know, like how we used to go fishing, shooting, piece together puzzles, and—"

"Live as a family," I finished. "Well, you should've thought about that before you killed Mom."

I slammed my fork on the table, shot up from the chair,

and stormed off to my bedroom. I didn't want to leave my half-eaten plate behind, but I also didn't want to discuss the subject with my father. And didn't ever plan to.

I held my head low as I sat on the edge of my bed, my stomach in knots. I knew it was only a matter of time before my father would bring up the past again. I dwelled on how harsh my words toward him were. They had to be, or else he wouldn't understand how I felt. I assumed he thought I was angrier with him than ever before, but that wasn't the case. I just didn't want him bringing up old feelings. He didn't deserve all the blame, though. If I hadn't returned home in the first place, he wouldn't have had the chance to try to reconcile our relationship. However, the guilt of not coming back to check on him would have haunted me until the end of time.

I dropped to my knees before my dresser and retrieved my old camera. My emotions were awash with sorrow. "I miss you so much, Mom. I'm sorry I couldn't protect you." As I closed my eyes, I rolled to my side and curled into a ball, attempting to picture us together one last time.

———

After I'd gotten dressed and was all set to go to the library for some research, the slam of the front door echoed through the house. It was two hours after breakfast. I hurried to my bedroom window and spotted my father approaching the F-150. Not wanting him to leave without me, I slipped on my shoes and bolted out the front door to catch up with him in the driveway.

I was reluctant to ask him for a ride, knowing we hadn't

spoken since breakfast, but I saw no other way to get to the library unless I were to spend money on a private car. However, I knew better than to pass up a chance to save some cash. So I just had to endure his unrelenting pleas for forgiveness if I were going to hitch a ride. When I sprinted off the front porch, my father spotted me, and he lowered the window as I approached the vehicle.

"You mind dropping me off at the library on the way?" I asked. After all these years of me being gone, I highly doubted he'd say no. He wouldn't dare miss a second chance at trying to get an acceptance of an apology out of me.

"Not a problem. Hop in," he said, just as I had predicted.

We were only a mile from the house and two stop lights in when he asked, "So, what's at the library that you can't find online?"

When he asked, I was two levels deep in a mind game on my cell phone. "I'm looking for some local history. A yearbook, to be specific."

The truck turned left at the light, causing my body to sway right.

"Is this for one of your videos or something?"

I paused the game and turned to him. "It is now. I'm researching the Camp Mercy suicide because I believe it's related to the murder of the guy I found."

"You really think some kid's suicide is related to a murder?" His eyes didn't budge from the road.

"There are so many forums online that say James didn't kill himself, Dad—that it was murder. And I believe it."

Before I knew it, the Ford eased to a stop in front of Tulsa City-County Library.

My father turned to me, resting his elbow on the steering wheel. "It's been thirty years, Kacy. If there *was* a killer, they'd surely be long gone by now."

"I know, I know. But that doesn't mean I can't look into the case. If anything, it'll help me come up with an idea for another video since the police confiscated my footage." I opened the door, stepped out, and turned back as he lowered the window. "Don't worry about picking me up. I've got a ride already." I lied. I didn't have a ride. Hadn't thought that far ahead. I focused more on finding out as much as possible about the case. Hitching a ride home was the least of my worries.

"Gotcha," he said.

Then he drove off down the block, disappearing behind a building after taking a right at a stop sign. Once he was out of sight, I headed toward the entrance. It was time to get to work. Opening the large double doors, I walked into the library and approached the help desk. "Excuse me?" I said to the elderly man who was fighting with something just below the counter. "Where can I find old yearbooks?"

The man rose and said, "Say again?" His hand was cupped around his ear as if he were hard of hearing.

I repeated my question.

"Ah, yes. Follow me. I'll take you to 'em." With his back hunched, he shuffled across the room as I followed. We walked past numerous bookshelves, turning left down a narrow corridor until we finally arrived at a door situated at the end of the hall. On it, a plaque read: COLLEGE AND UNIVERSITY ARCHIVES.

I thought to comment, seeing the title of the room. But instead, I waited to see what I'd find inside. He opened the door, showcasing three ceiling-high shelves, all stuffed with various-sized books. The room was tiny, as small as a janitor's closet—a place where people with claustrophobia wouldn't go. I gawked at the copious volumes from every school in the area, from universities to high schools.

"You should find everything you need here, all in alphabetical order," the old man said. "If, for whatever reason, you *can't* find what you're looking for, then most likely it's because we don't have it."

I ran my hand along a dusty shelf, then turned to the man. "Thank you for helping me. I appreciate it."

He grinned, his teeth yellow and crooked. "Anything for someone looking to broaden their horizons."

I smiled.

"Well, I'll leave you to it." He closed the door, leaving me by my lonesome. Upon his disappearance, I turned and scratched my head. I didn't know where to begin. But I knew I had to start somewhere. I first searched for the "M" section in Memorial High. My gaze fell to the shelf on my left, scanning it only to realize the bottom row ended with the letter "G". Then I skimmed through the books on the middle shelf opposite the door.

I dropped to my knees, sat cross-legged, and examined the bottom two rows. After running my finger along the collection of volumes, I stopped at a thin black hardback book with gold-foiled writing on its spine. It read: MEMORIAL HIGH SCHOOL YEARBOOK 1986.

Bingo.

I slid out the book and carefully opened it, its spine letting out a squeak. Despite the tinged pages and dust and grime that had accumulated in the crevices over the years, the book remained intact. Every page was. And that was all that mattered. I set the book aside, fished out my cell phone, and tapped on Eloise's contact. The phone rang through its cycle, ending at her voicemail box.

I tried again, and yet, I received the same result. So instead, I left a message. "Hey Eloise, it's Kacy. You're probably in church, sleeping, or whatever else you do on Sundays. I'm at the library right now, and I found the yearbook. So if you can, hopefully within the next thirty minutes, maybe come by, and we can go through it."

I ended the call and decided to wait, hoping she'd hit me back within a few minutes. However, after a few minutes with no response, I rang her again. And yet again, she didn't answer.

So much for getting a ride.

I slid across the floor and pressed my back against the right bookshelf. Opening the yearbook again, I skimmed through it until I stumbled upon a picture of Eloise. *Carpenter's her last name. Huh? She really lucked out on marrying someone with a similar name.*

Then I skimmed further, finding her husband, Charles, a few rows down. After a few more pages, I finally reached the end of the book. Turning back to the first page, I started over again. However, I only made it five pages this time before something caught my eye.

I tucked my hair behind my ear and looked again. I'd found my mother in one of the community group pictures. I searched for her name under the senior section, discovering she and my father were positioned beside each other. Her smile brought a sense of warmth to my heart, the memory of it resting heavily on my soul. I kissed my finger and pressed it against my mother's picture. *I miss you so much, Mom.*

Three minutes slipped by as I sat there, my finger still pressed to the page, sniffling. I couldn't seem to pull away, as if something had a hold on me. I had my time to grieve, but clearly, it wasn't enough. All those years had passed, yet it felt like it had happened yesterday.

I drew in a breath and closed the book. It was time to head home. I couldn't spend any more time dwelling on the past because I wasn't at the library for that reason. I retrieved my phone again and tried Eloise one last time. But to no avail; it was the same result. *Looks like I better start walking.*

Using the shelf as a prop, I pushed myself up from the floor. My backpack's zipper clacked against the metal shelving as I rose. I went to put the yearbook back but then had a second thought. Leaving it behind would only complicate matters since I had no idea how much free time Eloise had to meet with me here. And unfortunately, checking the book out wasn't an option since archived books were considered relics. So, I resorted to my usual course of action—breaking the rules.

I slipped the yearbook into my backpack and slid out of the room, down the narrow hall, and past the help desk, waving goodbye to the elderly gentleman as a kind gesture. Then I walked out of the entrance and headed home in the simmering heat, wondering when Eloise would call me back.

13 · Robert

Never did I think that I would find myself working on a Sunday. Sure, there were times when I conducted some research over the weekend from home, but being on the clock was never a part of the plan. Once I arrived at my office, I hastily gathered the notes I'd taken the night before, along with some pictures of James, and stuffed them into a manila folder to bring with me on my visit to the Edlin family estate.

I'd had no problem locating James' parents. Luckily, there was only one Edlin in the DPS (Department of Public Safety) database, where I found their address. Upon contacting them before leaving the precinct, I was concerned they'd not want to discuss the past, it having been thirty years since their son was last spoken of. However, when Mrs. Edlin said, "Thank God, you're looking into my son's case again. I thought we'd never get justice for him," I was taken aback.

I hadn't expected James' parents to still be so eager to find the truth after all these years. I believed they would have eventually lost hope and accepted the fact that their son was gone. Perhaps they were the ones back then who created the rumors of his apparent suicide being a lie—a cover-up, even.

I'd done my research, looking into any online buzz I could find about the event that took place in 1986. Much of it was complete nonsense, such as people saying James' death had been the result of aliens or the many slaughtered Aboriginals from the Osage Murders seeking vengeance from beyond the grave. Nonetheless, when I pulled into their neighborhood, I pushed the meandering thoughts away and prepared to talk business.

When I arrived at their address, I noticed three people sitting on the front porch. The older couple was engrossed in a conversation with the younger woman, who looked remarkably like James. I hesitated for a moment, unsure if I had the correct address or if I should even interrupt their family time. Perhaps the younger woman was James' sister. Yet, there was no trace of it in the DPS database.

"Good morning," I said, stepping out of my cruiser. "I apologize for the intrusion on this wonderful Sunday." I closed the door and headed up the driveway.

"It's not a problem whatsoever, Detective," Mrs. Edlin said. "We're just happy someone is looking back into my boy's case."

I extended a hand as I approached, greeting Mr. and Mrs. Edlin, and then—

"Hi," the younger woman said as I shook her hand. "I'm Doris, James' sister."

I had guessed right. Mrs. Edlin must have called her daughter following our conversation on the phone. Which meant Doris must have lived nearby. And from the looks of the ring on her finger, I could conclude she was married, which explained her absence from the database.

The Edlin family welcomed me into their home, offered tea and coffee, then asked me to join them in the living area. Catching a whiff of the lingering aroma of cinnamon wafting from the kitchen, I took them up on the coffee. That, coupled with hazelnut creamer, and the coffee topped what I'd had earlier at the precinct by far.

"So, I'm here because I have reason to believe your son's case was unjustified and might have ties to a more recent one," I said as I sat on their loveseat across from them.

"What's the more recent case?" Mr. Edlin asked.

"I'm sorry, but I can't disclose much on that. Just know it involves Camp Mercy and one of James' peers."

Mr. Edlin's hopeful look turned to an understanding one.

I took a sip from the mug they had given me, dwelling on how to start. My gaze shifted to Doris. If I had known she existed, I would have jotted down some questions for her as well, but with it being last minute, I only managed to conjure up one off the bat.

"If you don't mind, Doris, I'd like to speak with you first."

Doris nodded, and I continued.

"Are you older than your brother or younger?"

"Older."

"By how much?"

"Two years."

"Did you ever notice anything strange with James? Like, did he ever act depressed or down and out?"

"No. From what I can remember, he was the happiest boy I knew."

"What fifteen-year-old boy wouldn't be?" As I placed the manila folder on the coffee table and took another sip from my mug, I continued with my next question. "Did you attend the camp that summer alongside your brother?"

"Unfortunately, no." Doris' gaze shifted toward her parents, her expression emanating a sense of regret. "My parents suggested I get a job at the local grocer that summer. They said it would help build character." She balled her fists as we locked eyes again. "It still haunts me 'til this day. Sometimes I feel like if I was there to protect him, then maybe...just maybe, he'd still be here."

As tears pooled in her eyes, I struggled to relate, knowing I was an only child. However, witnessing her exude such loving emotion over the loss of her sibling tugged at my heartstrings. It was then that I knew Doris might know more about her brother since they were closer in age compared to their parents. But there was the off chance that she and James never confided in one another, never told each other things in confidence, as many siblings did. There was only one way to know for sure, though.

"Doris..." I paused, second-guessing myself. "I assume you looked after James in school occasionally since you mentioned something about wanting to protect him."

"I did," she admitted, drying the tears on her sleeve. "Even broke up a fight once between him and some other kid."

"Would you say he got into fights often or just once in a blue moon?"

Mrs. Edlin interrupted her daughter. "James was a nice boy. Didn't break the rules and didn't badmouth the teacher either—or anyone for that matter. He was innocent. Raised right."

"Duly noted," I said. Then to Doris, I added, "His fighting?"

"I only broke up two of his fights. One on school grounds and the other on a walk home one day."

Hmm. Occasional altercations. Noted.

"These *fights*...were they with the same kid?" I placed the mug down beside the manila folder.

"No. Two different people."

"Detective," Mr. Edlin said, standing from the sofa. "Is there a reason you're interested in these children my boy fought with?"

"I'm just covering all bases, that's all, Mr. Edlin." I leaned forward, sinking my elbows into my knees. "See, James' face was badly beaten when they found him. Even if he'd gotten into a fight with one of the kids, it surely would have been reported to the camp's staff. And if that were the case, then one of the counselors would have kept an eye out for James to ensure he was okay afterward."

I took another sip of my coffee. "However, after looking at the notes the original CI on the case wrote, there's nothing regarding such an incident having happened. This leads me to believe James was beaten to death. Possibly by someone who then covered it up."

Upon hearing my verdict on James' case, each of them began tearing up. They were tears of joy—a feeling of relief that should have been felt thirty years prior. I guess it was better late than never. Regardless, it was settled. I was going to reopen the Camp Mercy case to get justice for James. However, reopening it was only the beginning. There were many more hurdles to overcome if I was going to prove James Edlin's death was murder, let alone that it was somehow related to Charles Carter's.

To: Professor Carter (tulsauniversity.carter@gmail.com)
From: Jeremy Saunders (jsaunders1994@gmail.com)
Date: Tuesday, March 29, 2016 9:22:38 EST
Subject: Re: Re: Re: Re: Re: Re: School Project

That's a great idea! I already did some research over the weekend. If you can remember who else was involved or who might
remember anything from that night, I'd love to pick their brains.
I'll start writing up questions once I get home from class today.

To: Jeremy Saunders (jsaunders1994@gmail.com)
From: Professor Carter (tulsauniversity.carter@gmail.com)
Date: Tuesday, March 29, 2016 6:34:02 EST
Subject: Re: Re: Re: Re: Re: Re: Re: School Project

I'll see what I can do about getting in contact with some of my
old peers. In the meantime, continue with your research. I'll see
you in class tomorrow.

14 · Kacy

IT WAS four-thirty in the afternoon when my cell phone buzzed with a text from Robert.

ROBERT:

Still on for our date tonight?

I had completely forgotten I'd agreed to a night out with him, having been preoccupied with producing content for my YouTube channel and researching the case. However, now I remembered I was set to meet him at six. That gave me ample time to get ready. I replied.

Yes.

I began searching through my dresser for something to wear. And as the sun disappeared below the horizon, the pangs of hunger finally set in. Knowing I'd soon be sharing a quiet evening with Robert over dinner, I saw no reason to snack on anything I might find in the cupboard. So I drew my focus away from my growling stomach, back to figuring out how to explain myself to him without revealing too much about why I'd left so long ago. The weight of those thoughts hung over me like a heavy cloak, casting a shadow over the quiet, still evening.

I was finishing the last touches on my double-dutch braids when the doorbell rang. I wasn't even dressed yet. I glanced at the clock on my nightstand, which read half past five. *Shit! He's early.*

I suppose Robert wasn't early, considering we had planned to be at the restaurant by six o'clock. However, I still wasn't ready. I guessed mulling over how I'd apologize to him had caused me to lose track of time. I looked over my shoulder to find my room a total mess. Clothes were strewn across the floor. I needed to hurry up and get dressed. So, I quickly finished my hair, then desperately searched for a cute outfit through the pile of clothes on the floor. However, when I came up empty-handed, I realized my chest of drawers was my last hope.

I rifled through it frantically, hoping to find something remotely sexy. However, I'd packed nothing for the nightlife scene since I had no intention of going out. And though Robert and I had dated in the past, not having an outfit for the evening didn't resolve my anxiety. It only made the process more challenging. After eventually settling on a pair of light blue jeans and a plain white t-shirt, I examined myself in the mirror above my dresser. But I quickly shook my head.

Then, as I held up another shirt in front of the one I had

on, huffing and puffing away at my indecisiveness, the doorbell rang again. I buried my head in my sweaty palms before finally settling on the next thing I grabbed: a cherry-red ribbed tank top. I rushed out of my room and down the hall, almost tripping over the large area rug in the foyer and face-planting at the front door. Luckily, I'd caught myself on the doorknob before taking the fatal plunge, narrowly avoiding cracking my face against the floor. Upon impact, I probably would have broken my nose, forcing us to spend our evening in the emergency room instead of at a restaurant. Oh, how that would have been a shit show.

After quickly regaining my balance, I went for the doorknob and pulled. The door swung open so fast it blew his hair back. We locked eyes, but mine couldn't help but wander, drifting south toward the rest of his body. He looked like a young George Clooney, yet somehow more attractive and with less gray. And his baby blue eyes made me feel like I was drowning in a pool of water, like at any moment, he'd need to pull me out to administer CPR.

"Wow. You look...amazing," he said. "Not that you didn't the last time we saw each other, but..." He stopped and looked away, scratching the back of his head in embarrassment.

It seemed like he didn't want to risk digging himself into a hole, but to be honest, I wouldn't have minded if he did. I was almost hoping for it just so I could have the opportunity to turn the tables on him. After all, he had nearly drowned me with his captivating gaze.

I crossed my arms and leaned against the doorjamb. "You don't look too bad yourself, Mister." A bit of a lie. He looked phenomenal, and the urge to run my fingers through his freshly trimmed beard was almost overwhelming. But I couldn't let on that I was also fond of him, just as he was of me. So I held back, beaming with a coy smile instead. "But you're early."

He smiled back. "Got done with work sooner than expected. Figured it wasn't a big deal." Then his eyes trailed up and down my body. "You look ready to me."

I smirked. "Well, you're lucky that I am." *Barely.* "Because if I wasn't...oh boy..."

"Well, if you still need some time, then—"

"Nope, not at all. I'm ready," I lied again.

Though I was dressed and ready to go, mentally, I wasn't prepared to explain why I'd broken things off so suddenly. But memories resurfaced as I admired Robert in his snug-fitting khaki slacks and navy blazer. Images of all the good times we'd had together flashed before my eyes, like when we went hiking in the woods and saw a bear to our night at senior prom. Hell, even the time we'd first had sex. He'd been my first. And people never forget their first.

I struggled to snap out of it. *I can't do this with him again. I just can't.*

My life in Maine awaited me. Certainly, I couldn't leave it all behind. Plus, my father. I could never forgive him for what he'd done to my mother, to our family. I couldn't stay here. I couldn't rekindle my relationships. *It's just dinner, that's all,* I thought as I locked the front door and followed him to his car.

Once in the passenger seat, I buckled up, turned to him, and said, "Now, don't get any ideas, alright? We're just catching up, that's all."

He chuckled without bearing a glance.

Oh, God. I had a feeling that might happen. Maybe I shouldn't have said anything. Dammit, Kacy. Why'd you open your big fat mouth?

I regretted what I'd said. But there was nothing I could do about it now. Robert put the car in gear, backed down the driveway, and pulled onto the road.

————

"It's been a long time since I've been on a date," I said, staring at the menu in my hands.

I caught a glimpse of Robert's eyes peeking over his menu. "Long as in a couple of months or…"

I shot him a menacing glare. His curiosity was going to get him killed. However, I wouldn't actually kill him; I'd just stab him with my fork a few times. "Five years, if you must know. But that doesn't matter because it was by choice. My career was of greater importance."

As I perused the menu, trying to decide on an entree, my father suddenly appeared at our table, catching me off guard.

"Ah, look at you, out on a date," he said. "Well, I'll be damned."

I rolled my eyes. "Dad, please."

"Well, if it ain't the man himself," Robert said, turning to my father.

I had no clue when they had last seen each other. But you'd think they had remained friends way after I'd left with how they greeted each other. Hopefully, that wasn't the case because it would only make moving on much harder. "Looks to me like you guys still keep in touch." I tried to play it off.

"Eh...not as much as you think," my father admitted.

"If anything, we see each other less now compared to when I was a rookie on the force," Robert added.

My father rested his hand on Robert's shoulder. "That's right. I used to see him about every week or so when I first got this place up and running with all the people causing trouble and whatnot. But enough about that; what can I get you two?"

I glanced back down at the menu. There were so many options to pick from. The Poyha I'd had the day I'd arrived in town was out of this world, so getting it again wouldn't be a mistake. However, I wanted to try something different. "I'll get the Navajo Burger."

Robert chose the same thing. Perhaps he didn't want to venture too far into Native American cuisines or wanted to eat light. Whatever the reason, I quickly got back to the matter at hand. And that was keeping him talking, so I wouldn't have to.

"So, how's work?" I asked after my father left with our orders.

Robert exhaled. "I asked you out so we could catch up, not talk about work."

"But talking about what you do for a living *is* a part of catching up, wouldn't you say?"

He shrugged. "I guess you're right."

From there, he talked, and I listened. He broke down every little detail of what he did after graduation, from managing a fast-food restaurant to being a volunteer fire-fighter to making the outlandish decision to become an officer of the law. "I never thought I'd do it, you know, become a cop. But after almost getting shot one night when some man robbed me, I decided to put my foot down..."

A kid brought our food to the table and the condiments we had requested. I squirted mustard on my plate, and Robert poured ketchup on his.

"...And so, I joined the force. That traumatizing experience changed me. Thinking of all the other people that man had possibly injured or killed struck a chord in me. So, I made a vow. Entered the academy, and now, here I am—stopping crime and making sure people never have to experience what I experienced."

Robert's words made my heart flutter. Hearing who he had grown into and become made me think that if I hadn't left, maybe he wouldn't have become the great man he is today.

"That's deep," I said. "I don't remember you ever being so caring. I guess you have come a long way from that immature teenager you used to be."

Robert took a bite of his burger after dipping it in the mountain of ketchup on his plate. "Don't get me wrong, I still have my moments of fun," he admitted. "But enough about me. How have you been?"

I was reluctant to answer, afraid my nervousness might show in my tone. However, there was no reason not to explain why I had left long ago since he'd opened up to me. It only felt fair. "Well, I've been good, but nowhere near as well as you've been."

He tilted his head to one side and stared at me with concern.

"I mean, I've just had a lot on my plate lately. And you,

coming back into the picture, hasn't made things any easier. From my father's heart attack to Eloise asking me for help, I've just been a—"

He stopped me with a motion of his hand. "Wait! Mrs. Carter asked you for help? With what, exactly?"

Perhaps it was fate or a second chance allowing me to devise a better excuse for why I left. Whatever the reason, I took it. "Well, when I met her in the parking lot yesterday, she seemed pretty upset after you told her to go home. One thing led to another, and now I'm helping her solve her husband's murder."

"Why in the world—"

"Beats me." I waved my hands about. "It's crazy, I know. But I figured there might be a bigger story here. And I'm going to find out what it is."

He smiled as I took a massive bite out of my cheeseburger. With my mouth full, I added, "So if there's any information you can spare, it would mean a lot. And everything I find out, I'll share with you. Deal?"

Robert's gentle smile turned to a grim expression. He shook his head. "No deal. I get that you want to help and all, and that's great, but it's not that easy, Kacy. I took an oath, so involving a civilian in a murder investigation would go against everything I believe in. And even if I *could* rope you into this somehow, I wouldn't."

"And why's that?" I took another bite, landing a sliver of mustard from the patty on the left outer rim of my mouth. I quickly wiped it with my napkin.

"Because if anything bad ever happened to you, I wouldn't be able to forgive myself. So please...stay out of it."

Throughout our date, Roberts's blue eyes had been as

calm as the sea, but at that moment, when he'd told me to "stay out of it," they turned to a rushing storm as his tone clipped. I took a second, feeling mixed about being told what I could and couldn't do. I knew he cared for my safety, but that wasn't enough to stop me. So, I lied, crossing my fingers under the table as I said, "Okay."

15 · Robert

MONDAY WAS A NEW DAY, with new plans to check off the list I'd made the previous day. I was going to question my first witness in the reopened Edlin case. As I strolled down the hallway toward Sheriff Wells' office, a myriad of questions circled in my mind. Questioning someone who was once my superior regarding a case that had been closed thirty years ago was sure to be perceived as random. I doubted he'd remember much about the case, but I hoped talking through it would jog his memory a little.

When I reached his office, I drew in a breath and knocked before opening his door. "Sheriff? You have a minute?" I asked, poking my head inside.

"Ah, Robert, yes!" Sheriff Wells said. "Come on in."

As I entered the room, I found him sitting at his desk, his hands poised over the keyboard of his computer. I shut the door behind me and sat across from him.

As soon as I sat, he added, "I got your message last night. Sounded pretty urgent."

"It is," I said. "Pertains to the Carter case."

His brows raised in wonder. "Well, go on, spill it." His Texas accent came out a little.

"So, I looked at the statement you made thirty years ago in the Edlin case. Says you were hanging out with your girlfriend down by the lake when James was found. You were nowhere near the—"

"So, this is why you wanted to see me?" he interrupted. "What's this have to do with the Carter case?"

I leaned back in the uncomfortable, short-backed chair. "Well, Mrs. Carter believes James, the boy who was hanged, didn't die by suicide but was murdered. She also believes her husband was murdered by the same person who hung James."

"And that's because..."

"He was found at the camp, in the same cabin you, Charles, Victor, and James bunked in. Cabin number two."

"Hmm, I see." Sheriff Wells sank his head as he tapped his finger against the tabletop. Then he gazed out of his office window onto the rest of the precinct. "Well, that is quite the coincidence, ain't it?" He turned to face me.

I leaned forward, resting my elbows on my knees, and clasped my hands together. "Sure is. But that's why I'm here. So, it'd be greatly appreciated if you don't mind recounting the events leading up to the body being found. And I know it's been thirty years, so take your time. I'm in no rush."

"I don't know how much I can remember from that night," Sheriff Wells said, the lingering stench of tobacco on his breath slipping between his yellowed teeth. "Hell, I don't have much more to say besides what I said in my statement back then, but I'll try my best." He smiled.

I pulled out my notepad and pen and prepared to write. "How well would you say you knew James Edlin?"

"Well, we went to school together," Blake admitted. "We were in the same grade. Might have even shared a class or two."

I began writing as he continued.

"I don't remember exactly which."

"Well, tell me what you do remember," I said.

Sheriff Wells scratched at his bald head, the light from above reflecting off his scalp. "From what I can remember, it was a normal day much like today. We did activities, had burgers and dogs for lunch, and, well, nothing really happened that day besides..." He paused for a moment as if he was thinking of what to say. "Wait, I remember. There was a fight that night in the main cabin, where we gathered for supper. You know, before James was found. I remember pulling my friend off the kid. As a matter of fact, he was fighting James."

My eyes shot up from my notepad. "And who is this *friend* of yours?"

"I suspect you already know of him. He was one of the guys Reynolds spoke to when Charles first went missing. He was the one who found James, if I'm not mistaken. Name's Griffen Houser."

"Got it. I guess I'll reach out to him next, then." I stood and headed for the door. However, as I reached for the knob, I remembered something. I doubled back. "Speaking of already knowing people, why'd you neglect to mention to

Reynolds that you knew Charles prior to his disappearance? It wasn't in any of the notes from the other detective."

The sheriff shrugged. "Hell, I don't know. It probably never came up in conversation. That's not really a question you ask when it comes to a missing persons case. Now go on, get! I got work to do."

I left his office and went on with my work.

16 · Kacy

WHEN I WALKED into the police station Monday morning at eight, I expected to speak with only one person: Sheriff Wells. Not anyone else. However, upon my arrival, I was told he was in a meeting by the woman at the front counter. Could that meeting have been with Robert? I didn't know. Regardless, I was determined to speak with someone who was there the night of James Edlin's death.

Eloise told me she wouldn't be available to discuss the case until after five o'clock because that was when she got off work. But then I thought, why not go to her job and discuss the matter there? I knew intruding like that was a bad idea, but I was feeling impatient that morning. So, I barged out of the station, returned to my father's truck, and headed toward the food mart up the street. She was the store manager there.

The look she gave me when I walked through those sliding glass doors was pure rage. "I'm sorry to bother you,

Eloise," I said, approaching her and one of her coworkers mid-conversation, "But we need to talk."

"I'll show you how later," she told the young man she spoke with. Then to me, she added, "I told you I'm busy, Kacy. I can't be bothered with this right now."

She wrote something on her clipboard while her gaze was fixed on the canned goods. How she silently counted each shelf made me believe she was taking inventory.

I grabbed the sleeve of her shirt and pulled her aside. "I know you said not to, but the sheriff isn't available at the moment, and I have no other leads, so—"

"And you didn't think to sit and wait for him until he was?"

I slid my bag off my back and fished out the yearbook. "I can't, Eloise. My father will be heading to work soon, so he'll need the truck. Camp Mercy is my latest project. But with all that's transpired over the last week, I sort of need to help *you* in order to help myself."

She rested her hand on my shoulder. "Dear, I've been waiting for three months to hear something about my husband. I think I can manage to wait a few more hours to—"

"Here me out," I interrupted. "I borrowed the yearbook from the library yesterday. All I need from you are the names of everyone who bunked with your husband. That's all." I held out the book. "Then I'll get out of your hair. What do you say?"

She stood there with her hands on her hips, glaring at me while the clipboard she held dangled by a thread. It was clear she thought I wouldn't stop pestering her until she helped me. For a moment, I even believed it myself. But then her expression shifted to one of determination. As the store manager, she had the power to do as she pleased, including taking a few minutes to assist me.

I couldn't understand why she hesitated to help me find out what had happened to her husband. It made me wonder if *she* was somehow involved in his disappearance, but that theory didn't make any sense since she'd asked for my help in finding his killer. Before I knew it, Eloise snatched the yearbook from my hand and stormed down the aisle. I followed her without hesitation.

I sincerely cared about helping her find justice for her husband. However, I also wanted to find the truth for my fans. That was the only reason why I urged her to help me. We walked past the chilled produce as we traveled to the other end of the store. Then we went down a dimly lit hallway, past the bathrooms, and through a door labeled: STORE MANAGER.

Eloise sat at her desk and turned to me. "I hope you have a pen and pad handy because I plan to be quick."

I was skeptical of her recollection skills, considering she wasn't a detective, and it wasn't the 1980s anymore. It was hard to believe that she could remember details that well. Despite my doubts, I took out my phone and turned on the camera, ready to capture pictures of the people and their names as she pointed them out to me. This way, I could research them when I got back home.

Eloise quickly flipped open the book and skimmed through the pages, running her fingers along each face with impressive speed, almost like a high-speed printer. I had expected it to take longer, perhaps due to her age or eyesight, but I was sadly mistaken. In just two minutes, she had identified the last name of the ginger boy who she believed had discovered James thirty years ago that fateful night.

"Houser. That's Griffen's last name."

"Great!" I exclaimed.

I snapped a picture of him. Then Eloise continued her search. Shortly after, she pointed out Sheriff Wells in one of the community group photos.

"This is what the sheriff looked like at fifteen," she said, pressing her finger to the page.

He was in his football jersey. "He looks handsome," I said, examining his cute, babylike face.

Eloise scoffed. "You should see him now. He's really let himself go. Didn't make it in football, so instead, he went into criminal justice." She turned to the next page. Then suddenly, she stopped and began sniffling.

I leaned in over her shoulder in search of the reason, to find her running her thumb along a picture of her husband in another community group photo. I rested my hand on her shoulder. "We're going to find who did this to him. And we're going to make them pay." My hand remained on her shoulder until she eventually stopped sobbing.

Eloise wiped her tears on her collar. "I sure hope so."

"Don't allow the grief to burden you," I whispered in her ear. "We *will* find out who did this to him, I promise." Those kind words, followed by a gentle pat on the shoulder, got her moving again. It didn't take but another minute more before she identified another person who was there that night.

"This is the last guy. Name's Victor Pines."

I examined the picture of the boy. His slicked-back, dark

brown hair and boney face said it all. He looked like Fonzie from *Happy Days*.

"So, there were only four of them bunking together?"

"Yes. And since Charles and James are dead, there are only two left you can talk to. Victor and Sheriff Wells."

"And Griffen," I added.

"But that's if any of them remember anything from that long ago, let alone that night."

Eloise was right. Regardless of how much I wanted to find the truth, wait—how much we wanted to find the truth—it came down to whether the Sheriff, Victor, and Griffen could remember what happened back then. I snapped a picture of Victor in the yearbook, closed it, and returned it to my backpack.

Eloise stood from her chair. "Hopefully, you won't need to show up at my place of work again."

I zipped up my backpack and draped it over my shoulder. "Don't worry. It won't happen again." I followed her out of her office. "And if you want to ensure it won't happen again, you could take off work for the next couple of days," I suggested.

"I'll think about it."

Eloise slipped her hands into the cozy pockets of her sleek black trousers and led me out of the grocery store. Upon reaching my father's truck, I unlocked it and turned to find her bidding me farewell with a graceful wave. In return, I waved back before sliding into the driver's seat and firing up the engine. With the air conditioning on full blast, I drove home.

To: Professor Carter (tulsauniversity.carter@gmail.com)
From: Jeremy Saunders (jsaunders1994@gmail.com)
Date: Wednesday, March 30, 2016 2:45:51 EST
Subject: Another Question

Dear Professor,
The lecture you gave today was great. It wasn't too drawn out. I don't think any of my classmates even fell asleep. Regardless, I forgot to ask after class... did you have any luck reaching out to the others who were there when James killed himself?

To: Jeremy Saunders (jsaunders1994@gmail.com)
From: Professor Carter (tulsauniversity.carter@gmail.com)
Date: Wednesday, March 30, 2016 5:58:21 EST
Subject: Re: Another Question

Dear Jeremy,
Yes. I managed to get in contact with Blake Wells, the sheriff. He and his girlfriend—now wife—were there. He reminded me of the names of the others. Unfortunately, I couldn't get in contact with one of them, but he gave me a number for the guy who found James. His name's Griffen Houser.

17 · Kacy

A QUICK GOOGLE search of anyone's name can yield a plethora of results. Griffen's was the first name I looked up. Within a half hour, I had three addresses listed in Oklahoma under that name. *God, do I love the Internet.*

I powered down my MacBook, slipped on my shoes, and headed for the front door. I was prepared to meet the guy who had discovered James' body when my father stopped me in the foyer.

"I hope you plan on being home by ten," he said. "You know I need the truck for work." He was laid back in his God-awful orange suede recliner, watching TV.

I walked into the living area and came up beside him. "C'mon, Dad. You shouldn't even be working. The doctor ordered you to take it easy."

He used the remote control to mute the TV. "The restaurant isn't going to run itself, Kacy. I need to be there regardless of how I feel."

Frustration weighed heavily on my shoulders, causing them to slump in defeat. I was beginning to think my father had burned the candle at both ends, which ultimately led to his heart attack. I knew arguing with a man determined to run himself into the ground was pointless. There was no need to dispel any more of my energy. "I guess now we know what caused your heart attack."

"What do you mean?"

"Exactly what I said. You ran yourself into the ground. And now, based on your eagerness to return to work, you'll most likely do it again. There's no point arguing about it anymore. Is there any way I can drop you off at the restaurant instead, so I can use the truck for a little while longer?"

"Fine. Where do they live?"

What am I, sixteen? I'm grown! "That's the thing...I don't know exactly. I'm actually looking for someone who, I believe, lives in Flint. But I don't know for sure. They could live closer, in—"

"Does this person know you're coming?"

"Dad, it's too much to explain right now. It was just a simple yes or no question. Can I please borrow the truck again?" He stared at me blankly. I knew I was wrong for not explaining why I needed the truck. It was his vehicle, but maybe what I said had struck a chord within him.

A moment of reflection later, he stood, his knees cracking as he rose. "Kacy, if you really need to borrow the truck again to go look for someone who might not even be where you think they are, then by all means, go ahead. I can't stop you. Even if I didn't allow you to borrow the truck, you'd find another way to get there. You always did."

He rested his hand on my shoulder. "All I ask is that you be careful, okay?"

I couldn't help but smile. "Thanks, Dad. I will be. Now, let's get you to work."

My mind raced with the need to locate Griffen or anyone who might be willing to divulge information regarding the case. Time was of the essence, for the sooner I found the truth, the sooner I could send shockwaves through the Internet with such a newsworthy video. And from there, I could return home to Maine.

I left the house and got in the Ford as my father put on his shoes. After dropping him off at the restaurant, I headed toward the gas station to fuel up, then I set out to find Griffen.

————

The seventy-five-mile trip was further than I had wanted to drive, but I needed to be behind the wheel to find Griffen Houser. Luckily, one of the addresses was right on the way to Flint. So, after twenty minutes, I shot off the freeway and swung by that location first.

When I arrived at the residence and parked by the ditch out front, I wasn't expecting to find anyone around, given the time of day since most people worked conventional jobs. However, to my surprise, there was a short woman outside, loading something into the trunk of her SUV.

I opened the driver-side door and stepped out. "Excuse me," I said as I approached. "I'm sorry to bother you." The woman turned sort of abruptly as if I had startled her. A random person coming up behind me would have scared me too.

"Yes, miss?" the woman said, brushing her long brown hair out of her face.

I didn't want to steal any more time from the woman, especially after noticing a child strapped in a booster seat in the back of her vehicle, so I said, "Does a Griffen Houser live here?"

The woman hesitated for a second. Her facial expression went from puzzled to worried. "Are you the police? Is my husband okay?"

Police? Do I really look like a cop? I was wearing jeans and a collared shirt. Perhaps she believed I was undercover, but still. "Eh...I'm not police," I admitted. "I've just got a few questions for your husband about his time at Camp Mercy."

"Camp what?"

"Camp Mercy," I repeated. "The abandoned summer camp just down the road there." I pointed back over my shoulder in the general direction of where I believed the camp was located.

The woman reached for another bag on the ground and loaded it into the trunk. "I don't know anything about a Camp Mercy, miss. My husband and I just moved here a year ago."

A year ago? I must have the wrong person.

I fished out my cell phone, quickly pulling up the image of Griffen to show to the woman. "Is this your husband?" I tilted the phone so she could get a good look at him.

The woman squinted, cupping her hand around the screen to deflect the beaming sun. "That's not him."

I did have the wrong person. At least now, I could check

this address off the list, leaving only two remaining. Hopefully, the Griffen in Flint was the guy I'd been searching for.

"Sorry to bother you, ma'am. You enjoy the rest of your day." I turned and walked back to my father's truck.

Getting back onto the freeway was easy. However, dealing with the idiot drivers that traveled it was another story. Traffic wasn't too heavy, thank God. If I had taken the drive on the weekend, it probably would have taken me even longer, but luckily, I made it to Flint within forty minutes of leaving the first address.

The second location reeked of sketchiness, and I immediately went on high alert. The mailbox near the road dangled precariously from its post as if it had been viciously struck by a vehicle and crudely hammered back into place by its negligent owner. It was evident that delivering mail was not a priority for them. And the not-so-well-maintained gravel road that curved to the left and disappeared behind some brush made me think the place resembled the setting of a horror movie.

Why didn't I check Google Maps before I left?

When I finally mustered up enough courage to drive down the length of the property, I found something far from a pretty house at the end of the road. It was a rusty, doublewide trailer stationed on a few cinderblocks, the surrounding land looking damn near the size of a four-acre lot with a forest of trees surrounding it. God, did I wish I had a gun to protect myself with. There was no telling what went on out here in the boonies. Nevertheless, I took a deep breath, pulled the key from the ignition, and opened the driver-side door.

Bang!

A gunshot startled me, sending me falling on my ass right as I stepped out of the truck. My heart almost exploded out of my chest. Someone had shot at the road in front of me. If I had been standing two feet to the left, I would have been no good—ankle shot, body on the ground, pleading for help. I would have been a sitting duck, for sure. Then another shot rang out, but this one struck my father's truck, shooting out the driver-side headlight.

"Don't shoot!" I yelled as I threw my palms to the sky. "I'm unarmed!"

I examined the trailer, searching for any sign of where the shooter might be, my body riddled with anxiety in fear I might catch a bullet between the eyes. But I persevered. Another shot came at me, blowing right past my face. But I didn't budge.

"I'm looking for a man named Griffen Houser," I shouted.

"What do you want with Griffen?" a hillbilly voice shouted back from somewhere I still couldn't identify.

I've got to choose my words wisely. Don't want to say the wrong thing, or else I'm a goner. "He's not in any trouble. I...I just want to ask him a few questions about..." *I shouldn't say.* "I just want to ask him a few questions."

My fate rested entirely in the hands of God now. Having already stated my purpose, if the person on the opposite end of that gun wanted to silence me, it would surely be my last day on Earth. Fortunately, the shooter emerged from the shadows with his rifle pointed at the ground in a sign of surrender. As I lowered my hands, I exhaled in relief.

"Sorry 'bout that, miss," the man said. "Not too many

people come 'round here. So, I always send off a couple warning shots."

I took a few steps toward him. "You must be Griffen."

I said it like I was unsure but knew it was him. Despite the long goatee and sunburnt freckles that bore his cheeks, he looked the same as his high school picture.

The man nodded. "I am. What's this 'bout?"

"Well, my name is Kacy, and I'm a student at the University of Oklahoma. How're you doing today?"

His menacing stare was daunting. I was taken aback by his lack of a response to my courteousness. However, I wasn't offended. The whole thing about me being a student was a lie. Hopefully, he bought it.

"You think we can go inside? It's kind of hot out here," I suggested.

Griffen wiped the sweat from his forehead and spat whatever was in his mouth onto the yellow grass. It was probably chewing tobacco. Whatever it was, it was undoubtedly gross.

"Not a chance in hell," he said.

"Well, can I speak with you on the porch? You know, so we can get out of the sun?"

Griffen mumbled something as he turned and headed up the porch steps and inside his house. As I climbed the creaky steps, I overheard some noises coming from inside his place as he opened the door and disappeared into the shadows. It wasn't music or kids running about but a constant buzzing sound. Perhaps he had multiple circular fans spread about the inside of his place.

I awkwardly stood beside the entrance as he shuffled around inside. I peered in through the screen door, discovering six circular fans, all going simultaneously. I was right. He did have fans. Maybe going inside wasn't such a good idea after all. The constant buzzing made it hard for me to hear my thoughts. And I was outside. I couldn't imagine what it would be like inside his trailer.

I set my backpack down, fished out my camera, and began piecing it together as he came back outside. "You mind if I record this?" I asked.

He sat in his rocking chair. "You still haven't told me what this is 'bout."

I tapped the record button and set the camera beside me, then aimed it toward his lower half, preventing his face from being seen. "I'm doing a summer school project on the different people of Oklahoma."

He nodded, like he understood, but still carried a look of curiosity as if he wondered why I'd want to speak with him of all people.

Action! "So, what is your name, sir?" I sat and crossed my legs.

He cracked open a can of beer he must have grabbed from the refrigerator inside. The can fizzed for a second before he answered. "Name's Griffen Houser."

I typed his answer in on the notes app on my phone, giving the illusion that the camera was off. "And what high school did you go to?"

"Memorial High."

"Would you say you had a pretty decent childhood growing up?"

He nodded.

"So, that's a yes," I said as I typed into my phone,

knowing the camera couldn't see his face. "Were there any great experiences from your teenage years?"

He took a swig. "Besides losing my virginity at prom, no." The way he smiled at me after making such a comment gave me the notion he'd taken a liking to me.

I smiled back, not wanting to be rude. However, inside, I was disgusted, not because he was ugly, but because of his lack of hygiene. His face looked as if he had layers of dirt and soot caked on his skin. It was possible he hadn't showered in days. I couldn't tell if the putrid odor that lingered about his home was coming from him or whatever was inside his trailer. Regardless, I was all alone, far from civilization. If Griffen were to try and take advantage of my innocence, thinking I was just like every other woman, he'd surely have another thing coming. For if he were to make a move on me, I'd reach in my bag and pull out a can of pepper spray, dousing his face in the burning liquid.

But as he didn't budge from his rocking chair, not acting on what I believed was his temptation, I typed his answer in my notes and moved on to the next question. "Were there any *bad* experiences from your teenage years?" This was it. I had asked the question I'd come all the way out to Flint to ask. Hopefully, he'd mention Camp Mercy in his answer.

Griffen gulped down the beer in his mouth and shot me a look. "What are these questions for, exactly?"

I don't know if my question had rubbed him the wrong way or if he was just curious. He didn't seem as willing to answer that question for whatever reason. Feeling worried I'd lose my chance, I saw no reason not to come clean.

"I'm studying the hanging at Camp Mercy," I admitted. At that moment, I knew he wasn't going to say anymore.

The way he glared at me and squeezed the beer can in his hands so tight that it crumpled told me it was over.

"I think it's time you leave, miss," he said, reaching for his gun beside him.

I grabbed my camera and pleaded, "Please, I just have a few more questions. If you don't mind—"

"Leave!" he yelled. "Get on and don't come back."

I jumped and skidded off the porch, my bag hanging halfway off my shoulder. I feared looking back as I headed toward the pickup, thinking Griffen would be staring me down through the sight of his rifle. So, I didn't turn around until I touched the door of the Ford and opened it. And when I did, he was just staring at me in an awkward silence.

What is he hiding?

18 · Kacy

GRIFFEN WAS A DEAD END. But at least I found out where he lived and where I could find him again. There was no doubt in my mind he refused to talk about James, given the swift ejection from his property after mentioning Camp Mercy. The question remained: did he kill Charles Carter? If so, why did he let me leave alive? Perhaps he thought someone knew where I was. And that if anything happened to me, he'd be the prime suspect. I couldn't imagine him wanting more blood on his hands if that were the case.

As I drove home, my thoughts were consumed by a barrage of questions, one of which caused my fingers to tremble against the steering wheel. The fear of almost having gotten shot made me shudder. Nonetheless, I'd crossed one person off my list, and that was something. The next name on my list was Sheriff Wells. With that in mind, I charted a course for the police station, determined to seek him out. Afterward, I'd return home and resume my search for any relevant information about Griffen online.

After an hour's worth of traffic on the freeway back to Tulsa, I made it to the station a quarter after noon. I was in such a rush, hoping he'd be available, that when I pulled into the spot, I could quickly tell I had parked on an angle from how close I was to the vehicle on my right. Regardless, I hurried inside. Sadly, Sheriff Wells wasn't available *again*. However, this time, the woman from earlier said he was out for lunch instead of in a meeting, so things were looking up.

As I waited on the bench in the lobby, I felt a twinge of relief, hoping that the sheriff would return soon and give me a few minutes of his time. However, my mind quickly wandered, and I found myself lost in thought. The more I postponed finding the truth, the longer I would be stuck in Tulsa. And the longer I stayed in Tulsa, the more my father would pester me about the past, and the more likely Robert would ask me why I left. I was reluctant to forgive my father, let alone discuss the loss of my mother. I also wasn't prepared to discuss why I'd left with Robert. Even after nine years, the unresolved issues still hung over me like a dark cloud.

"Do you have any idea where I can find him?" I asked the woman politely after returning to the counter.

I believed she could sense the desperation in the tone of my voice. And because of that, I also believed she wouldn't likely release that information to me. I couldn't blame her; if a wide-eyed woman stood before me, asking about the sheriff's whereabouts, I wouldn't provide that person any information either. It'd be too much of a risk. And the next thing you know, there'd be a picture of the sheriff on the news later that afternoon stating he'd been shot and killed by some crazed woman.

"Sorry, but I can't give out that information," she finally answered. "I recommend you try back in an hour. Or if you'd like, you could sit and wait for him...or perhaps even make an appointment?"

I rested my hands on the counter and lowered my head. "Of course. You said that last time." Then, suddenly, my name was called, prompting me to turn around. Robert was standing behind me, looking like a tall and handsome prince.

"What are you doing here?" he asked.

"I came to thank the sheriff for something he did for my father, but of course, he isn't here." I didn't want to lie to Robert, but I had to because I knew he didn't want me digging further into the case.

Robert took a sip of his drink and gulped. "Well, you just missed him. Left no more than"—he glanced at his watch—"ten minutes ago. Went to grab a late lunch at the Seven-Eleven down the road. If you're quick, you might catch him."

I beamed and wrapped him in a bear hug. "Thanks." Then, I dashed out the door, rushing back to the truck and racing out of the parking lot toward the gas station.

———

My heart raced as I arrived at the Seven-Eleven. I parked beside a police cruiser, expecting to find the sheriff in it.

However, the vehicle was empty, which meant he must have still been inside. I got out of the truck and entered the establishment, only to discover the cashier at the front, standing behind the tempered plexiglass that barricaded the counter.

I ran my hand along the assortment of chips and pretzels that lined the shelves as I sauntered down the snack aisle. *Where did you go, Sheriff?*

A screeching noise caught my ear, followed by the foul stench of rotting intestines. I turned to my left to find the sheriff stepping out of the restroom into the next aisle. *God, is he in desperate need of a colon cleanse. Maybe even an enema.*

Eloise was right about one thing: the sheriff had changed. The man who stood before me bore little resemblance to the person I saw in his high school yearbook photo. He was still clean-shaven, except for a mustache that looked like it had been glued to his upper lip, but his head was now completely bald. He'd also put on a considerable amount of weight, most of it settling around his thighs and waist. But despite his physical transformation, I was determined to get some answers from him about James' apparent suicide.

"Excuse me," I said, crossing over to the next aisle, holding my breath as I passed the putrid-smelling restroom.

He stopped and turned to face me. "Why hello, miss. What can I do you for?"

"My name's Kacy. I'm a student at the University of Oklahoma, and I'd like to speak with you about Camp Mercy." I told him the same lie I'd told Griffen. That was my way in. The only difference this time was that I had included the words Camp Mercy to see if it would yield better results.

The sheriff raised a brow. He probably thought that Robert and I were conspiring against him, assuming he and Robert had already spoken about Camp Mercy. Upon my request to speak with Sheriff Wells on the matter, I never would have imagined him saying something as promising as what he went on to say. I assumed he'd say, "I don't have the time," or "You'll find everything you need to know online."

But after he glanced at his watch as if implying I was intruding on his lunch break, he came back with, "Tell you what, dear. Come by the precinct 'round six, and I'll answer all the questions you have. How's that sound?"

"I'll be there."

He nodded, then turned and headed toward the counter to purchase whatever he'd ordered for lunch. Which only made me realize that I, too, had grown hungry. Rubbing at my gurgling stomach, I walked to the heat lamp near the register. Then I slipped on a disposable plastic glove and pulled out two slices of pepperoni pizza. The tiny, triangular-shaped cardboard box was barely big enough to fit both pieces. However, I managed to make it happen.

"I'll see you at six," I said to the sheriff as he walked out the door, but he didn't seem to hear me. He didn't even acknowledge my presence with a nod or a gesture.

It took the cashier waving his hand in front of my face before I finally peeled my attention away from the sheriff. The cashier probably thought something was wrong with me—like I'd gotten lost in oblivion or had the hots for the sheriff—but I didn't care.

"That'll be three ninety-two," the cashier said.

I pulled a five-dollar bill from the wad of cash I carried in my pocket and paid the man. Then I returned to the truck and ate my lunch.

19 · Kacy

For thirty long minutes, I sat in the parking lot, eagerly anticipating the arrival of six o'clock. My eyes remained glued to the dashboard clock in my father's pickup, watching the seconds tick by like molasses. When the time finally arrived, a wave of anxiety washed over me like a tidal wave. My mind was in a daze. Even though I'd gone home and relaxed, I still felt uneasy about everything. And at that moment, I forgot the questions I'd prepared to ask. Regardless, I was still determined to move forward. So, I got out of my father's truck and headed inside.

"Good afternoon," I said to the same woman from earlier, hoping she wouldn't tell me off. "The sheriff said I could come by around six."

She ran her hand along the desk, plucking a yellow sticky note from the pile of paperwork that cluttered it. "Yes, got the note right here."

The woman handed me a visitor's pass to pin to my shirt, then said, "Follow me."

I followed her down the hall, then around a corner, stopping at a door with a gold plate on its face. It read: SHERIFF BLAKE A. WELLS. I was finally going to be able to make some progress. Real progress. All I needed to do now was walk through that door and ask the right questions.

The woman knocked, then opened it, beckoning me through.

"Thank you again for seeing me, Sheriff," I said upon entering.

"Thank you, Sarah," Sheriff Wells said to the woman. Then to me, he added, "Anything for a student." He smiled and motioned for me to take a seat.

Sarah closed the door and left, the clacking of her shoes permeating the hall.

"So, Kacy...when you first approached me, you mentioned something 'bout Camp Mercy. I find it odd that you're still looking into it, being that you're the witness who discovered the body."

I gulped, surprised at the fact he knew who I was. "Eh... you're right! It is odd. But like I said at the gas station, I'm doing a school project on the camp, which explains why I was there in the first place." Feigning a lie as I had left me awash in nervousness. I feared how he'd respond, knowing there was a good chance that he'd read over the statement I'd given.

"Stranger things have happened," he finally said, breaking the daunting silence. "What is it that you'd like to know?"

Knowing he was at the camp that fateful night, I

wanted to ask him what he was doing when Griffen found James. However, doing so would mean revealing information that I knew wasn't readily available online, which would only spark a red flag. So, instead, I said, "I want to put in a request to look at the case files, so I can get better insight into the event that shut that place down."

"Public records requests don't go through me, Kacy."

"Oh, my apologies, Sheriff. I didn't know. I'm still trying to figure out which avenues I can take to help improve my understanding of the matter. I've already exhausted my options at the library, and of course, I didn't get a chance to finish scoping out the camp."

"It's fine," he said, reaching for the phone and dialing a number. "I can direct you to someone who can help you with that."

I had to act quickly if I was going to get the information I sought. "Well, actually...before you do that, by chance, is there anyone I could speak with on the matter? You know, someone who might have been there, perhaps? Maybe I can cite them in my work."

The sheriff returned the phone to the hook and leaned back in his chair, his bulging belly poking out from under the desk. "Well, there is someone."

"Wonderful! Who?"

"Me."

"Really?" My eyes widened as if in surprise.

"Sure was."

I grinned. "I'm definitely going to get bonus points on my project now."

"That's *if* I'm willing to talk," he added.

"Well, are you?"

"I will if you have some questions on hand."

"There's a few that come to mind. But first, do you mind if I record this?" I fished my camera out of my backpack and began to piece it together. "It's just so I can listen back to the information, that's all. If you want, I can aim the camera away so I don't capture your—"

"I do mind, Kacy," he interrupted. "Things such as photographic and audio recording equipment are prohibited on station grounds. I'm sorry, but you gon' have to put that away."

"My apologies," I said, returning my camera to my bag.

Who knew that was a rule? I certainly didn't.

Wondering how to continue from the awkward silence that followed me putting away my camera, I began spewing questions.

"What were you doing at the time James was found?" Just like Griffen, I had to be quite meticulous with my questioning. Any wrong word might spook him, and I didn't want to get kicked out of the station and dismissed by the only person I'd been able to get answers from.

"I was down by the lake with my wife when he—"

"Wife?" I interrupted.

He cleared his throat. "Yes. She was my girlfriend then, but now, she's my wife. Been married twenty-seven years."

At that moment, I had a revelation. There was another person at the camp during the hanging that I could question: Mrs. Wells. However, I believed the odds of discussing the matter with her were not in my favor. But at least now I had someone else to add to the list. Someone Eloise had forgotten about or should have mentioned.

I typed Mrs. Wells in the notes on my cell phone, under

my experience with Griffen, then motioned for the sheriff to continue.

"Like I was saying, we were down by the lake when he was found."

"And who found him?"

"Some kid who was in another bunk. His name was Griffen Houser."

"Would you say you were good friends with James?"

"I'd like to say so. I mean, he was one of my bunkmates, after all."

"So, there were others who experienced the same trauma as you? Bunkmates, I mean." That was my chance to verify all the names involved in the case.

He nodded. "Yes. There were four of us: Charles, Victor, James, and myself."

"And, of course, the boy who found James."

The sheriff shook his head. "No. He was in a different bunk like I said."

Bingo. Everything is coming together with one extra person to add to the list. "Geez, the trauma you four endured—especially at a young age, assuming you were still in high school—must've been horrible."

"It was. But, sweetheart, that's life." He leaned forward, readjusting himself in his chair a little. "Honestly, I believe I got the worst of it, though, being the sheriff's son and all."

Sheriff's son? My eyes narrowed. "Your father was the sheriff back then?"

He mhmm'd. "Taught me everything I know. And I plan on doing the same with my son."

Typing as fast as I could into my phone, I said, "That's sweet."

"There any other questions you have, Kacy?"

My head shot up from the phone in my lap. "Now that you mention it, any chance I can speak with your wife?"

"I don't know if she'll remember a thing from that night, but I'll speak with her and see if she wants to talk. How's that sound?"

"Sounds wonderful!" Then my phone buzzed with a text message from my father.

DAD:

You available? I'm done with work. Come
pick me up.

On my way.

I slipped my cell phone back into my pocket and stood from the uncomfortable chair. "Thank you again for your time, Sheriff. I appreciate it. Unfortunately, my father needs me for something. So, I've got to run." I turned and headed for the door with my backpack in hand. But then I remembered something and doubled back. "One last question—do you happen to know where I can find Victor or Griffen, by any chance? I'd love to hear their sides of the story."

Asking the sheriff if he knew the whereabouts of the two would tell me one thing: whether he'd stayed in contact with either Victor or Griffen. Because, as of right now, the sheriff remembered his bunkmates' names. I might have just been phishing, but I had my reasons to. Anyone on the list of suspects could have done it. Any one of the kids who were stationed at Camp Mercy when James died could have killed both him and Charles Carter.

"Unfortunately, I don't. Sorry."

"It's not a big deal whatsoever. You've given me more than enough to work with. And hopefully, I'll learn a few more things from your wife if she's willing to meet with me."

"Yes, *if* she's willing."

"You enjoy the rest of your evening, Sheriff," I said, holding the door half open.

He nodded. "You too."

Then I left his office and headed to the restaurant to pick up my father.

To: Professor Carter (tulsauniversity.carter@gmail.com)
From: Jeremy Saunders (jsaunders1994@gmail.com)
Date: Thursday, March 31, 2016 7:45:33 EST
Subject: Interviewee

Dear Professor,
I want to thank you again for allowing me to interview you and your wife. It's really helped me gain some insight into what it was like hours before James Edlin's death. Now, all I need to do is question the sheriff and Griffen to see if I can squeeze any more information out of them.

To: Jeremy Saunders (jsaunders1994@gmail.com)
From: Professor Carter (tulsauniversity.carter@gmail.com)
Date: Thursday, March 31, 2016 6:02:52 EST
Subject: Re: Interviewee

Dear Jeremy,
It's no problem, Jeremy. I always make sure my students have the help they need. Based on your eagerness to find out more, I believe your report will be a great example to use for future class projects. Hopefully, you'll allow me to hold onto it after the semester is over.

P.S. I've informed the sheriff and Griffen that you will be reaching out to them to conduct interviews. They shouldn't give you any trouble. If you have any other concerns, don't hesitate to email me.

As I LEFT work to grab dinner, I thought back to all the information I'd gathered on the case. Something still wasn't adding up, and I suspected that Mrs. Carter and Sheriff Wells weren't sharing everything. If the sheriff had been such good friends with Griffen, why would he not have kept in contact with him? As for Mrs. Carter, if she was present the night James was murdered, why hadn't she developed her theory about who had done it long ago? She could have possibly seen someone acting fishy or fidgety after the crime.

Perhaps, if I sat them both down in a room and had them discuss what they remembered from that night, it might shed some light on things. It might even bring up some old feelings. However, I highly doubted either of them would be willing to do such a thing.

I stopped at a traffic light and scratched my beard, mulling over their statements from thirty years ago. Sheriff

Wells and his now-wife were down by the lake staring up at the stars, probably getting intimate like most teenagers, and Mrs. Carter was with Charles in the main cabin alongside a few others, playing Texas Hold 'Em. However, one question had eluded me.

Where was Victor at the time? His statement said he was asleep, but could anyone verify that? Then, another question loomed. Griffen's statement never went into detail about what he was doing in the woods before he came across the body. It was then that I decided that he was next on the list of people to visit. Hopefully, he'd remember something from that day.

I pulled my phone from my pocket and called in a favor.

"You've got Leonard!"

"Hey, Leonard, it's Robert. Need a favor. Two, actually."

"Shoot!"

"Give me everything you have on a Griffen Houser in the state. Spelled H-O-U-S-E-R; address, phone number, and social security too, if you can find it."

"Got it. And the second?"

"Victor Pines. Spelled—"

"No need, Robert," he interrupted. "Should have 'em both to you in a few."

I assumed he would have gone home by now, with it being after six, but from the sound of his urgency, I must have caught him on his way out. I felt glad that I could count on Leonard whenever I needed him.

"That's what I want to hear!" I said. "Call me back when you find it."

"Sure thing, boss."

Then I ended the call.

21 · **Kacy**

WHEN I PULLED into the Navajo Bar & Grill parking lot, I was met with a mountain of regret as my father walked out and almost had another heart attack on the sidewalk.

"What the hell, Kacy?!" he shouted, grabbing his head in shock to what he saw.

I had completely forgotten about the headlight being shot out during my run-in with Griffen. *Dammit. I hope he's not too pissed.*

"What in the world happened?"

I hesitated to answer as my mind raced with possible responses. I didn't want to risk causing my father any stress that might lead to another heart attack, let alone give him a reason to chase down Griffen for damages. However, I couldn't lie to him either.

"I...I got shot at, Dad," I said, stumbling over my words. I couldn't lie to my father. No matter how much I wanted to, I just couldn't.

"What?! Are you okay?"

"Yes. I'm fine."

"Good."

"I'll get the headlight fixed after I solve the—"

"No!" he shouted. "Whatever you're trying to do here involving Camp Mercy, it's over! Done with. I don't want you getting hurt." He snatched the keys from my hand and headed for the driver's seat.

"Just like how Mom and I didn't want *you* to get hurt!" I shot back. "And now she's dead, all because you couldn't stop drinking!"

My father was halfway in his seat when I brought up his biggest mistake ever. And he didn't take it lightly. He slammed the truck door closed, marched up to me, and said, "That's right! I couldn't stop. But now I'm sober!"

Janet came storming out of the restaurant. "What's going on?" She must have overheard the commotion from inside.

"This is none of your concern, Janet," my father said. "Go back inside and tend to the customers."

"Don't speak to her that way!" I yelled, tears bubbling in my eyes.

Janet rushed to my side, probably to prevent me from getting worked up. However, I didn't want to be calm. In the heat of the moment, I wanted to tell my father off. Tell him what was on my mind, why I'd been so distant all these years. Though he already knew the reason, I felt I needed to remind him.

"Don't touch me," I screamed as Janet locked me in a bearish grasp.

"Shhh," she whispered in my ear. "Calm down, Kacy. I

know you're angry. I was, too, some time ago. But your father knows what he did wrong. He's been drowning in that guilt for some time and probably will for the rest of his life."

I tried with all my might to break free but to no avail. I was weak. Even with adrenaline coursing through my veins, I still wasn't strong enough to escape my auntie's grasp. "Let go of me!" I yelled again, tears wetting my cheeks.

"Not until you calm down."

"I am calm!" But I wasn't. I was nowhere remotely close to feeling at ease, but I liked to have believed I was.

My father grabbed Janet's shoulder. "Let her go, Janet. It's okay."

Once Janet released me, I didn't fight my father like I thought I would. The entire time I was in her embrace, I felt like balling my fists and hitting him. I believed that if only I could break free from her grasp, I would beat him senseless like a gorilla for killing my mother. But instead, I hugged him as tears poured from my face, unrelenting like a tropical rainstorm.

"Why didn't you just let her drive that night?" I pled, sensing his heartache, pain, and regret upon our loving embrace.

His tears crashed against my forehead as he answered. "I don't know, dear. I don't know."

22 · Robert

ONE HOUR PASSED before Leonard finally called. I had just left the restaurant where I'd grabbed dinner and was sitting at a stoplight on my way home, patiently waiting for traffic to ease forward.

"Whatcha got?" I asked.

"Found them both. Didn't take long at all."

"Great!"

"I searched for the one thing both names had in common."

"And?"

"Their high school. Memorial High."

Hmm. So, all five suspects attended the same high school. Perhaps James' death was a group effort.

"Griffen's got a rap sheet longer than the Nile. I'm talking aiding and abetting a fugitive, burglary, insurance fraud…" Leonard paused for dramatic effect. "The list goes on and on. I'm surprised this guy's not in prison now, or at least has a warrant out for his arrest."

"Well, stranger things have happened, Leonard."

"You've got that right," he continued. "You'll find Griffen in Flint. Victor's still in town. I'll text you both addresses."

"Thanks." Then I ended the call, expecting to receive a text message with both addresses shortly after. Within seconds, my cell buzzed with a notification from Leonard. There I was, a mile from my home, with all the information I needed to approach Griffen and Victor with at my disposal. Even though my day had ended and I was ready to settle down in my Lazy Boy with a cold beer while Grey's Anatomy played on the TV, I felt the urge to skip the mundane pleasures and visit Griffen instead. So, I deliberately bypassed the turn that led back to my apartment and continued straight toward the interstate.

23 · Kacy

As I sat on the edge of my bed and stared at the camera my mother had gotten me, my father suddenly appeared outside my open door. He leaned against the jamb with a look of desperation on his face.

"I am truly sorry, Kacy. If I could take it all back, I—"

"Don't say it," I said through sniffles.

He inched into my room and sat beside me, sinking the bed even further. "But, I *would* take it all—"

"Dad, you can't look me in my eyes and say that you'd do it differently. I know you wouldn't have. We tried so hard to get you to stop drinking, but you just wouldn't."

He began tearing up as he reached inside his pocket, retrieved a coin, and handed it to me.

I set aside my camera and examined it. "What's this?"

"My sobriety chip."

I flipped it over to find the number six planted on the other side.

"Been sober six years, Kacy. Haven't had a single drop."

I looked at him, feeling amazed at his accomplishment. In all my years, I never believed he'd quit drinking. I never thought he'd want to, especially after my mother died. He always claimed he would before she did; he just didn't want to. But now, I guessed the guilt had taken its toll.

"Even in the beginning, when the restaurant wasn't doing so well, I still didn't relapse," he continued. "I have Janet to thank for that. I couldn't have done it alone."

Janet? Maybe she pushed him to quit, especially after he killed her sister and all.

I handed over the coin. "This still doesn't make up for what you did, Dad, but I am proud of you for committing to stay sober."

He grabbed my shoulder and roped me into a hug. "I know nothing I do will ever make up for breaking up this family, but just know that I *am* sorry for everything I put you two through. From all the drunk arguments to the missed school performances to that fateful night. Will you ever forgive me?"

It was then, within his embrace, listening to his admission of guilt and wrongdoings, that my heart grew warm. Was it a yearning for something more? Maybe. Should I have forgiven him? Certainly. But did I want to? Not exactly. Ultimately, I did in the end because no matter what distance I put between us—no matter how much time I spent grieving—my mother would never return. And the understanding that she was gone and that my father was responsible for it would forever linger in the back of my mind until the day I died. It was then that I realized there was no point in dwelling on the past any longer. There's no point in holding onto such anger when you can reconcile the time you left with someone.

Because, in the end, we all die.

24 · Robert

When I arrived at Griffen's place, the moon was clearly visible above the nearest mountaintop. The sky had turned from blissful blue to a sorrowful purple haze—almost black. I hesitated to pull onto the property, thinking I should have called for backup. But it was too late for that now. I was experienced and prepared. And that was all I needed to do my job. I knew I could handle anything that came my way, at least for the most part.

I drove down the eerie graveled path until I reached a trashy trailer. Yellow lights poured from its windows as fireflies lit the building's surroundings. The tan and brown trailer had seen better days. I could only imagine what the inside looked like; disorganized, rotten smelling, smokey. But I was on a mission, in search of answers. So, how it looked didn't matter.

I put the car in park, pulled the keys from the ignition, and stepped out. A shadow zoomed across one of the windows, snatching my attention. I drew my Glock-9 and hugged the car door, being cautious of my surroundings, knowing it was late and dark. As I closed the car door, I inched closer to the front of the trailer, my finger resting on the trigger guard, ready to pull it at a second's notice. I stopped approaching when the door suddenly flew open, followed by the screech of the screen door. A man emerged, muttering nonsense, as he walked out onto the uncovered porch. He didn't notice me as he wobbled to the right and sat in his rocking chair.

He must be drunk.

Despite the lack of alcohol odor, I could tell from his actions—the wobbling, the muttering, and the apparent disregard for his surroundings—that he was heavily inebriated. I re-holstered my weapon under my blazer and clicked the lock button on my key fob, sending the headlights on my cruiser to flicker. It was at that moment that Griffen spotted me.

"What are you doing on my property?" he demanded slurredly.

I cautiously continued my approach. "I'm sorry to bother you so late, sir. I'm just looking for someone. Griffen Houser. I assume you're him?"

"Why yes, I am. What's it to you?"

"My apologies. I'm Detective Stone. You spoke with one of my colleagues on the phone months ago regarding a missing person." I climbed the steps of the porch and flashed my badge. Then I extended a hand. However, Griffen didn't shake it; instead, he stared at me in disgust.

"Eh...missing person?" he slurred, standing and wobbling back inside, leaving the main door open so we could communicate through the screen. "I don't remember no missing person. Why are you here?"

I wanted to step inside, but I wasn't invited. And entering without being invited would only permit him to shoot me on sight for whatever reason. "I just have a few questions to ask you regarding your time at Camp Mercy in eighty-six."

Instantly, he started sputtering nonsense again, as if I'd said something triggering. "First, it's that woman...now you. What the fuck is it with you people and that camp?" He hiccuped. "Thirty years, and I'm still having to keep my mouth..." He hiccuped again.

Woman? Could he be referring to Kacy? Mrs. Carter, perhaps? I peered in through the doorway to catch the tail end of what he was saying, but sadly, I missed it.

Griffen shuffled over to his sofa and plopped down, the light overhead creating a silhouette. He tilted his head back. "Go away! I...I don't talk to police."

"Please, Griffen. If you give me just a few minutes of your—"

"No! Now leave before I shoot you!" His voice was getting louder now.

I'd have a shootout with this guy if I wasn't careful. And that would only end badly—for him, not me. *I guess I'll return tomorrow when he's sober enough to know the difference between threatening a trespasser and an officer of the law.*

But I was being optimistic. From the looks of the inside of his place and the lingering odor of cheap liquor, I doubted he'd ever sober up enough to distinguish the two. That alone told me he was the type to stay inebriated for the better part of a day—the true definition of a functioning alcoholic.

"Understood," I said. "I'm leaving now. If, for whatever reason, you change your mind, then—"

"I ain't gon' tell you again. LEAVE!"

Instead of pressing my luck, I fished out my card with my contact information from the interior pocket of my blazer and slid it between the screen door and the jamb. Then I backed off the porch and returned to my car.

In hindsight, I should have gone home and watched TV instead of visiting Griffen. But then, I wouldn't have overheard him complaining about something I wish I could have heard entirely. "Thirty years, and I'm still having to keep my mouth..." Seemed likely he was going to say, "Keep my mouth shut."

What was he keeping quiet about?

25 · **Kacy**

I HAD JUST FINISHED GRABBING lunch at the gas station the following day when I decided to visit Eloise. I'd tried calling her twice while eating, but she didn't answer, which led me to assume she was working.

I walked into the food mart and approached the first cashier I spotted. "Excuse me, where can I find your manager...Eloise?"

"She's not here at the moment," the teenage boy said. "Is there anything I can help you with?" He looked so innocent in his red, short-sleeved button-up. And he was so polite.

"No," I answered. "I'm just a friend who's concerned, that's all. I tried calling her a few times, and she didn't answer."

Another employee, on the register behind the boy, butted into our conversation. She looked older, maybe close to Eloise's age. "Eloise took off for the week," the woman said.

"Thanks. I'll check to see if she's home."

I headed to Eloise's place next, hoping to find her there. However, when I rang the doorbell, I received no answer. Immediately, my mind was bombarded with fears. Could she have been kidnapped? Murdered like her husband? Or was she asleep? I rang the doorbell again, standing there impatiently, worried for her safety. The look on her face when she finally opened the door didn't surprise me. She didn't seem fully aware of her surroundings, as if she'd just woken from a nap.

"What's going on?" she asked, letting me into her home. "I was sleeping."

"I can see that," I said, noticing the fresh bags under her eyes. "I have a lead. And I need your help looking into it."

I was eager to solve the case. I knew that every second spent wasting time, not searching for answers, only meant the killer was still roaming the streets of Tulsa. That was if the killer hadn't already skipped town.

"I think Griffen is hiding something," I continued, following her inside and into the kitchen.

"What are you talking about?"

"I visited him yesterday. And as soon as he found out I wanted to hear his side of the story, he quickly kicked me off his property."

Eloise sat in a chair and crossed her legs. "That *does* sound suspicious."

"Got any idea about how I might get him to talk? Maybe he has a past trauma, or you have a picture we can use for blackmail?"

Eloise shot me a *what the fuck* look.

"What?" I questioned as I sat opposite her and crossed my arms. "I'm not afraid to go the extra mile to solve the case, Eloise. And you shouldn't be either."

"Well, I am. For all we know, the killer could still be in town. And if that's the case, I don't want to be targeted for trying to get justice for Charles."

I scoffed. "Eloise, you want to know what happened, right?"

She nodded.

"Then you're going to have to be willing to do whatever it takes to find the truth."

"I...I...can't."

"I understand, Eloise. I really do. Your husband...James...It all hits close to home. I get it. But remember, you asked for my help. I can only do so much on my own. I'm going to need you for some things. Like I said, I already tracked down Griffen and talked with him. I'll look up Victor after we speak with Griffen again today. Then we can visit him next."

She averted her gaze out the nearest window, biting her bottom lip seemingly in hesitation. "Well, maybe he might talk if we approach him together." Her eyes darted back to mine. "You know...since I'll be a familiar face and whatnot."

"Now that sounds more like it," I said, standing.

"Come back around five, and we can ride to—"

"Eloise, it'll be better if we go now."

"Now? Kacy, I need to go grocery shopping."

"You should have thought about that before taking a nap," I joked, heading for the front door. "C'mon, I'll drive."

As I sat in my father's truck, with no idea how long

Eloise would be, an ounce of shame arose—like I was being a real pain demanding she up and drop everything to come with me. But what else was I supposed to do? I had fans waiting.

After five minutes, Eloise hurried out of the house and jumped in the truck. Then we left.

———

The drive to Flint wasn't too bad this time. There was no need for air conditioning with the windows down and the gentle breeze flowing through my hair, carrying all the scents mother earth had to offer—cow manure and all.

When we finally arrived at Griffen's place, I stopped at the beginning of the gravel road and turned to Eloise. "I don't know when you last saw him, but I want you to be prepared."

"*Prepared?* For what?" she questioned, her face showing concern.

As much as I wanted to keep Eloise in the dark, I knew that wouldn't be fair to her. If we were going to make any headway as a team, there had to be total transparency. No secrets, no holding back. "Well, he might shoot at us," I hinted.

Her grip tightened around the edges of her seat, then relaxed a little as her eyes moved over my shoulder.

I turned to find her examining the poor repair job on the mailbox. "I know what you're thinking. Why not just replace it entirely, right? But you'll understand why he didn't once you see his place." I put my foot on the accelerator and continued down the road until we reached the end.

Eloise kept quiet the whole way. When we pulled up, Griffen was sitting on his porch, cleaning his rifle.

"Don't panic," I said, putting the truck in park and pulling the keys from the ignition.

My nerves were on edge as we approached Griffen's house. My mind raced with images of him unleashing a barrage of gunfire at the truck, just like the day before. I expected to see shattered glass, punctured metal, and chaos all around. But to my surprise, Griffen simply set his weapon aside and stepped off the front porch.

My heart sank to the pit of my stomach as he approached us. I even thought I heard Eloise swallow the lump in her throat. I feared what would happen next, not knowing Griffen's true intentions. Regardless of how sick and perverted his intentions might have been, I just wanted answers. I hoped that with Eloise here—being a familiar face and all—Griffen would be more inclined to discuss Camp Mercy with us.

I kicked open the truck door and jumped out.

Griffen stopped in his tracks. "Now, miss, I told you never—"

"I know, I know," I said, throwing my hands about. "You said not to come back, but I have questions that need answering." Then the passenger door opened, following a screeching squeak as if its hinges were in dire need of oil. "And I've brought a friend this time."

Griffen looked at Eloise, and a subtle form of recognition followed as if he wasn't sure whether he remembered her.

"Long time no see, Griffen," Eloise said, closing the door

and cautiously approaching him. "What's it been? Ten... twenty years?"

He squinted as if trying to figure out who the Black woman standing before him was. Then I saw the realization sink in.

"I'd say that's 'bout right, Eloise."

I relaxed my shoulders. *He's not going to shoot anyone now. At least, I hope not.*

"You haven't changed a bit," she said. "Even with the goatee, you still look the same."

He tipped his hat off to scratch his head and looked at the ground. "I wish that were true, but honestly, I look like shit." Then he looked back at me. "How you know this woman?"

"Eh, it's kind of a long story."

"Well, if you want me to tell you mines, I'm gon' have to hear yours first." He spat on the ground, then turned and headed up his porch steps. "C'mon inside, so we can get started."

Eloise and I followed Griffen up the front porch and inside his trailer to discuss how we met, why we were searching for answers, and where we were in the case.

26 · Kacy

AFTER AN HOUR of explaining what had happened to Eloise's husband, why we were interviewing people, and who we had spoken with so far, Griffen began breaking down his accounts of what happened the night James Edlin died.

He took a swig of his beer, belched, then inhaled deeply. "Man, has time passed."

"Yes, it has," Eloise added.

"So that morning, I had scored some bud from my bunkmate. Had won it in a bet to see who could get a kiss from Sally Mae first. Man, was she something."

He locked eyes with me and licked his lips. But I didn't do the same, instead shuddered in disgust.

"I remember her," Eloise said, sitting beside Griffen. "She was the one who died in a car wreck three weeks after James died, right?"

"Yep. Sure had."

"That's terrible," I said.

"Damn shame it was," he added. "But back to that night...after all the fun and games of the day, many of us gathered in the main cabin for dinner. That night was pizza. I remember it like it was yesterday." He took a big whiff as if he were there, inhaling the scent of oregano, thyme, and garlic as it baked in the oven. "I wanted to smoke beforehand but didn't. Looking back, I should have 'cause I got into it with James shortly after. He took the last slice of pineapple. It took a couple of people to get me off him, even with the help of a counselor. Man, was I pissed." A fly buzzed around the room, landing on the arm of his sofa. He swatted it away without any effort. "Afterward, I went for a walk to cool down, using the joint to do so." He downed the rest of his beer, followed by a heavy gulp. "It was 'bout a quarter after seven when I heard some rustling in the trees nearby. Some said it was the weed I smoked, but I know what I saw."

He paused as he stood and grabbed another beer from the refrigerator. He might have done it for dramatic effect; I wasn't sure. I was curious to hear what he saw or *who* he saw with him in the woods. But Griffen didn't say a single word when he sat back down. Just popped open the can, leaving the release of fizzy pressure to fill the awkward silence.

He took a sip.

"We're waiting," I urged. The suspense gnawed at my gut.

His eyes darted to mine.

"What did you see out there?" Eloise asked.

Griffen placed his beer on the floor, pressing his elbows to his knees. He exhaled as if he was unsure of what to say. "Not exactly sure what I saw. All I know's that I heard some talking. When I got close enough to see who it was, I heard a scream. Next thing I know, I see James hanging in a tree."

"You had to have noticed something or seen someone else in the area," I suggested.

"As a matter of fact, I did," he admitted. "Granted, it was dark out, but from what I could see, it sort of looked like Victor running off."

"Just one person?" Eloise asked. "It couldn't have just been him."

"Hey, I'm just telling you what I saw. You can draw your own conclusions from that." He grabbed his beer and stood. "Now go on, get out, 'cause I've got guns that ain't gon' clean themselves."

"Wait! What about a motive?" I urged. "Can you think of any reason why Victor would want to hurt James? A hate crime, maybe."

"Look, I don't know. Now, I done answered your questions, now leave."

"Just one last question, then we'll leave," I pled.

"Fine."

"Have you seen Victor recently?"

"Yeah, 'bout six months ago. Now go on, get out!"

Eloise and I exchanged glances. Could it have been that easy to find the truth? Could Victor Pines be responsible for the murder of James Edlin and possibly Charles Carter? I didn't know. Hopefully, questioning him would give me that answer. I tapped the button on my camera to end the recording, returned my gear to my backpack, then thanked

Griffen for his time. Then Eloise and I exited the trailer and got back in the Ford to head home.

————

Once we returned to Tulsa, I planned to drop Eloise off at her home so she could retrieve her car and most likely go grocery shopping. After pulling into her driveway, I parked beside her sedan, and she got out.

She turned back to lean in as I lowered the window. "I'll call you after I get back from the store so we can go over your interview with the sheriff."

I nodded, then Eloise headed inside.

I continued home, knowing my father would contact me in a few hours to pick him up from the restaurant. Once I pulled into the driveway of my childhood home, I grabbed my backpack and went inside. With the place to myself, I got to work, dumping all the footage I'd collected from my interview with Griffen onto my computer.

I reviewed it twice, studying his words and mannerisms when answering each question. Then I thought back to the sheriff's answers. *There's no way both of you are telling the truth. It just can't be that easy.*

Griffen's claim made me think it was so. But without the others' recounts of the events, I was undecided about whether Victor had murdered James and Charles. Or even one of them. I required more information to make a solid conclusion. I trimmed the clips from Griffen's video, exported some, and uploaded them to YouTube as a short trailer to give my fans something for their patience. But I blurred Griffen's face in the video, not to trouble myself with more problems or incriminate him.

The comments on the video I'd posted explaining what I was doing had reached a mere 3,000, but the views were close to 250,000. And that was on a clip that was only a minute long. My subscribers were rooting for me, wanting me to give them the truth. All I needed now was to solve the murder. And to do that, I fished out my phone and tapped on Robert's contact. As I waited for him to answer, I powered down my MacBook. Then I rolled over onto my stomach, kicking my feet in the air.

Three rings later, he answered.

"Hey, Kacy," Robert said. "I'm surprised to hear from you."

"Well, I was just thinking about you," I said with a giggle.

"Just wanted to hear my voice, huh?"

You're half right.

I bit my bottom lip. "You could say that."

"Well, now that I've got you on the line, I do have a question for you."

"What is it?"

"What were you doing in Flint, visiting Griffen Houser?"

I caught my breath. *Shit. He knows!*

"Rob, I can explain—"

"Kacy, I told you not to get involved. And you said you wouldn't. Why did you lie to me?"

I jumped to the edge of my bed. "I didn't want to lie to you. I just—"

"Wanted to?" he questioned, his voice getting a little

louder. "What good reason could you possibly have to lie to me?"

Sweat beaded up on my forehead. I didn't want to tell Robert I was also chasing leads for YouTube, along with helping Eloise get closure for her husband. It sounded idiotic—reckless as if I was doing this purely for likes. But I wasn't. I had told my fans so much already; I couldn't turn back now.

I couldn't explain myself. All I could do was apologize. "I'm sorry for lying to you, Rob. I...I just feel obligated to help Eloise get some closure, that's all. You know what I mean?" I didn't even give him a chance to answer. "Like, I know you're very busy saving the world and all and can't answer all her questions or be there for her in her time of grief. Which is why I took it upon myself to be there for her." I tried to end it on a positive note, so he wouldn't chastise me. Then, amid the silence, I asked him a question. "But look...the reason I called was to see if you wanted to join me for dinner again. Tonight."

There was nothing but silence on the other end of the line, as if Robert was in a state of shock. I couldn't blame him. After all, I was the same woman who had rejected his advances countless times. But now, out of the blue, I was asking him out. It was a confusing situation for him, I'm sure. It felt somewhat strange to me as well. But that was to be expected. There was no other way I'd manage to milk him for every drop of information he had on the case. God knew he wouldn't tell me if I'd asked. And I couldn't wait for Eloise to ask him because he probably wouldn't tell her either.

"Robert?" I called, the line still silent.

"Sorry," he said. "Someone came into my office. Dinner? Tonight? Sure. Where at?"

"You pick since I picked the last time."

"I'll pick you up at seven."

Then he ended the call.

My phone buzzed immediately after I hung up. It was a text from my father, prompting me to come pick him up.

To: Professor Carter (tulsauniversity.carter@gmail.com)
From: Jeremy Saunders (jsaunders1994@gmail.com)
Date: Monday, April 4, 2016 10:45:11 EST
Subject: Interview w/Sheriff

Dear Professor,

I just left the police station. I must say, I learned quite a few things from the sheriff. I even asked to speak with his wife. Unfortunately, she wasn't available and wouldn't be until after the due date on this project. I feel like I'm going to receive an A+ on this report. Lord knows I need one to pass this class.

To: Jeremy Saunders (jsaunders1994@gmail.com)
From: Professor Carter (tulsauniversity.carter@gmail.com)
Date: Monday, April 4, 2016 1:02:05 EST
Subject: Re: Interview w/Sheriff

Dear Jeremy,

Good. I'm glad to hear your interviewing process is panning out. As for your grade in this class, you're doing fine. Even if you weren't to receive an A+ on this assignment, you'd still pass.

<h1>27 · Robert</h1>

THAT WAS UNEXPECTED. I never thought Kacy would call me out of the blue like that, let alone lie to me. I wondered what else she'd lied about. But at least making plans with her had given me a second chance to win her over. That was all that mattered in my eyes. I couldn't help but feel like she was brought back into my life for a reason. Hopefully, I wouldn't waste it this time.

I slid my phone back into my blazer and turned into the parking lot of Heritage Point, an assisted living facility. There weren't many parking spots available, which I found pretty strange for a Tuesday afternoon. But eventually, I secured a spot and then headed inside. As soon as the sliding glass doors opened, the stench of old people crept up my nostrils. It was the same smell hospitals had—the kind that used astringent cleaning products with an herbal scent. But it didn't truly smell of herbs in any way.

"How can I help you, sir?" a woman's voice called out

from behind the front counter opposite the entrance. She was dressed in all white, crimson hair pulled back in a ponytail, with skin as white as snow.

I approached the counter and flashed my badge. "I'm Detective Stone. Called earlier about speaking with one of your patients regarding a case I'm working on."

The woman looked at me strangely, thrown off by what I'd said, as if she wasn't aware of the situation. Before I could say anything else, she picked up the phone, pressed a button, and paged someone.

"Linda? I have a detective here. Says he called earlier about speaking with one of our patients."

I couldn't hear what Linda was saying to her. But after a second more of silence, she returned the phone to the hook and stood.

"Right this way." She gestured for me to follow her down the hall.

I had much appreciation for them being overly cautious with their security measures. It made me think of putting my parents here once they were incapable of living alone. I followed the woman down the hall, taking a right at the end.

"If you don't mind me asking, what's the case regarding?"

"I'm not at liberty to say. But I'll put it this way—it's a very *old* case."

Suddenly the woman started giggling. She probably thought I was trying to be funny, using *old* as the pun for the joke. But that wasn't my intention. We turned down another hall.

"And here we are," she said, approaching a door at the

end of the hall. She opened it, following a knock, and motioned me in. "Good luck," she whispered before closing the door behind me.

Good luck? What's that supposed to mean?

As soon as I turned around, I found two people inside: Victor, sitting about a foot in front of me, in a wheelchair beside a woman who was dressed in the same all-white outfit as the lady who had escorted me here.

"Hello, Detective. I'm Linda," the woman said, extending a hand. "I'm the person you spoke with earlier on the phone. I'm also the leading coordinator here at the facility."

"Yes. It's a pleasure to meet you," I said, then to Victor, I added, "Hello, Victor. I'm Detective Stone."

Victor didn't move a muscle. Just continued staring at me. Then, seconds after, his grim stare turned to a joking smile and a muted laugh. He lifted his arm and shook my hand. I glanced at Linda, then back at Victor, joining him in laughter. What an odd introduction.

"I hope someone has told you I'm here to ask you a few questions about your time at Camp Mercy in eighty-six."

Victor tilted his head slightly to the side as if he didn't know what I was talking about.

Then Linda butted in. "This is why I'm here, Detective. See, Victor isn't capable of answering your questions verbally. He doesn't remember much either."

"Remember? How come?"

"Because he had a stroke. A pretty bad one, rendering him unable to walk or communicate easily."

My gaze drifted back toward Victor as he rolled over to his bedside table, where a small whiteboard and dry-erase marker lay. As he jotted down something, I approached him, my ears still tuned in to what Linda was saying.

"We've worked with him, but we can do only so much. Luckily, we've managed to get him writing again, even if his choice of words aren't ideal."

Linda came up beside me as I stood over Victor's shoulder, squinting to see what he was writing. Victor spun and showed me the whiteboard. It read: CAMP MERCY?

I was thrown askew. *This must be a joke. Surely, this couldn't be the perp who killed Charles Carter.*

"What is your name?" I asked.

I waited to see what he'd write down. Lo and behold, he wrote his name. It was Victor, for sure. However, I couldn't fathom why he'd repeat the camp's name. Had his stroke dispelled his childhood memories? I was now riddled with a new dilemma. How would I get his recount of what happened thirty years ago if he couldn't even remember what he had for breakfast?

I exhaled my troubles, sat in the chair in the corner of the room, and pressed my elbows against my knees. This case was far from cut and paste. Dammit. Why did I even think of reopening James's case? Why did I even believe Mrs. Carter could be right? That both cases could be connected? It's been nothing but headaches from the start.

———

So far, I've had no genuine leads—not one thing that could point me in the right direction. I only had a hunch that Griffen was hiding something. But what? Having a hunch wasn't enough. Yes, I could get Leonard to search the database for any registered firearms in Griffen's name, but that was only if they were registered. Knowing him, they could all be illegal.

I could get a warrant to search his place, hoping to find the murder weapon. However, without probable cause, the judge wouldn't sign off on it. So, I was back to square one. Even with Griffen's criminal record, what could have been his motive for killing James Edlin? Let alone Charles Carter? All the emails Charles had traded with his student only mentioned Griffen and Blake's names—nothing else.

Sheriff Wells wasn't much better, either. Yes, I'd worked with him for a few years, so I knew what he was like—how he handled things. If he were responsible for Charles Carter's death, let alone James', I strongly believed he'd know how to get rid of the evidence. His willingness to answer my questions and quickly remember everyone's names was a little concerning. Granted, it was a traumatic experience for a teenager, so it made sense. However, even haunting traumas could be forgotten in time.

Then came Mrs. Carter—the first suspect on my list of people to investigate. She was a widow, and they were always the first person of interest in a homicide. But the only reason she had for killing him would be that he was cheating on her. But the M.E. report didn't mention anything out of the ordinary. If she had murdered her husband, there likely would have been multiple gunshot wounds or stab wounds to his body, showing signs that it was a crime of passion. But there weren't any. Only his badly beaten face. But that wasn't enough evidence to convict her.

And last but not least, there was Victor. As I sat,

thinking of ways to question a suspect who wasn't necessarily credible, Linda came up beside me and rested her hand on my shoulder. "There are a few exercises we do with patients who suffer from memory loss and dementia to try to get them to remember things."

"Exercises like what?"

"Doing these might not be how you'd typically question a suspect, but we can give it a shot." Linda turned and headed for the door. "I'll be right back.

Once she left, I sat in silence alongside Victor. When she returned, she had a small portable table under her arm and a plain brown rectangular box in her hand. I shot up from the chair and assisted her in unfolding the table. As we did, I noticed Victor getting excited from out of the corner of my eye, as if he knew what he was about to do.

"Are you ready, Victor?" she asked, opening the box she held.

Victor started clapping and smiling beyond belief.

When Linda opened the box, a chess set was inside.

"Grab a seat," she instructed, pointing over at the one in the corner of the room.

Victor rolled up to the table as I grabbed the chair. Then I sat opposite him, feeling uncertain about how this would go. But what did I have to lose? Nothing. I was desperate. At this point, I was willing to do anything for a lead.

I let Victor begin, him moving a pawn first. After many more rotations, I'd lost three pawns, a knight, and a rook. I hadn't expected Victor to be so good, but then again, chess wasn't my game. As we continued playing, I watched him more than the board in front of me.

"So, Victor, what did you have for breakfast?" I asked.

He moved his knight, taking another one of my pieces, then grabbed the whiteboard and jotted down his answer.

eggs and pancakes.

So he did remember what he had eaten. Perhaps I could go back even further. I turned to Linda beside me. "How much do you think he remembers?"

"I have no clue. But it doesn't hurt to try."

I turned back to Victor. "What year did you graduate from high school?"

I knew what I was asking for was a lot—a giant leap, really—however, I didn't have time to ask questions that weren't related to the case. Once I knew he could remember when he graduated, I could mention names—the names of the other suspects. His bunkmates. And from there, hopefully, the truth would be revealed. However, when he showed me what he'd written, I exhaled a sigh of agitation. Victor couldn't remember the year he graduated, which meant he likely wouldn't remember the names of his fellow peers either.

Again, I had reached another dead end.

28 · Kacy

At seven on the dot, the doorbell rang.

Robert's here! And he's not early, thank God.

Even if he had been, I would have been prepared. I was hungry, dressed, and ready a quarter after six. He wasn't going to catch me by surprise again. Not this time. I sauntered down the hallway in my rose gold dress and matching high heels I'd picked up from the mall earlier in the day and answered the door.

"Who's at the door?" my father shouted from somewhere in the house, his voice permeating the hallway.

"Just my date," I shouted back.

I imagined him sitting at his desk, his eyes glued to the computer screen, while he worked on expense reports or ordered supplies for the business. Honestly, it didn't matter where he was because my attention was squarely on Robert, pondering on how I'd convince him to reveal the details of the case without alarming him.

"Date?" my father questioned, his head popping into the hall as I opened the front door.

"Hey!" I said to Robert with a smile.

"Hopefully, I gave you enough time to get ready," Robert joked.

I tucked my hair behind my ears and giggled.

"Two times in one week," my father said, coming up behind me. He pulled the door from my hand, opened it wider, and leaned against it. "You both must have a *lot* to catch up on, huh?"

Oh, God, please save me.

I cringed at what my father said, afraid it might remind Robert that I never explained why I'd left so long ago on our first date.

"We sure do," I said, gently shoving Robert out the door as quickly as possible.

"You two have fun now."

I rushed Robert off the front porch, not wanting him to spend a second more in my father's presence. Once we got in his car, we were off. The ride to the restaurant was filled with hilarious jokes and flirtatious compliments I wasn't prepared for. Perhaps I'd made a mistake in leaving him behind years ago. Maybe I should have given him a chance —gave us a chance.

When we finally arrived at the restaurant, I couldn't help but gape in amazement. It was like something out of a fairy tale. The building resembled an enchanted cathedral or a royal palace, with its illuminated sign gleaming in the night sky. The outdoor seating area was equally stunning, with warm, inviting lights that shone like stars above each table. This was not your average Applebees. When I'd asked

Robert out for dinner, I wasn't expecting to be wined and dined like Julia Roberts in *Pretty Woman*. If I didn't know any better, I'd say he was trying to get laid tonight.

I guess I'm not the only one with a hidden agenda.

————

As we followed the waiter to our seats, I dreaded where he'd place us. The bar in the center of the restaurant was a little crowded, just like the rest of the place, which I felt was not great for us to discuss the case. And though the outside seating area was fairly empty, I didn't want to go there either. As we approached the patio door, I couldn't help but think how romantic it would be to sit outside under the moonlight. However, I knew that wouldn't be wise for me or my current situation. I had to stay focused on getting information from Robert, and being in such a dreamy atmosphere would only make it more challenging to keep my emotions in check. Unfortunately, the waiter passed the last table, opened the door to the patio, and guided us out.

Dammit. Now I really have to focus so I don't get caught up in this luxurious evening.

After we sat down, the waiter took our drink order. Then moments later, he returned with our beverages and took our entree orders.

"So, how's your week going so far?" I asked awkwardly, hoping to get things started on the right foot.

Robert leaned back in his wrought-iron chair and scratched his head. "Eh, it's been one of those weeks. I assume yours has been better."

"Better?" I repeated, remembering how I got shot at by a

raging hillbilly and decided to pay him another visit the following day. "I wouldn't say that exactly, but it was definitely interesting."

"How so?"

I hesitated to respond. Robert knew I'd visited Griffen, so telling him about the gunfire would only dampen the mood. As much as I wanted to discuss the case, I had to be smart about how I approached it if I wanted to extract information from him. "My dad's truck got damaged, that's all. It's still functional, though."

"What got damaged?"

Dammit. I shouldn't have said anything. He's a detective; why did I think I could sneak one past him?

"The driver-side headlight. Someone shot it out."

"Shot it out?" he said, concern plastered on his face.

There was no point in hiding the truth from him now.

"Yes. When I visited Griffen, he shot at me."

His look of concern switched to agitation. "This is why I didn't want you getting involved, Kacy. There are too many unknowns. We don't know who killed Charles Carter, let alone if they're still in town. I can't protect you if you're—"

"I don't want you to protect me. I can handle myself."

Robert paused for a second as if to reiterate. "I know you can handle yourself, Kacy. But I need you to be careful. No matter how many times I tell you not to do something, I can't stop you from doing it. If you feel the need to help Mrs. Carter, then that's your prerogative. However, please keep in mind...first, it was the headlight on your father's truck. The next one could be you."

I could sense Robert's frustration. He might have cared for

my well-being way more than I thought he did. I couldn't help but think Robert had never gotten over me. After all, I'd left him. I couldn't blame him, though. Deep down inside, I felt I still had some feelings for him too. Despite the night having just begun, and my failure of an attempt to extract information from him, it seemed like our conversation had hit a dead end.

Then suddenly, amid the awkward silence, he changed the subject. "You remember prom night, right?"

"And all the fun we had," I added, running my foot along his leg under the table.

"Well, I was thinking...maybe we could go dancing after dinner."

"Dancing?" I repeated as if I'd heard him wrong. "No. I can't." I retreated my leg. And as soon as I did, he reached for my hand.

"Kacy, the last I remember, you were better at it than me. Hopefully, that's still the case, unless—"

"It's probably not the case. Sorry, Rob, but I haven't danced in years." Honestly, I hadn't danced since that fateful night. However, I would never admit it. The closest I came to dancing was being a wallflower at a few weddings over the years. But that was also way too embarrassing to share. Regardless, my gut hinted at the feeling that he was leading up to something bigger. Perhaps, asking me why I'd left.

But just as he was about to share something, our waiter returned with our food. God, it smelled amazing; the aroma of stewed tomatoes and fresh garlic. I couldn't wait to devour it, but before I knew it, Robert had already beaten me to the punch, catching a glimpse of his fork leaving my plate as I unwrapped my silverware. I couldn't believe he'd do such a thing.

"Mmm," he groaned, pulling his fork from between his lips in a playful manner.

"Looks like you're enjoying it," I said. "Better be careful, though. I don't want to have to do the Heimlich on you."

He chuckled, almost choking right then and there. I cringed at the thought of seeing his face turn blue because a meatball got lodged in his throat. That'd be so romantic, wouldn't it?

Robert swallowed with a gulp, then spoke. "If you like, you can try some of mine."

I was already reaching for a piece of his steak when he said it. "Oh, I was planning on it."

Robert took a sip from his glass as I chewed the tender steak. "I must say, Kacy, it's been great having you back in town, even though I can sense that you don't want to be for some reason, but still. Honestly, I wish you'd never left." He paused as he looked away, glancing at the dim lights overhead, then back down at me. "But I know you had your reasons."

We locked eyes.

There it was. He was leading up to the question I had been dreading ever since I'd returned home.

"And if I never find out why, it won't be the end of the world," he finished.

His words hit me in a way I never could have imagined. They touched my soul, reaching deep into the inner depths of my loins. Had he just forgiven me for leaving him without an explanation so long ago?

I was in disbelief.

Robert *had* changed.

And for the better at that.

Our time apart was worth it. Perhaps coming home wasn't such a bad thing. Maybe I could see us building a life together after all.

———

Our date was short-lived, but only because we scarfed down our entrees like neglected dogs. Afterward, we returned to his car so we could go dancing. He insisted on taking me dancing, even though I'd made it clear that I wasn't too keen on the idea. But then he said something about dancing where no one could see us, and suddenly I felt more at ease about the whole thing.

As we drove, I found myself deep in thought. *I can't believe I failed at milking him for more information on the case. But this night hasn't been all bad. I've enjoyed his company, his jokes, and his positive vibes. Even though I'm still a little worried about what his reaction might be to my horrible dancing.* I drew in a breath. *Oh, and I can't forget about his cologne. God, does he smell amazing.*

When he stopped the car and pulled the key from the ignition, I noticed we were sitting in the parking lot of a dingy apartment complex. "I thought we were going dancing?" I said warily.

"We are." He grinned. "We're going to dance where no one can see us...inside my apartment."

I went stale-faced. What a clever ploy to lure me back to his place. Kudos to him.

"I know what you're thinking, but you'll see once we go inside, I promise," he finished.

He opened the door and stepped out. I did the same, even though my mind said not to. It was like he had me in a trance—a gravitational pull of some kind. With my hand in his, he guided me up the heavily eroded concrete stairs onto the second landing. From the looks of the black trash bags piled up at the end of the walkway, and the remnants of cigarette butts and marijuana roaches spread about the ground, I'd say the place looked grungy.

I thought detective's made more money. I stood corrected. Perhaps, he was transitioning into buying a house, and his time living here was only temporary. Once we reached his door, he fished the keys from his pocket, opened it, and ushered me in.

"I know it's not much, but it's temporary," he confirmed, flicking on the light switch.

"You saving up to buy a house or something?"

"Yes, I am. Can't rent forever, you know."

Thank God this trash heap isn't permanent.

As I stood awkwardly near the door, not knowing where we would dance, Robert shed his loafers and went to the stereo across the room beside his TV. He tapped the button, powering it on, slid in a CD he'd snatched off the shelf, then turned the volume knob up a tad.

I had no clue what was about to play over the speakers. However, when Michael Jackson's '*Break of Dawn*' came on, I knew we were about to have a good time.

"I didn't know you liked Michael," I said as he grabbed my hand. "I love oldies. Modern music is such trash."

He chuckled. "Take your heels off."

I didn't want to, fearing I might catch a fungus from the outdated carpet in his place, but I did anyway. Then he pulled me out into the middle of the living area and spun me around. When Michael began to sing, Robert pulled me into a tight embrace and gripped his hand close to my ass. *You better watch it!*

We locked eyes.

"Follow my lead," he whispered in my ear with confidence.

Then we started to move.

He guided me left and right as our hips swayed to the beat. Fearing I'd step on his toes, or worse, he'd step on mine, I clung tight to him like a koala to a tree. Then he spun me again, but when he pulled me in this time, he immediately sent me into a dip I wasn't expecting.

Crash!

I had slipped from his grasp. The carpet cushioned my fall.

"Kacy!" he exclaimed. "You okay?"

I couldn't help but burst out in laughter from the look of worry on his face. Perhaps he was afraid I was hurt—that I'd broken something. However, once he realized that I wasn't hurt in any way, his look of worry turned to a grimace. Perhaps he was concerned that he'd ruined his last shot at getting back with me.

"I'm fine," I said, reaching for his hand. "Now, help me up." He extended his hand. But when I grabbed it, I yanked him down on top of me to be funny. I laughed some more as he started to do the same. Then as our laughing spell ceased, we locked eyes again.

"I miss this so much," he admitted.

"I do too." Then suddenly, he pressed his lips to mine, pulling me into his warm embrace. *Whoah!*

Was I expecting it? Somewhat. Did I entice him into kissing me? Yes. Were we going to have sex? I didn't know, but I certainly wouldn't mind.

Amid his eagerness to feel me up, I inhaled deeply to catch my breath. My nipples stiffened as I gave in to his advances. I reached for his chest, unbuttoning the first few on his silk shirt. Then he slid off his blazer and finished unbuttoning the rest. I anxiously unbuckled his belt as he shed his outerwear and ripped off his undershirt. Through all the dancing and laughing, I'd definitely become horny. And I could tell he was, too, by the large knot that protruded from under his belt line. God, was I ready. I hadn't had sex in such a long time. But with all the stress I was under lately, I definitely needed a release.

"Take me, Robert."

"I'll take you when I'm ready, princess," he said between kissing breaths.

I was so ready to feel him inside me that I didn't even try to remove my dress—just slid it up my thighs and pulled my panties to the side. Amid the removal of my underwear, I noticed an oozing sensation coming from my—

Wait! No, why now?

I quickly slid my panties back in place and pulled down my dress. But by the time I did, Robert already had his pants around his ankles and his throbbing cock out, ready to give me what I'd asked for.

"What's wrong?" he asked, watching me jump from the floor like a gymnast.

"Where's your bathroom," I asked through panicked breaths.

He pointed to a door across the room. And in an instant, I was there as if I'd teleported. I slammed the door shut, locking it before rushing to the commode. A minute later, the door received a gentle tap, followed by his calming voice.

"Kacy, you okay? Did I do something wrong?"

"No...no, Rob. It's not your fault. You didn't do anything wrong. It's me."

Then the door rattled with a thud. It was probably his head hitting against it in aggravation. Even though I didn't plan on having sex with him beforehand, we both wanted to toward the end of the night. But unfortunately, my body had other plans.

29 · Kacy

GETTING my period right before having sex couldn't have come at a worse time. Never in my life had I experienced such a thing. God, was it embarrassing. Luckily, I'd cleaned myself up with some toilet paper to slow the bleeding long enough for Robert to get me home so I could use the proper feminine hygiene products.

"Are you sure you're okay, Kacy?" Robert asked, pulling into the driveway of my childhood home.

I had remained silent the entire ride home. "I'm fine, Rob. It's just the start of my period. Amid everything going on in my life, it must have slipped my mind. I'm sorry about how our night ended."

"Oh, well, there's nothing to be sorry about. It's a part of human biology. If anything, I appreciate you being so considerate."

I poked a smile, knowing how gracious Robert was being. Even though I'd ruined his chances at getting some, I couldn't help but think he wasn't upset in some way. Perhaps he was putting on a front, or maybe, he truly understood. Regardless, I kissed him on the cheek, then got out of his vehicle and headed inside.

Despite how well our date went, my night was much worse. I couldn't even fall asleep after Robert dropped me off because the wrenching pain in my abdomen was unbearable. Every few minutes, I'd toss and turn, trying desperately to find a comfortable position where I could pass out. It wasn't until around four a.m. that I finally fell asleep.

When I finally woke up, I found a note on the kitchen counter that my father had left behind for me.

Tried to wake you at seven for breakfast, but you were out cold. Went to the grocery store. If you want something, shoot me a text.

After eating breakfast and cleaning the kitchen, I went to the bathroom to take a warm bath. Ten minutes later, my cell phone rang. Assuming it was my father, I darted from the bathroom back to my bedroom to answer it. But when I checked the caller ID, it read: UNKNOWN NUMBER.

Now, who could this be?

"Hello?" I said warily.

"Is this Kacy Roe?" the raspy male voice on the other end asked.

"Speaking."

"You'd better be real careful with what you dig up from the past, 'cause if you aren't…you might just disappear."

Then the line went silent as if he'd ended the call.

I gasped and dropped my phone. It hit the floor with a thud. That call had to be a joke—a prank or something, perhaps even a wrong number. But then I thought, *How'd he know my name?* It was at that moment that it sank in. My heart almost burst out of my chest. *Who was that, and how'd he get my number?*

There was no way I could guarantee my safety now. Even if I were to solve the case. Whoever was on the phone wanted to halt my pursuit. And if I didn't stop, they'd make me disappear entirely. I had to tread carefully if I was going to continue investigating the case.

———

An hour later, I stood in front of the police station. I had dropped my father off at the restaurant shortly after he'd returned with groceries, then headed here. I feared walking inside and telling Robert that someone had called, threatening to kill me if I didn't stop looking for answers. However, I believed if I didn't, it would only make things worse. At least between us, since I'd blatantly disregarded his request not to get involved in an ongoing murder investigation. But I had to do something because my life was at risk.

I walked inside and stormed up to the counter. "Excuse me. Can I please speak with Detective Stone? It's urgent."

I knew the man recognized me. The look he gave me said it all. I'd spoken to him a few days earlier when I came to pick up my equipment after Charles's body had been identified. Hopefully, he wasn't going to give me any problems this time.

As the man picked up the phone to ring Robert's office, I added, "Tell him it's Kacy." And to my surprise, that was precisely what he did. No hassle this time, thank God. A minute later, Robert came trudging down the hall. I could hear his leather shoes clacking against the linoleum.

"Kacy, you know I'm busy," he said, towering over me. He pulled me aside and whispered. "If this is about last night—"

I pressed my finger to his lips to shush him. "It's not that, Rob," I whispered back. "It's about the Carter case. I think someone's trying to kill me."

He scoffed in disbelief. "You're joking, right?"

I shook my head. "No. I got a call an hour ago, telling me to be careful with what I dig up or else I might disappear."

"That can't be right."

"Why can't it be?"

"Because I thought you and I were on the same page, Kacy." His voice got a little louder, but he quickly caught himself, reverting to his *inside* voice. "I thought you weren't going to help Mrs. Carter anymore, that you were going to leave it for the police to handle."

"I hadn't done anything with her since yesterday before we went out to dinner." Robert grabbed me by the arm and yanked me down the hall and into the elevator.

He pinched the bridge of his nose in agitation as the elevator doors closed. "Great. You got involved, and now you might be in danger. I was afraid this would happen."

"I'm sorry," I begged.

"It's too late now. Someone already knows you're involved. And even if you *were* to stop, they'd still keep an eye on you. At least that's what I'd do if I were trying to cover my tracks." He turned away and punched the metal wall. "Dammit, Kacy. Why didn't you just listen to me from the start?"

I came up behind him and wrapped him in a bear hug, resting my head in the middle of his back. "I did it because I was curious and wanted to help. But also...because I wanted to know the truth. It's not your fault." As soon as I loosened my grasp on him, he turned to me with an exhale of acceptance. Then he grabbed my wrists and looked me in the eyes.

"Look, you're going to come stay with me 'til this thing blows over, okay?"

What?! Oh, God. Did he just say what I thought he said?

Staying with Robert in his grungy apartment was going to be a total nightmare. I knew having sex was probably the last thing on his mind at that moment, but it was still there, lingering somewhere in the back of his head. It had to be, or else he wouldn't be offering me safety in the confines of his home. However, what was I to do? I didn't want to end up like Charles, my body left decaying in some long-forgotten place, or like James, hanging from a tree waiting to fall like a rotten apple as worms and insects ate at it from the inside out.

And then I thought about my father. *I hope he's not in any danger.*

I gasped. *Eloise.*

I was afraid to find out. But I had to warn them just in case. But before I could retrieve my phone to call them, I needed Robert to release me from his unyielding grasp. And for him to do that, I had to agree to stay with him until the case was solved. Despite not wanting to stay with him, the way he demanded it made me think I had no choice. And this was neither the time nor place to argue with him about it, so I agreed.

The elevator doors opened, and a few people walked in.

"Let me see your phone," he demanded.

"Why?"

"Don't question me right now, Kacy. I'm doing this to protect you. Got it?"

I relinquished my cell phone and let him toggle through it. I didn't know exactly what he was searching for, but when he fished out his cell phone and snapped a picture of my screen, I knew it was for a good reason.

"Go straight home, grab all your stuff, and wait for me to come get you. Got it?"

"Got it."

He returned my phone and left the elevator, leaving me to ride it back down to the first floor. But before the doors closed, he spun and added, "And, Kacy...don't go anywhere."

I nodded as a subtle warmth built within me. It seemed like Robert had genuine feelings for me—feelings that had matured over the years. Perhaps he was the man for me, someone who could protect me in times of crisis. The thought of giving in to temptation circled my mind as the doors closed and the elevator descended.

Once I landed on the main floor, I exited the lift and headed toward the lobby of the station. While on my way out, I ran into Sheriff Wells, leaving the men's bathroom.

"Sheriff?"

"It's Kacy, right?" he asked. "What can I do you for?"

I knew it was probably the wrong time to ask—my life

being in danger and all—but I still needed answers, still wanted to help Eloise, and still wanted to solve a murder for my fans. Because the sooner I found the killer, the sooner I could save my own ass, and the sooner things could go back to normal.

"Did you ever ask your wife if she would meet with me to answer a few questions for my school project?"

He rubbed his hands together, probably to dry the last few drops of water those cheap air dryers failed at catching. "Ah, yes. 'Bout that. I don't know what your availability is like, but—"

"I'm free anytime," I admitted, interrupting him.

"Hmm, I see. That makes sense, seeing that you're a student. You must not have a job."

"I do, but it's an unconventional one."

He nodded. "Okay. Well, then, how 'bout tomorrow evening? You can come back then. I'll have my wife stop by 'round six. Sound good?"

"Sure does. Thank you." We went our separate ways, him most likely returning to his office and me heading out of the station and back to my father's truck.

___

I dialed my father's number when I returned to the Ford, hoping he'd answer. However, he didn't. Fearing the worst, I tried again and again. Luckily, on the third try, he finally answered.

"Is everything okay, Kacy?" he asked.

His tone carried an ounce of concern. He probably wondered why I was calling and not texting him.

"Dad, listen...I'm going to spend some time at Robert's for a little while. Don't ask me for how long because I don't know. But just make sure you stay safe, okay? I'll leave the truck at the house, so if you can, get Janet to take you home tonight since—"

"What's wrong, Kacy? You sound—"

"I'm fine, Dad. It's just..." I paused, wondering whether I should tell him the truth or not—that someone had called me with a death threat.

*No, I can't worry him. He's already under enough pressure. Throwing this on top will only make things worse. But I also can't run the risk of him getting hurt because of me, either. God, if something happens to him...*I shuddered, unable to finish the thought.

I exhaled and continued, "It's just this case I'm working on. I'm getting close to solving it, and I think the killer is still in town. Keep an eye out for anything strange, okay? If anyone comes knocking on your door, don't open it."

I expected my father to start spewing questions upon questions, wondering why I was still chasing this ghost of a killer. I felt he'd try to guilt me into stopping, using the broken headlight as an example. But when he didn't say a peep, I was at a loss for words. The line remained silent for longer than necessary.

"Dad?" I called, breaking the daunting silence. "You still there?"

"I'll keep an eye out, Kacy. Just stay safe, okay? Don't do anything stupid."

"I won't; I promise."

Then I ended the call and raced home to pack my things.

To: Professor Carter (tulsauniversity.carter@gmail.com)
From: Jeremy Saunders (jsaunders1994@gmail.com)
Date: Wednesday, April 6, 2016 11:51:02 EST
Subject: Questionable Death

Dear Professor,
How well do you know the sheriff and Griffen? The reason I ask is because I think James didn't kill himself. After doing tons of research online, and interviewing the two, I've found quite a few claims that say otherwise. I think James was murdered and someone covered it up. I'm going to meet with the sheriff again and ask him a few more questions about it. I might need to speak with you and your wife again too.

To: Jeremy Saunders (jsaunders1994@gmail.com)
From: Professor Carter (tulsauniversity.carter@gmail.com)
Date: Thursday, April 7, 2016 6:48:30 EST
Subject: Re: Questionable Death

Dear Jeremy,
I'm well aware of the different articles online that claim James was murdered. The police did all they could back then. Technology was limited at the time, so forensics could only do so much. I highly doubt James was murdered, though. It is a good idea to throw that thought into your project. It'll make for good discussion among the class.

30 · Kacy

With all my belongings packed and ready to be moved, I sat in the living room, curled up on the sofa, waiting for Robert to come and get me. I nervously bit at my cuticles as I eyed the front yard through the window. I'd sent numerous texts to Eloise an hour ago, warning her about the death threat I'd received and that she should be on the lookout. However, when I didn't receive a reply from her, I became worried.

I hope nothing has happened to her.

I wouldn't know what to do if she had been killed or kidnapped. Granted, I didn't know her all that well, but she seemed like a nice lady—someone I could befriend. The need to know if she was okay gnawed at my neck. I pulled my phone from my pocket, pressed her contact, and waited for her to answer. *Dammit, Eloise. Pickup.*

"I'm napping, Kacy," Eloise said immediately after answering. "What's up?"

"*Please*, tell me you got my texts."

"Texts?" she questioned. "What texts?"

Dammit. Either she hadn't received them at all or just hadn't read them yet. Hopefully, it was the latter. "Listen, someone called me with a death threat, saying I'd disappear if I didn't stop looking into the case. I'm calling you to—"

A gasp on the other end cut me off.

"I had a feeling this would happen. And now we're both in danger."

I whisked my hand through my hair as my gaze averted from the window. "I'm sorry, Eloise. Please be careful."

"That's all you can say? Be careful." She scoffed. "You've now put my life at risk too."

"I'm not the only one who wanted answers, Eloise," I shot back. "Remember...you came to me asking for help? Well, this is what it's come down to." I was pissed at how inconsiderate she was being. "I didn't call to be chastised and blamed. I called because I felt I should warn you, that's all." I paused, expecting her to cut me off again, but when she didn't, my pause ended up being for dramatic effect instead. "So if you want to bring this shit to an end, be ready to visit Victor tomorrow so we can get to the bottom of this."

"Maybe we should just leave it to the police, Kacy."

"No! We're too involved at this point."

"Fine. I'll be ready come tomorrow."

"Good. Stay safe."

Then I ended the call.

31 · Robert

It was 5:20 p.m. when I pulled into Kacy's driveway. She may have doubted my intentions, but I meant every word when I told her she had to come stay with me. Through all the years we had known each other, I sure wasn't going to let anything happen to her.

When I exited my car and headed toward Kacy's front door, it swung open with a flourish. She must have been watching me from the window. With a massive purple suitcase trailing behind her and a black backpack slung over her shoulder, she looked prepared for the long haul.

"You ready?" I asked.

"As ready as I'll ever be," she answered with a crack in her voice.

She was clearly nervous.

I grabbed her suitcase and lugged it over to my car. When I glanced over my shoulder to see if she was following me, I found her taking her sweet time locking the front door. Perhaps she was having doubts about coming to stay with me. Regardless, she knew there was no other option. I opened the trunk, tossed her luggage in, and got in the driver's seat. A second later, she joined me in the car, squishing the backpack on the floor mat between her legs.

"Okay. Next stop, Regional Heights." I put the key in the ignition and brought the motor to life. Then we pulled out of the driveway and onto the main road.

As I drove through the city, I kept glancing at my mirrors, afraid we were being tailed. Call me paranoid, but a black Lincoln Town Car had been trailing us for the past ten miles. It'd turned down the same street as us—three times. And that was way more than I would have liked. When I glanced over at Kacy, her eyes were doing the same as mine —peering out the side-view mirror.

Does she think we're being tailed too?

To test my theory, I parked in front of the post office, conveniently pulling into the parallel spot right behind a minivan. As expected, the car I was surveilling drove right by. Now we just had to sit and wait for a little while, making sure no one suspected anything, before pulling back out into the flow of traffic.

I had expected Kacy to say something about why I'd stopped, but she didn't. Then suddenly, she said, "Smart move pulling off like that. That Lincoln had followed us for far too long."

She had a good head on her shoulders—good enough to know what was happening around her. And before I could respond, she continued with a question.

"How much more of this case is there to solve?"

"What do you mean?" I answered her question with another.

"I mean, have you narrowed down your list of suspects? Have you spoken with Victor yet? What about Griffen, the Sheriff, or his wife?"

The fact she knew the sheriff's wife was involved had thrown me for a loop. I hadn't thought to speak with Meredith Wells on the matter, let alone thought I needed to. But maybe I should.

"Kacy, I've spoken with everyone," I lied. "No one seems—"

"And you still haven't found the killer yet?"

"It's not that easy, Kacy. I can't just convict who I think did it, okay? Certain measures need to be taken to solve a case. There's a lot that goes into this. Things like finding clues, questioning suspects and witnesses, to even looking up phone records. Now please, give it a rest."

She sighed. "Robert, I can't."

"You can and you will, Kacy. I can take it from here."

"Well, did you at least look up the number that called me?"

"It didn't come up with anything. It must've been a burner phone," I regrettably said. As much as I hated to admit it, I failed to uncover the person who had sent Kacy the death threat. It was a bitter pill to swallow, especially since I had all the resources I needed to succeed. Yet, despite my best efforts, I came up empty-handed.

After a few minutes passed, and there was no sign of that Town Car in our midst, I pulled back out into traffic and continued to my place, the two of us sitting in silence the rest of the way.

When we arrived, I parked, unloaded her luggage, and helped her settle in. "You do realize you're not allowed to leave, right?" I said, grabbing a glass from the cupboard and running it under the kitchen faucet to fill it.

"Yeah, yeah, I know," she said, clearly irritated.

Kacy began unpacking some things from her suitcase onto my coffee table. She sounded pissed, as if she didn't want to be here. I couldn't blame her, though. My place wasn't the Ritz Carleton, but it was something. However, it was temporary. And she knew that. She also knew the sooner I solved this case, the sooner she could return to her father's.

I was perched against the sink when she stood from the sofa and went to the bathroom to put away a tiny bag she'd pulled from her suitcase. I took a sip of water. "I know it sounds like you're being held hostage, but I'm just doing this for your safety, Kacy. That's all."

"I know, Rob, I know. Enough already."

She shuffled through the medicine cabinet behind the mirror, probably putting away her toothpaste or something. Then she came back out.

"You can take the bed. I'll sleep on the couch." That was when she just stared at me as if I'd brutally beaten someone to death in front of her. Had I said something wrong? I hadn't the slightest clue. "What?" I asked, wondering what was going through her mind.

"Oh, nothing," she said with a smile. "What's for dinner since I'm not *allowed* to go out?" She giggled.

My friendly gesture must have lightened the mood a little. Perhaps the look she gave me was one of surprise, not fear, as if she thought I'd never offer up my bed to her. I downed the rest of my glass and answered her.

"Pizza. Harry's Pizza."

"That place is still open?"

"Sure is. You call it in, and I'll go pick it up." As she pulled out her cell to look up the number, I placed the glass in the sink and headed for the door.

32 · Kacy

WHEN I AWOKE the following morning, I didn't expect to be all alone. I lifted my head and instantly winced at the pain. There was a crook in my neck that I believed had probably come from Robert's old mattress. God, was that thing stiff. Sliding out from under the covers, I got out of bed and peered out the bedroom window, where I spotted his car leaving the parking lot below. The sudden jarring of the front door was probably what had woken me up.

Knowing that Robert would be gone until five o'clock, I had plenty of time to search for Victor's whereabouts so that Eloise and I could visit him. I went to use the bathroom, then returned to bed to snuggle back under the covers. I glanced at the digital clock on his nightstand as I got comfortable again. It read: 8:37 a.m.

I hope Eloise is up.

I reached for my phone next to the clock and sent her a text with Robert's address, telling her to be there at ten a.m.

Then I set the phone aside, pulled my MacBook from my backpack that I'd stored under the bed, powered it on, and searched 'Victor Pines' on Google. With my location services turned on, it yielded fewer than ten results. Hopefully, there was only one Victor Pines in Oklahoma.

After twenty minutes, I found him. It was easier to find Victor than Griffen, thank God. But how I had found him was surely unorthodox. It was through his daughter, on her Facebook page, in one of the many pictures she'd posted on her account. Who knew he had a daughter?

Upon further inspection of that picture, I noticed they were standing in the courtyard in front of a building. I zoomed in on the photo to make out the name of the place. However, only part of it was visible. All I could read was 'Heritage P' on the sign. After checking the date the photo was posted, I discovered it was from three weeks ago. Hopefully, Victor was still there, not somewhere else, or worse—dead for whatever reason.

I quickly scrolled up to the search bar, highlighted everything I had typed, and hit the delete button. Then I entered 'Heritage P' to find the name of the place. Luckily, the name auto-filled with Heritage Point. Thank God for technology. However, I encountered another problem. There were two locations, one in Oklahoma City and the other in Tulsa. Despite my success in locating Victor, I still faced a fork in the road. Visiting both locations was an option, but that would only waste time and gas. Then I thought, why not call the place?

I picked up my phone and dialed the number for the Tulsa location first. It rang twice, then a woman answered.

"Hello, this is Heritage Point, where we make the most

of each and every day. How may I help you?" The woman's voice was chipper and uppity sounding.

I put on my polite voice to match her tone. "Hi, good morning. I'm just calling to see what your visiting hours are for today and to find out whether I need to make an appointment to see a friend?"

"Our visiting hours are from ten a.m. to five p.m., and as for an appointment, you don't need one. If this is your first time visiting, we'll just need a copy of your driver's license, and that's it."

I fell back onto the pillows I'd stacked together to improve my back support. "Wonderful! Thank you. Oh, and eh…I just flew in yesterday evening, and I don't know whether my friend is at your location or the one in Oklahoma City. Do you mind confirming for me?"

"Not a problem. What's your friend's name?"

"Victor Pines."

I listened intently as the woman typed, her fingers clacking against the keyboard. Then the tapping stopped.

"Ma'am…he's here at our location."

"Oh, what a relief. Thank you so much."

"My pleasure. Now you enjoy the rest of your day, okay?"

"Thank you! You too."

Then I ended the call.

With Victor's location confirmed, I was all set to question him about his time at Camp Mercy. The only thing standing in my way now was the lack of transportation to get there. However, with Eloise kindly agreeing to be a lift, that had also been sorted out.

I had one hour to get ready before she'd arrive. I felt that was plenty of time to get myself together, so I could spruce up and look presentable for the woman at the front desk. I just hoped we wouldn't encounter any obstacles getting in, particularly since my license was from out of state. However, I had faith that Eloise's credentials would be enough to smooth things over.

Nevertheless, I got up and made Robert's bed, tucking in the sheets under the sides of the mattress and folding over the top lip of the comforter, making his entire bed resemble a beautiful spread out of a Better Homes & Gardens magazine. It was the least I could do for him since he was keeping me safe at his place. A kind gesture for sure, which only increased my desire to get back with him.

Regaining my focus, I dropped to my knees and sifted through my suitcase. I pulled out my black jeans first, then a burgundy shirt. With no clue as to what could accentuate that top, I went without another piece of clothing and finished off the outfit with my white-checkered Vans. Then I headed to the bathroom to brush my teeth and wash my face. I looked in the mirror to examine my looks. God, did I look awful. I was tired—exhausted. The bags under my eyes said it all. Mainly from the lack of sleep due to everything on my mind. However, I still managed a smile. I had to if I was going to finesse my way into an old folks home to speak with the possible Camp Mercy killer.

After completing my daily hygiene routine, I walked out of the bathroom and back into the bedroom to finish getting dressed. Then I headed to the living area and got comfortable on the sofa as I waited for Eloise to arrive. Before I knew it, my phone buzzed with a text from her saying she was outside.

33 · Robert

WHEN I ARRIVED at the precinct, I didn't expect to find a shit ton of paperwork on my desk—stuff that had nothing to do with the Carter case that had dribbled over into a closed suicide investigation from thirty years ago. I understood that other cases demanded my attention—court hearings I needed to attend and simple files I needed to email. However, knowing Kacy's life was still in jeopardy, I couldn't deal with those things. Knowing I was here stuck at work and she was back at my place unsupervised made my stomach simmer with unrest.

I knew that the sooner I solved the case, the sooner she'd be out of harm's way. At least, that was what I'd liked to have thought. So instead of sitting at my desk, I left my office and marched over to the sheriffs'.

I poked my head into his room. "Hey, Sheriff? You have a sec?"

"Sure, c'mon in," he answered, wiping his mouth with a napkin. "Make it quick."

I found Meredith sitting in one of the chairs opposite his desk as I entered. They were sharing a large slice of pie she must have brought in for him.

"Oh, my apologies. I didn't mean to interrupt."

"You're fine, Robert. What's this 'bout?"

"Well, I was thinking back to our little conversation and...I need to speak with your wife to get her recount of the events that took place that night in eighty-six."

They both exchanged glances.

"Dear, what's he talking about?"

"Camp Mercy, honey," the Sheriff said. Then to me, he added, "Give us a sec. When we're done here, I'll send her your way."

"Thanks, Sheriff. Much appreciated."

As I turned to leave, he called my name. "Robert?"

"Yes?"

"You were there that night, weren't you? When that girl uncovered Charles Carter's body?"

"Yes, I was. Is this about Kacy?"

"Yes. She came 'round here asking to put in a request to see the case files on Camp Mercy. Said something 'bout being a student at the university."

"Which was why she was out there exploring the camp in the first place," I added, knowing all too well I hadn't planned on covering for her. "She mentioned something about that when I questioned her."

"Just checking. I find it odd that you are both looking into the case simultaneously."

I shrugged my shoulders and smiled. "Stranger things

have happened." Then I left the room, heading straight for my office. Despite Kacy's lack of experience and knowledge on how to be a good detective, I couldn't ignore the fact that she'd managed to be so conniving. She was definitely relentless.

———

Twenty minutes after my short talk with the Sheriff, there was a subtle knock at my door.

"Come in," I said, sifting through the last of the paperwork.

The door opened, and Meredith Wells entered.

"How're you feeling today, Meredith?"

"Oh, I'm doing just fine, Robert," she answered. "How're you?" She closed the door and inched closer to my desk as I beckoned her to sit in the short-backed chair. She draped her purse over its back, then sat and crossed her legs.

"I'd be better if I didn't have this case to deal with, you know." I set some papers on the bin rack behind me. "Other than that, I'm better than ever."

"Perhaps you should look into a career change."

"No, I can't do that. I'd be doing myself *and* this state a disservice." She remained silent as if she didn't know how else to respond, so I continued. "So, the night James Edlin died, where were you around six p.m.?"

She put her hand to her chin, thinking of what to say. "At that time, we were probably all eating supper in the main hall. Don't ask me what we were eating, though, 'cause I don't remember that."

I jotted down what she said on my notepad and continued. "Blake mentioned a fight between Griffen and James."

"Yes. Those two fought. Don't know what over, though. Never found out. All I remember seeing was Blake jump up from the table to help break it up."

"And then?"

"And then, after everything cooled down, we finished eating. Blake and I took a stroll to the lake afterward. We did that every night after suppertime. It was our form of *relaxation*."

"Form of relaxation, in which you mean you two went to the lake to smoke weed?" I joked. My joke fell flat. The way her forehead creased up proved that she didn't find my humor amusing. I tapped my pen against the notepad. "My apologies. I'll keep it professional."

"If you must know, Robert, we were quite sexually active teenagers."

"You two weren't the only ones back then, I can imagine."

Meredith brushed her blond shoulder-length hair behind her ears. "Regardless, do you have any more questions?"

I flipped through my notepad, glancing at the sheriff's answers compared to his wife's. There were no discrepancies between their accounts of what happened. "Yes. Charles Carter. You remember much about him?"

"Of course! How could I forget him? How could I forget anyone that was involved?" Meredith looked away and readjusted herself in the chair. "Charles was my friend. When I heard what happened to him, I—"

"When did you hear what happened to him?" I interrupted. "And from whom?"

She hesitated, catching herself in a pickle. Sweat began to bead on her forehead. "I...Blake told me when he was found."

Hmm, interesting. "So, if you and Charles were friends, then I can assume you were with his wife too?"

"Why, yes, I am. She and I talk occasionally. Not much recently, though, given everything going on and whatnot."

"Well, the last you saw her, did you notice anything unusual?"

Meredith shook her head. "Sorry. Like I said, I haven't seen her in a while. About a month before her husband was found was the last time."

"Understandable. Thank you for your time, Meredith. It means a lot."

She didn't respond to my courteousness as she stood from the chair, sweat still beading on her forehead. She grabbed her purse and left my office. Seeing her sweating like that made me wonder. *Is she really friends with Mrs. Carter?*

I'd known the Wells family for some years now. Had even gone over to their home for dinner, and not once had they mentioned a supposed friendship with the Carters. Perhaps I was overanalyzing it, but I couldn't help but think it would have come up in conversation at least once. If not, I would have at least seen them conversing at the state fair. However, I couldn't recall such a sight. Then I thought back to Blake. During our time together, fishing and shooting the shit over dinner, he never mentioned Charles, Griffen, or

Victor. Something seemed off. I just didn't know what exactly.

I fished out my cell and called Mrs. Carter to test my theory.

"Detective?" she said after answering. "Now's not the best time."

"I just have a quick question, if you don't mind. Are you friends, or have you ever been friends with a woman named Meredith Wells?"

"If you're referring to the sheriff's wife, then yes, I know of her. We attended the same high school. However, we've barely talked."

Her answer said it all. Meredith had lied. Now I just needed to find out why.

"Thank you. I'm sorry if I have inconvenienced you in any way."

"No inconvenience whatsoever. I'm just a little busy at the moment, that's all."

Then I ended the call.

To: Professor Carter (tulsauniversity.carter@gmail.com)
From: Jeremy Saunders (jsaunders1994@gmail.com)
Date: Friday, April 8, 2016 3:40:51 EST
Subject: SAFETY CONCERNS!!!

Dear Professor,
I'm getting a little worried. There was a car that tried to run me off the road today on my way home from class. I don't know if it had anything to do with my report on Camp Mercy, but I'm really concerned. I tried to meet with the sheriff, but he was busy. I hope I can meet with him sometime tomorrow.

To: Jeremy Saunders (jsaunders1994@gmail.com)
From: Professor Carter (tulsauniversity.carter@gmail.com)
Date: Friday, April 8, 2016 5:55:11 EST
Subject: Re: SAFETY CONCERNS!!!

Dear Jeremy,
Tread carefully, Jeremy. I also just encountered someone on the highway who tried to make me wreck. I don't think it's a coincidence. I think someone's trying to scare us. Maybe James was murdered.

34.

It was ten a.m. when a black Lincoln Town Car pulled up outside Griffen's residence. Griffen was napping out on his front porch, the morning sun baking his freckled skin.

The car door opened, and a heavyset man dressed in all black stepped out. His pores sweat from the heat, and his skin glistened in the sun's rays. His bald head even reflected the light. The man examined his surroundings, then approached Griffen's trailer. With each step he took, the gravel under his feet crunched.

When he reached the steps to the porch, he balled his fists tight enough for each of his knuckles to crack. Then he began to climb. The old wooden steps creaked and flexed as he did, but each step's sounds weren't loud enough to wake Griffen. When the man finally reached the top, landing on the main porch, he found Griffen fast asleep.

Griffen was sure in for a surprise.

The man nudged Griffen's foot with the tip of his boot.

Griffen's snoring ceased, and his eyes shot open.

"Eh, haven't seen you in a while. What are you doing here?" Griffen asked, rubbing the sleep from the corners of his eyes.

"I'm here 'cause you couldn't keep your mouth shut," the old man said, drawing a Glock-9 from his holster and aiming it directly at Griffen's forehead.

Bang!

35 · Kacy

ROBERT NEVER GAVE me a key to his place. But it made sense. I didn't need one in his eyes because I wasn't going anywhere. However, with Eloise patiently waiting outside, I realized I had a problem. How could I lock up the apartment without locking myself out?

I knew that once Robert returned home to find me stranded outside, it would be clear that I'd left without his permission. The thought of leaving the door unlocked made me uneasy, knowing it would leave his belongings vulnerable to theft. And if someone had broken in in my absence, I wouldn't be able to forgive myself. So I decided to take my chances and lock up, hoping that I could explain away any confusion later.

With my backpack hanging halfway off my shoulder, I trekked down the crumbling staircase and got into Eloise's car. Once strapped in, I typed the address for Heritage Point of Tulsa into the GPS on my cell phone, then off we went.

We arrived after a short ride across town. The place fell short of my expectations. I had expected it to be bigger, multiple levels even. But sadly, it wasn't. But I still hadn't seen the inside of the facility, so my opinion of the place could still improve.

"You ready?" I asked Eloise as she parked in a spot and turned off the vehicle.

"I'm ready," she answered.

She opened the door and stepped out, and I did the same. I took a deep breath as we crossed the parking lot onto the sidewalk. We were steps away from the entrance when I felt a headache begin to build.

"This is it," I said, exhaling the deep breath I'd taken. "I'll ask all the questions, okay? See if I can trick him into confessing."

Eloise nodded.

As we walked through the entrance, the sliding glass doors opened, and we were greeted by a stunning display of colors. Maple wood cabinets gleamed in the bright light, while the light-gray tiles beneath our feet offered a soothing contrast. The walls were a blend of white and beige, lending a warm and inviting feel to the space. And then there was the scent—the tantalizing aroma of lemon cake, teasing my senses and making my mouth water.

As I was lost in heaven for a second, I caught Eloise inching forward from out of the corner of my eye. She reached the counter before I could move.

"Excuse me," she said to the woman behind the counter. "I'm here to visit a friend. Name's Victor Pines."

I joined her, coming up on her right side.

"I just need both of your driver's licenses, please, and fill

227

this out," the woman said, her voice different from the chipper one I'd spoken to earlier.

The woman pulled a clipboard from under the desk and held it out. I grabbed it, trading my license for the clipboard, and skimmed the page as Eloise dug through her purse for her driver's license. I filled out every line marked with a red X next to it—information such as my name, telephone number, address, and the reason for my visit. After Eloise handed over her license and filled out her information, the woman retrieved the clipboards, then guided us down the hall and to the left.

As we made our way down the dimly lit hallway, my anxiety started to bubble up inside me like a pot boiling over. My breaths came in short gasps, and my chest felt like it was being squeezed in a vice. I had never experienced such fear before, and it was disorienting. Was this really what anxiety felt like? No matter how hard I tried to calm down, I couldn't shake the feeling. My heart pounding in my ears only increased my sense of dread. To make matters worse, a splitting headache added to my discomfort, making it hard to think clearly. I was trapped in my mind, and I couldn't seem to escape.

Then the woman stopped at the door at the end of the hall, and my heart did the same.

She knocked and opened it. "Victor, you have another visitor."

Another visitor? Who was the first?

Then, as the door opened fully, I saw a light-skinned girl poking her head out from around the corner. *Wait a second, that's Victor's daughter!*

What were the odds she'd be here at the same time as us?

The woman left to return to her post as we entered.

"Hello, I'm—"

"Kacy Roe!" his daughter exclaimed.

In my attempt at introductions, his daughter leaped from the chair beside his bed and dashed toward me.

"I'm a huge fan," she admitted. "I watch *every* video you post. Got the notification bell clicked too."

I was at a loss for words, caught off guard by her reaction. It was unbelievable that the daughter of the man we sought out was a fan of mine. I couldn't believe my luck. And with that, I knew I could use it to my advantage.

She immediately enveloped me in a tight hug as I extended a hand. Her grip was so firm I could sense her heart beating rapidly against my chest. She was clearly thrilled to meet me, and I couldn't help but feel a surge of excitement as well.

"Sorry, I...I just never thought I'd meet you...like ever," she admitted, releasing me from her fan-girlish grasp.

I beamed. "It's no big deal."

"No big deal? You're a superstar! Of course, it's a big deal!"

I started to blush. "*Please.*"

"What are you even doing here, Kacy?"

"Well..." I paused, not knowing what to call her.

"Sorry, I didn't even introduce myself. I'm Lulu."

Lulu was a pretty name. And she was a pretty girl. I glanced at Victor, noticing the resemblance. She was the spitting image of his teenage self.

"Hello, Victor. I'm Kacy."

A thought immediately struck me about Victor and his situation. *Why is he in this facility in the first place, let alone in a wheelchair?*

Then I remembered Eloise standing in the corner. "Well, Lulu. Since you already know me, let me introduce you to my friend." I pointed to the door. "Her name's Eloise."

"Hi, nice to meet you," Eloise said, extending a hand.

"Eloise is here because she was friends with your father in high school and was there the night of the hanging at Camp Mercy."

Lulu's eyes lit up in shock. "So, that's why you're here."

Did she even realize her father had attended Camp Mercy years ago? Perhaps he'd never mentioned it. Lulu glanced at her father, then back at me, noticing the bag draped over my shoulder.

"So, we're hoping to ask him a few questions, if that's alright with you?"

"Anything for you, Kacy," she said. "But I don't know if he will be of much help."

"What do you mean?" I asked, making my way over to the windowsill to unpack my camera equipment.

"Well, my dad had a stroke four years ago and doesn't remember much of anything."

It was at that moment it clicked. Victor having a stroke explained it all. Why he was in a wheelchair, and why he was in Heritage Point, to begin with. If Victor had had a stroke four years ago, he couldn't have kidnapped and murdered Charles because that had happened three months ago.

I fished out my camera, attached the lens, and placed it on the sill. Then I aimed it toward Victor. As I continued setting up the microphone, I asked, "Is it okay if I record your father?"

"Of course," Lulu answered.

Eloise inched toward Victor, smiling and waving. "Hello, Victor. Do you remember me?"

I turned to see if he did. But he didn't answer her.

"Dad?" Lulu said, coming up beside him. "Do you remember Eloise from high school?"

Victor shook his head.

"Do you remember Camp Mercy? James Edlin or Charles Carter?" Eloise asked.

He shook his head again.

"Can he speak?" I asked Lulu.

Lulu sank her head and rubbed Victor's shoulder. "Unfortunately, no. I can barely afford this place, let alone rehab. At one point, I thought I was going to have to live in my car in order to keep him here."

"What about your mother?" Eloise asked.

Lulu kicked back against the wall and crossed her arms. "My parents never really got along. Got divorced when I was twenty. One year later, he had the stroke." She sniffled. "I believe that's what caused it."

Once my camera was set, I tried cheering up Lulu with a friendly hug. "I'm sorry. I can somewhat relate." Eloise didn't waste a second before melding into the embrace, her limbs encircling the two of us with ease. And as we shared that moment of solace, my mind slipped away.

Though my father's transgressions had been many, he'd taken ownership of them and made a concerted effort to right his wrongs. There was a possibility that Lulu's mother could return and redeem herself too. Despite the chances being slim to none, regardless, there was always a chance for someone to come back into your life.

And just as quickly as we had come together, we dispersed, leaving me with thoughts of Victor swirling through my mind. What if he had no memory of the past? What if he couldn't provide any information that could help us solve this case? I couldn't bear the thought of all our hard work going to waste. But I had to remain optimistic.

I shifted my gaze to Victor. Judging by the shape he was in, he looked nothing like a killer or someone who'd harm anyone. His cheesy smile with those gleaming pearly whites underneath, his short spiky hair, oiled to the max, and his fragile frame were the picture of a helpless old man. He couldn't be the killer we were looking for. He could have killed James in eighty-six, but certainly not Charles three months ago. However, with Victor's current state, there was no way to prove that he did. So we were back to square one. More than a week into the case and we were back at the beginning.

"Do you know if anyone else might've met with your father, Lulu?" I asked, fetching my camera.

"The office told me a detective came and spoke with him yesterday."

Mmm, a detective... it must've been Robert.

Eloise broke my train of thought. "You think it could be Detective Stone?"

"Most likely," I said. Then to Lulu, I added, "Do you happen to know if that *detective* managed to get any information from your father?"

"No clue. All they said was that he stopped by."

What Lulu said proved that Robert was covering all the

bases. At least, all the bases that I knew of. I wondered if he'd spoken to Griffen yet, before us or after. I wasn't sure, and I didn't want to ask him because that would only reveal that I was still searching for the truth despite my life being in danger. Nevertheless, I loaded my camera into my backpack and zipped it closed because there was nothing else Victor could do for us.

"I'm sorry for interrupting your daddy-daughter time," I said. "We're going to get out of your hair." I draped my bag over my shoulder and turned to leave.

"Wait!" Lulu called. "You're not going to ask him any questions?"

"If he doesn't remember Eloise, he most likely won't remember anything else from that time."

Lulu frowned. She might have been disappointed for me, for having come all this way to see her father only to hit a dead end. Perhaps, she feared we might never bring about justice. Regardless of the reason, I refused to give up.

36 · Robert

AFTER SIXTY LONG minutes of tirelessly checking off task after task, I had finally reached the end of my to-do list. Every single email had been answered, including the all-important one that revealed my court date for the following morning. Now, it was time to get down to the real business at hand: confronting Griffen and extracting the truth from him.

I marched out of my office, headed to my cruiser, and then hit the highway.

Despite investing so much time and energy into the case, I had yet to make any significant headway. Instead, I had found myself tumbling further down the rabbit hole of Camp Mercy's dark past. Looking back on my interactions with James' family, Eloise Carter, Sheriff Wells, his wife, and Victor, it became clear that only two of them posed a significant problem: Griffen and Victor.

Though I hadn't had the chance to question Griffen

thoroughly, he was my only remaining lead. Victor was useless due to his stroke, and there was no hard evidence linking Mrs. Carter to the case. The other leads had yielded no tangible evidence, leaving me with no other option but to press on and hope for the best.

An hour later, I pulled onto his gravel road. Clouds of dust flowed in the Tulsa wind from beneath my vehicle. Being careful with how much pressure I put on the accelerator, I crept down the path, trying my best to dodge every pothole Griffen had neglected to fill until I reached his trailer. Surprisingly, I found him outside, napping in his old rocking chair. The place looked remarkably bright in the daytime, though he had no foliage to accent his decrepit trailer. I didn't necessarily expect him to be the type to grow anything, but you'd think he'd want something green since the place otherwise looked like a total desert.

I turned off the car, opened the door, and stepped out. I expected Griffen to have been aware of my presence by now, yelling at me to leave or else he'd shoot, especially considering I wasn't keeping quiet. But he didn't wake. I hoped he wasn't in another drunken coma.

"Hey, Griffen," I said, approaching the front porch. "It's Detective Stone again. I don't know if you remember me, but I'm here to finish our conversation about your time at Camp Mercy."

I crept up the steps, each one creaking terribly. I expected Griffen to have responded or lifted the straw hat covering his face. However, he didn't move an inch. I could tell he was out of it with the way his limbs dangled over the arms of the chair as if he were dead. When I reached the top step, a fly buzzed and landed on his shirt, then flew upward toward his face, disappearing under the hat. When he didn't budge from that, I knew something was wrong.

"Griffen?" I called, reaching for the hat and lifting it to reveal his face. When I did, I found him in worse shape than before.

Fuck.

Griffen was dead.

He'd been shot. There was a bullet hole right between his eyes, brain matter dangling from the opened wound in his skull. Maggots were beginning to form.

Son of a bitch. The only possible suspect I didn't get to question is now dead.

I released the hat, causing it to recover his dismembered face. Then I pulled out my cell and called it in. It wasn't until after I ended the call to my team that I noticed something right under his seat—a gun. I knelt down to get a closer look.

It was a Glock-9.

37 · Kacy

AFTER OUR FAILED attempt at retrieving information from Victor, Eloise and I said our goodbyes to him, and Lulu then headed back to the car.

"It looks like we're back to square one," I said, disappointment weighing heavily in my tone.

"Not exactly," Eloise interjected. She tapped the unlock button on her car's key fob. "You remember what Lulu said, right? That Victor had a stroke four years ago?"

We each stopped at our respective doors.

"Yeah, I remember. So?"

Eloise rested her hands atop the roof of her sedan. "Well, that means what Griffen told us was a lie."

"How so?"

"He said the last time he saw Victor was six months ago. However, when we mentioned Griffen's name to Victor, he had no recollection."

"You're right. He didn't. Perhaps Griffen *did* lie to us. But why?"

My eyes widened in realization as the pieces of the puzzle finally began to click into place. Griffen's behavior during our last conversation suddenly made sense; he had abruptly ended the discussion after revealing that he'd seen Victor fleeing from the tree where James was found hanging. Perhaps that was just a diversionary tactic to get us off his trail. But what really struck me was his claim of having met with Victor recently, which seemed highly unlikely given Victor's current condition. While it was possible that Victor might have simply forgotten, I couldn't shake the feeling that there was more to this.

"Probably because he felt we were on to him," she answered.

"You're probably right," I said, opening the passenger door and getting in. "Which means he probably killed your husband. Let's pay him another visit to find out why he lied to us." As soon as I buckled my seatbelt, Eloise opened the glovebox in front of me and wrapped her hands around a .38 special.

"What are you doing with that?" My voice cracked.

"I purchased this yesterday after you told me about the death threat."

"Isn't there a wait to purchase a firearm?"

"Not in the state of Oklahoma," she said with a smile.

"Well, do you even know how to use one of those?"

"The place I bought it from showed me how. Haven't fired it yet, but I'll be ready to once we confront Griffen."

A wave of anxiety swept over me, flooding my veins with worry. While I was no stranger to handling weapons, I was wary of being in close proximity to someone who wasn't. And to make matters worse, Eloise had implied she would shoot Griffen. I couldn't bear the thought of witnessing a murder, let alone being an accessory to one. And as we left the parking lot and headed for the freeway, I couldn't help but feel apprehensive about how the day would end.

An hour later, we arrived at Griffen's residence. But this time, we weren't the only ones there. We couldn't even pull into the eroded driveway because there were too many cops and forensics personnel trudging the premises. Police officers from both Tulsa and Flint appeared to be present.

Eloise passed Griffen's place, swung the car around, and parked on the side of the main road, opposite his driveway.

"This doesn't look good," I said.

"Not one bit," she agreed. Eloise tucked the revolver back in the glove box and closed it. That was a smart move on her part. I didn't want the police to assume we were responsible for what had happened here. When we finally left her car and started walking toward the yellow tape, an officer stopped us.

"I'm sorry, ladies, but you can't be here," the officer said. "This is an active crime scene."

"What happened?" Eloise asked. "We just saw Griffen. Is he okay?"

A sense of disbelief swept over me as Eloise's confession sank in. I couldn't believe she had revealed something that could implicate us both. Even though I wasn't a detective, I knew better than to make such a mistake. The officer's eyebrows raised in suspicion, and I could sense trouble brewing. As the scrawny cop leaned in to whisper something to his colleague, I had a feeling that we were in for a round of questioning.

He turned back to face us and flipped out his notepad. "When did you say you last saw Griffen Houser?"

"Tuesday at around one o'clock," I blurted out. "We came to ask him a few questions about something. Is he okay?"

The officer ignored our questions.

"And this something was?" the officer asked.

I hesitated to answer, not wanting to say exactly what we asked him about, fearing it would evolve into something larger than it needed to be. Or worse, incriminate us even more. If Robert ever caught wind of me being outside, away from the safety of his apartment, I'd never hear the end of it. Then I gasped upon another realization. Could he be here now? If he was somehow here, lurking around the premises, he'd surely put me in a holding cell at the station until everything blew over. I shuddered at the thought before being snatched back to the situation in front of me.

"What he could remember from his experience at Camp Mercy in eighty-six, the year James Edlin was hanged," Eloise said, admitting the truth to the officer.

I guess the truth is out. And the way the officer looked at us made me think he knew it too.

He turned just as a cruiser approached the entrance to leave the scene. I didn't think anything of the vehicle at first. But when the officer lifted the yellow tape, allowing the cruiser passage, the car abruptly stopped right after going under it, skidding a few feet in the gravel beforehand.

The driver-side door flew open, and Robert jumped out.

"Kacy? Mrs. Carter?" he said, as if unsure if we were real.

His expression turned from shock and awe to grim and disappointed. He stormed up to us. "I thought you were going to stay put. I can't keep you safe if you're out here, running around doing God knows what."

Robert's anger was palpable and showed in his wild gestures as he towered over me. I was frozen in place, knowing there was no escaping his wrath. I'd been caught red-handed, and now I'd have to face the consequences.

"I...I'm..." I choked. Nothing I could say would improve the situation. So instead, I said nothing at all. I just gave him some puppy dog eyes as my heart beat uncontrollably.

Then Robert pinched the bridge of his nose and glared at Eloise. "And Mrs. Carter, why do you insist on putting yourself in harm's way trying to solve your husband's murder when I'm paid to do such things?"

Robert sure went easy on her compared to me. But I wasn't angry. I knew exactly why he was so hard on me. It was because he loved me, was in love with me, and had never stopped loving me. Even after I'd left years ago. That was the only plausible reason I could come up with at that moment. Perhaps I had made a mistake in leaving years ago. Maybe coming back home was something that needed to happen. A divine intervention. I exhaled, thinking now was the time to start over, piece together my broken relationship with my father, and rekindle my love for Robert.

"Kacy?" Robert said, snapping his fingers in front of my face to grab my attention.

I swatted his hand away. "What?"

"Get in the car. I'm taking you home." He headed toward his cruiser.

"But I can't! I need to know what happened to Griffen."

Robert doubled back. "Kacy, he's dead!"

I'd never seen Robert so angry before. He wasn't livid per se but undoubtedly agitated and disappointed. I couldn't blame him, though. The case was complicated, and my recklessness only added to his stress. The fact that someone was out to get me made things even worse.

Then amid the troubling thoughts, something clicked. "Why are you here?" I asked. "We're not in Tulsa. Is it because he was one of the suspects in the case?"

Robert stopped pacing and turned to face me. He inhaled deeply and answered. "I came to ask Griffen a few questions. But when I arrived, I found him with a hole in his head." He turned away and kicked his foot at the dirt, sending a puff of dust into the wind.

"If it helps, we questioned Griffen on Tuesday about the case," I admitted, creeping toward him and placing my hand on his shoulder. "He didn't give us anything but lies."

"Lies?" he repeated, turning to face me.

"Yes, lies," Eloise said. "He told us that the last time he spoke with Victor was six months ago."

"Which led us to think Victor did it," I said. "But when we met with him today—just an hour ago—and found out he'd had a stroke *four* years ago—"

"We realized Victor couldn't have killed Charles," Eloise added.

"So yeah, it's possible Victor could have killed James, but we may never know," I finished.

"Hmm. Then perhaps Griffen killed your husband, Mrs. Carter. And maybe he couldn't take the guilt anymore." Robert scratched his beard. "We'll have to wait for forensics to process the weapon I found to know for sure. In the meantime, Mrs. Carter, please go home." Then to me, he added, "Kacy, get in the car, so I can get you back to my place, where I know you'll be safe."

I fell into a slump and gave in. "Okay, Rob. Just let me grab my backpack from Eloise's car."

He nodded, then turned and headed for his cruiser.

I retrieved my bag, said goodbye to Eloise, and followed after him.

To: Jeremy Saunders (jsaunders1994@gmail.com)
From: Professor Carter (tulsauniversity.carter@gmail.com)
Date: Tuesday, April 12, 2016 3:40:12 EST
Subject: Missing Class

Dear Jeremy,
You missed another great lecture in class today, Jeremy. Hopefully, you finished up your report this past weekend because it's due on Thursday. If you don't show up and present, I'll be forced to give you an incomplete grade, which will result in your average dropping down to a D+. I'm looking forward to seeing your presentation.

38 · Robert

As Mrs. Carter headed home, Kacy and I headed back to my place, leaving the team of forensics to handle all the particulars, such as digging around in the filth of Griffen's place to gather whatever evidence hadn't been eaten by bugs and wildlife or burned to a wilting crisp from the hot sun's rays.

"This has been one hell of a case," I said, pulling onto the highway.

"You can say that again," Kacy joked. "But at least now, it should all be over with, right?" She turned to me with a smile.

"Well, that's only *if* forensics can link the gun I found back to Charles Carter's body."

"True," she agreed. "And that'll most likely take a few days, right? You said it yourself when I wanted my equipment, which means you get a few days to rest."

I chuckled at her hopeful thinking, realizing how ignorant she was about my job. Crime never ceased. The city never slept. Domestic abuse, drug dealers, corrupt politicians, you name it. Bad shit always happened. That was why the precinct was open twenty-four hours a day, seven days a week. Even though I sometimes wanted to, I couldn't just kick back with a beer in my hand as I waited to hear the verdict from forensics. I had other responsibilities to take care of, emails to send, and court hearings to attend. And I couldn't forget the myriad of cases that had been piling up on my desk over the past two weeks. Those didn't just disappear. Those other cases needed to be looked into and hopefully solved as well.

I was going off internally, angry at how Kacy didn't know a damn thing about police work. But then, I thought, *She doesn't know any better.*

When Kacy's glossy fingernails landed on my thigh, I exhaled all of my aggravation and glanced over at her. Even though she might not have known much about how police conducted business, she still had that way about her; that look of innocence, followed by an eagerness to learn anything she didn't quite understand.

"I wish I could take a few days," I said wearily. "But you said it yourself...crime never sleeps."

"Well then, maybe tomorrow, I'll just have to hide your car keys," she said, her hand inching closer to my crotch. Then she leaned in and whispered, "And in order for you to find them, you'll have to interrogate me. Maybe even do a strip search."

I grinned. Being assertive and putting my foot down was the key to getting her to open up. Perhaps that was what she liked—to submit to a man of power. Then I glanced out the window at the sign above the interstate to verify which exit I needed to take to continue west toward Tulsa.

Forty-five minutes later, we pulled into the parking lot of my apartment complex. My bladder was ready to explode. I'd been holding it since I got to Griffen's place. I rushed inside and bolted to the bathroom. A knock on the door followed shortly after.

"Hurry up, Rob," Kacy said. "I need to pee too."

"Okay, okay, I hear you," I shot back, re-zipping my fly and flushing the toilet. I washed my hands and opened the door to find her leaning against the frame with her arms crossed, bearing an expression of annoyance.

"What are we doing for dinner?" She closed the door and did her business.

I glanced at my Rolex, then quickly realized her question was baffling. "It's only three o'clock. Don't tell me you're hungry already."

"A girl's got to eat. And I missed lunch." And then, suddenly, she blurted out something completely unrelated to our conversation. "Shit! I completely forgot."

There was the sound of a flush, then a constant stream of water as she washed her hands. Then she pulled open the bathroom door and hurried to the kitchen. "I had set up a meeting to speak with the sheriff's wife about her time at Camp Mercy for six tonight."

"Well, if it were a few hours ago, I'd say you weren't going. However, do you still think it's necessary due to the recent events?" I crossed my arms and perched against the sink. "I've already questioned the sheriff's wife. She seemed a little skittish during the interview. Even lied to me about being friends with the Carters."

"She lied to you?"

"Yes. Perhaps she and the sheriff were covering for Griffen in some way. If that's the case, then they'll be facing some charges. Possibly some time, too, if we find any evidence that proves they were. But I can't say for sure until it's been verified that Griffen shot Charles Carter."

Her head tilted to one side as she squinted in thought. "I guess there's no need to speak with her now." She pulled out her cell from her jeans pocket. "What's the station's number so I can call and cancel?"

I gave her the number, and she punched it in. I didn't expect Kacy to cancel her appointment so easily, but I guessed she, too, believed that Griffen had murdered Charles and possibly James, so there was no longer a need for her to meet with Meredith.

After Kacy hung up, she said, "So what now?"

"We wait," I answered.

39 · Kacy

THE BEAMING sun shone in my eyes the following morning, Friday, prompting me to wake from my slumber. I groaned. *Robert must've opened the blinds again. Why must he do that?*

Call it a pet peeve, but I believed if anyone were still in bed, the blinds would remain closed until everyone was awake. I couldn't be mad, though. It was my fault. I shouldn't have invited him in to sleep with me last night. But it only made sense since we had almost had sex the other night. At this point, I felt it was only right that he sleep in his bed.

I glanced at the clock on his nightstand, which read: 8:51 a.m. "Guess it's time to get up," I muttered, sliding out from under the thick covers.

I kicked my feet over the edge of the bed and sat up, my head bobbing as it struggled to stay afloat. I was tired. My mind was too; foggy, sluggish, and slow. Having to share the bed this time, I hadn't gotten much sleep. I stumbled out of bed and shuffled to the bathroom to knock out my morning routine, then I got dressed. After a cup of freshly brewed coffee, I was wired, feeling ready to take on the world, starting with a follow-up video for my fans on the current status of the case at hand. Reaching for my back-pack under the bed, I fished out my camera and attached the lens. Then I hit the record button, turned it on myself, and beamed.

Action! "Hey, guys! Kacy here with another update on the mysterious murder of Camp Mercy. As of right now, the case has come to a close. Due to recent events, one of the suspects I questioned—the person I believe murdered James Edlin thirty years ago—has died unexpectedly. I don't know how, but the police are hinting at suicide. Don't know if the Police believe he was the alleged person respon-sible for the murder of Charles Carter—the man whose body I found at the camp over two weeks ago—or not." I tucked my hair behind my ear as I continued. "As of right now, I can't say much more because I don't have all the details. But once I learn of everything, I'll compile a full recap of all the footage I've captured and post it for you guys to watch. Stay tuned for the final product." *And scene.*

I tapped the button to end the recording, then went through the usual motions to get it posted online. I hoped my subscribers would be satisfied with another short video. At least until I could find out whether Griffen had actually killed Charles.

40 · **Kacy**

As Robert trudged through the door of his home, the weight of the day's events still heavy on his shoulders, a sense of eager anticipation built within me. I knew the long hours spent in court and the intense focus required to navigate the legal proceedings had left him exhausted and drained. The way he exhaled a great sigh of relief backed up my assumption. And as my gaze fell upon him, my mind couldn't help but wander to the intimate moment we had both been yearning for.

It wasn't just because my menstrual cycle had nearly passed; I was craving the physical release that only he could provide. It was also because I knew, deep down, that he'd been thinking of nothing but me all week, too, just as I had of him. And at that moment, it simply made no sense to deny him the pleasure we both craved. Especially since our last attempt at intimacy had been interrupted so abruptly.

I approached him as he sat on the sofa to untie his shoes. "Close your eyes, Rob. I'll take care of those for you."

"What?" he said, glancing up at me.

I smiled and shoved my hand in his face, covering his eyes as best I could. "Just close your eyes and relax. You've had a long week, and it's time for me to take care of you."

"Whatever you say, Kacy."

I pulled my hand from his face, dropped to my knees, and started unlacing his dress shoes. God, did he look sexy in that dark gray suit with the way he accented it with those light brown shoes and matching belt. I couldn't help but imagine Ryan Gosling in the mall scene of *Crazy, Stupid, Love*. The only thing missing was a slice of pizza in his hand.

"No peeking," I said, slipping off his shoes and setting them aside. Then I stood and snuck over to the kitchen counter, where he'd placed his car keys beside his handcuffs, and slipped them into my bra.

"Kacy?" he called out from the sofa, probably wondering why I'd stopped touching him.

"Gimme a sec."

"What are you doing?"

"Shhh, don't worry. You'll see in a few."

Robert exhaled another long sigh. That was when I returned to him and tossed something into his lap. His eyes shot open. He looked down, puzzled at the sight of his handcuffs. Then he glanced back up at me. "What's with these?"

I shifted my weight to one hip, crossed my arms, and smirked. "I've stolen something of yours. You're welcome to question me. And if you ask the right question, I might just let you strip-search me."

Robert shot up from the sofa and began his investigation as I took his place, throwing my arms up along the backrest to stretch out. I knew role-playing was a hit or miss, especially with a kink like cops and robbers. Since he did investigative work for a living, I doubted he'd want to include it in his sex life. However, by the look of his eagerness to play along, I'd say he'd never done such a thing before. There was always a first time for everything.

After a few minutes, he returned to me on the sofa and began his interrogation. "Where were you when I arrived home from work?"

"In your room, lying down," I said, giving him a seductive look.

He nodded, then went for another question, trying to trip me up, I believed. "Lying down or playing with yourself?"

"Well, aren't you dirty-minded?"

He smiled. "Oh, you haven't seen anything yet, Kacy. Now, after you removed my shoes, you disappeared off somewhere. Where'd you go?"

"The kitchen."

He paced the living area, circling the glass coffee table. "If I were a woman, where would I hide an item that I stole?" he muttered, his fingers combing his beard. He stopped and turned to me. "There are only a few places you can hide something *if* you were to hide it on your person."

"Emphasis on the *if*," I added with a kinky smile, leaning forward onto my knees to display my breasts a little, to hint at where his keys were located.

Robert approached me, the hunger and desire clearly visible in his eyes. They mirrored the emotions that were coursing through my body. "I'm going to need to do a strip search. Please stand and assume the position."

I bit my bottom lip, stood, and spun around so he could pat me down.

"Spread your arms and feet for me," he whispered in my ear.

"Yes, officer."

Then Robert snuck his hands—beginning at the nape of my neck—down to my ankles, feeling up my breasts as he passed over them. It was clear that he knew what I'd hidden from him. The way I winced at the keys digging into my breast as he felt them gave it away. I never thought role-playing could get me so hot. Just like him, it was also my first time.

"Be a nice girl for me and lift your arms," he whispered, blessing my cheek with a kiss.

I adhered to his request and let him remove my shirt. I shut my eyes and absorbed the rustling sound of fabric as he lifted it over my head. Then I heard it soar through the air and land on a surface nearby. His arms then snaked around my midsection. His fingers glided over the curves of my hips with ease. Without warning, he gently tugged at my waistband, popping the button on my jeans with a satisfying snap. Then he continued to free me from my clothing, unzipping my jeans with practiced ease.

Robert had me dripping like a leaky faucet. His hands were so lush against my skin, as if they were made of cotton. And his warm breath against my shoulder made me drool. Before I knew it, my pants were around my ankles, and I was helpless. He helped me undress as he slid my feet from the holes of my pant legs. As suddenly as it had begun, his touch vanished, replaced only by his frantic footsteps pounding against the floor. No doubt, he had gone to fetch a condom from his room. I had stumbled upon a pack of them earlier in the week hidden in his nightstand. Despite my desire to chase him down, I held still, allowing him to continue his search since he still hadn't found what I'd stolen. I was in my bra and panties and socks now—nothing else.

Suddenly, he pulled my arms behind my back and locked me in his handcuffs as he said, "You've been a bad girl." Then he reached around and yanked out the keys from between my breasts.

My eyes shot open, giggling at what fun we were having. "You caught me."

With alarming speed, he smothered my mouth with his hand, stifling any protests I might have made. Then he hurled his keys across the room, the metallic sound echoing throughout the space as they landed on the carpet. In a single motion, he yanked my panties down to my ankles, leaving me bare. I didn't know if he'd even shed his slacks yet, but I didn't care. All I wanted was to feel him inside me and to be taken from behind on the sofa.

Robert gently pushed my head down onto the plump cushion.

I bit my lip again, waiting.

Listening.

His belt unbuckled, and his slacks fell.

"You do have a condom on, right?" I asked as he squeezed my ass cheek.

"You know I do. Now shush."

As he slipped two fingers inside me, I couldn't help but

shiver in anticipation. His fingers were cool to the touch, but they quickly warmed. He moved them in and out, rubbing around, searching for that sensitive spot that would send me over the edge. My body tensed, and my legs quivered as he zeroed in on my G-spot.

And then, with a knowing smile, he looked down at me and asked, "You ready?"

I nodded, unable to speak, my body trembling with desire. And with one smooth motion, he pulled his fingers out of me and replaced them with his throbbing cock.

He began to thrust in and out, his hands gripping the short chain that connected the cuffs around my wrists. I could feel my orgasm building, my body arching up to meet his every thrust. And then, with a cry of ecstasy, my body convulsed with pleasure. As the waves of pleasure subsided, I looked back up at him, my breath coming in ragged gasps.

His expression was pure focus, and I knew he was just as caught up in the moment as I was. He leaned down and graced my lips with a fiery, passionate kiss. It was then that I knew this was only the beginning of an unforgettable night.

"Yes!" I moaned.

He had just enough pubic hair to cushion every blow he gave me. Every thrust was followed by a grunt. *God, does he know how to work me.*

He increased his speed.

"Fuck, yes!" I yelled.

I was teetering on the brink, unsure of how much more I could take. The release was imminent, creeping up on me at an alarming rate. It had been ages since I'd experienced such intense pleasure, and I was on the verge of exploding.

My toes curled, and my eyes rolled back into my head. I even drooled a bit—it was that good. But then, unexpectedly, Robert withdrew, and I gasped for air. It was too late, though; I'd already climaxed.

My body quivered with euphoria.

He pulled me up, spun me around, and kissed me. His cock was still hard between my legs as it brushed up against my thighs. We were lost in each other's eyes. At least, I was in his. However, it was in that moment of clarity that old thoughts resurfaced.

I had done him wrong.

I never should have left.

He deserved to know the truth.

He deserved that much, especially now that we were more than just old friends catching up. "Can you un-cuff me, please?" I asked, pulling my face away from his chest and gazing into his blue eyes. "I need to tell you something."

"No can do. I'm not done with you yet."

Not done with me?

His words ignited a spark within me, a burning desire to wrap my arms around him and have him carry me off to his bedroom for round two. However, I knew that there was something more pressing that needed to be addressed. I had been carrying a heavy burden for nearly a decade, and it was time to finally let it go.

"I'm serious, Rob," I insisted. "Please."

He ran his hand down the right side of my face and said, "Okay."

He retrieved the keys from the floor and released me from the metal bonds. Then we both sat on the sofa. At first,

I hesitated, not knowing how to start the conversation. However, how he gazed deep into my soul reassured me that I would get through it.

I grabbed his hand. "You deserve to know the reason why I left, Rob. Why I didn't say goodbye. It wasn't because I was angry with you or upset about something you did." I paused, looking away as I second-guessed telling him the truth. *No. I have to tell him. It's only right.*

I'd come this far, so it made no sense not to finish. I turned to face him. "I left because if I had stayed, we would have gotten married right out of high school. And I didn't know if that was what I wanted." I scooted closer to him, my thigh rubbing against his. "Following my mom's death, my dad went off the rails. See, my parent's relationship wasn't the best. You only saw them on good days. But my father was an absolute drunk, and my mother hated him for it. And since we were still finding ourselves—us being young and all—I was afraid if we'd gotten married and you grew into someone I didn't like, I'd regret marrying you. That I would repeat the cycle." I turned away again, releasing his hand. "I had already gone through that life once. I wasn't going to do it again. So, I left. Left everything behind...including you."

Robert wrapped his arms around me and pulled me into his embrace.

"I'm sorry," I said, tearing up. "I'm sorry I didn't tell you sooner." I anticipated him to say something in response, but he remained silent. Instead, he shifted his hand from around my body to my head and comforted me.

His touch was soft and soothing, a feeling that warmed my soul.

41 · Robert

THREE DAYS LATER, I walked into my office, feeling anxious to read the ballistics report on the weapon I'd found at Griffen's. I felt uneasy about the whole situation. If he'd thought we were onto him because he had killed James and perhaps even Charles, why didn't he just skip town? Crossing over state lines would have sufficed if he knew to keep a low profile.

I sat at my desk and checked my office phone for any messages, then my email, finding the M.E. report on Griffen's body. I opened it and read through the pages, taking note of everything.

TIME OF INJURY: APPROX—1035
PLACE OF INJURY: Decedent's home.

I grazed over a few more sections, like the decedent's address.

IMMEDIATE CAUSE: Penetration brain injury.
UNDERLYING CAUSE: Gunshot wound to head.
DID TOBACCO USE CONTRIBUTE TO DEATH: No.

Then I read the most important thing, the Medical Examiner's description of how the injury had occurred and the manner of death.

DESCRIPTION: Decedent had contact wound to center of forehead.
MANNER OF DEATH: Suicide.

It was confirmed. Griffen had killed himself. But what reason would he have to do so? If he was responsible for both murders and got away with it, why kill himself now?

The traded emails between Charles Carter and his student collected from his computer were vague—not specific in any way. Perhaps Charles had found something Griffen didn't want coming out. And so, Griffen had killed him. That would serve as a motive for why Griffen committed the crime if the gun had his prints on it. However, that still didn't explain why he hadn't run instead of killing himself.

My first instinct was to rush down to the lab and uncover the results. But when I arrived, I was surprised to find that no one was there.

"Morning, Robert," a familiar voice called out from behind me.

I turned to find Leonard and Rachel walking up, each holding a cup of coffee. "I was wondering where you were," I said to Rachel.

She shrugged. "Sorry. I went to grab coffee with Leo."

"How's it taste today? Was thinking about grabbing a cup myself."

"It's better than yesterday's pot," Leonard joked.

I let out a chuckle.

"I guess you're here to get the ballistics report on the Glock?" Rachel suggested.

"Mhmm." I opened the door to her office to allow her through.

"See you later, Leo," she said, passing through the door into the lab.

I trailed behind Rachel, my eyes sweeping over the heavy-duty microscope on the counter where she placed her steaming coffee. With swift movements, she grabbed a manila folder that rested beside her keyboard and began to click her fingers across the keys. Griffen's criminal file appeared on screen, revealing his fingerprints, age, height, and the amount of time he spent behind bars. Then Rachel doubled back to me, placing the folder on the counter and promptly flipping it open.

"So do you want the good news or the bad news first?" she asked.

I hesitated to answer. But then she shot me a funny face.

"I'm just joking, Robert. It's all good news."

"You really need to stop playing these games, Rachel."

"I can't help it. I'm in here all day by myself. If I don't play games with people who stop by, I'll go crazy!"

That could have explained why she hadn't emailed me the ballistics report so I could come down to the lab and keep her company. It explained much more than that, really, but I was more focused on getting the answers I so desperately had been waiting three days for.

"So, despite being unable to run the gun's serial due to it being scratched off, I still pulled the dead guy's prints from it," she said, flipping to the second page of the report. "As for the two bullets recovered from both bodies, along with the casings found at each scene, I can infer that both had come from the pistol. Looks to me like you've successfully solved another one, Robert." She patted me on my shoulder.

I leaned onto the counter, putting all my weight onto my hands. "It sure doesn't feel like it."

She took a sip of her coffee. "I feel like the more you do it, the less rewarding it becomes. At least, that's how I feel when I uncover something in a case. *Unless* the case is unique in some way, like when the killer uses a pipe bomb or something. That's when it gets exciting." She laughed.

"I guess," I said. "Anyway, thanks for the report. I'll talk to you later."

"Enjoy the rest of your day, Robert," she said as I left her office.

As I trekked back down the hallway toward my office, I fell deep in thought. A few questions still lingered in the back of my mind. *Why didn't Griffen run? He could've easily killed me, Kacy, and Mrs. Carter when we visited him, then fled the state. Why didn't he do a better job disposing of Charles Carter's body? Why leave it at Camp Mercy at all? Could Charles Carter finding out about Griffen murdering James have been the motive?*

None of it added up. It was just the surface of a murder-suicide that made sense—nothing else.

I couldn't bring myself to file the paperwork and close the case. Something about the whole situation just didn't sit right with me. So without hesitation, I drove across town to Saint Francis Hospital, determined to examine Griffen's body and find the answers I was seeking. It was worth the drive, knowing it held the potential to put my doubts to rest.

When I arrived, I pulled into the parking lot and found a spot. After I stepped out of my cruiser, I walked across the lot and through the sliding glass doors of the front entrance. In all my time as an officer of the law and then a detective, I'd never been to the Medical Examiner's office. I never needed to since most of my cases were cut and paste. But unfortunately, this one was far from it.

As I entered the building, I immediately made my way to the front desk and inquired about the location of the morgue. Then, following the directions provided, I walked down the hall until I reached the designated room. I knocked on the metal door, but there was no response. Undeterred, I waited patiently, knowing that it was important to pursue every lead, no matter how small. Eventually, the door creaked open, and I stepped back, feeling eager to find the answers I sought.

"Hello," I said, greeting the old man who had emerged from the room. He was short and lanky and looked as if he were at least fifteen years past his retirement age.

"Sorry about the wait," the old man said, shedding his latex gloves and tossing them in the tin trash can by the door. "I'm kind of hard of hearing. How may I help you?"

I pulled my badge from my blazer's pocket and flashed it. "I'm Detective Stone. Are you Clive?" I'd gotten his name from the autopsy report.

"Why, yes, I am. Come in."

Clive held the door open and gestured for me to enter. As soon as I crossed over, a wall of sheer ice smacked me in the face. It was freezing in the room. The sudden temperature change dried my eyes a little.

"So, which is the body in question?" Clive asked, guiding me further into the dimly lit office space.

"In question?" I repeated, unsure of what he meant.

"Which body are you here to see? I assume you're here to see one, right?"

"A suicide. Came in Thursday."

"Suicide, huh?" He tilted his head to the side as he inched closer to the rack on the wall to grab something. He sifted through some papers on a clipboard. "I don't have one of those here."

My brows raised in wonder. "Huh? I was told you had examined the body of Griffen Houser, the man who shot himself in the head."

"Oh, yes...him. My apologies. Old age." He motioned to his head. "I sent his body out to be cremated two hours ago."

"What?!" I exclaimed. "How's that even possible? The case hasn't been closed yet."

"Well, technically, after forty-eight hours, the body of a criminal can be disposed of if—"

"Who signed off on that?" I demanded.

"Nobody."

My anger ceased, and my fist unclenched. How could

something like this happen? Now I had no chance to inspect Griffen's body. Granted, I didn't know exactly what I was looking for, but I still wanted to see it for myself. The second best thing was to question Clive. But I highly doubted he knew anything because he was just M.E.

"I need a moment of your time," I asked.

"I'm sorry, but I'm swamped. I have a few more bodies coming in today and need to make some room." He entered another room labeled: COLD STORAGE, his hands pushing open the saloon-style doors.

"Clive," I said, reaching for his arm as he vanished behind the doors.

He turned to face me with a look of annoyance. It was only because I'd followed him into an area that was off-limits to non-hospital staff. "What else must you need?" he asked.

"I just need to ask you a few questions, that's all." I let go of his lab coat's sleeve.

Clive wobbled over to a body on a table, slipped on a new pair of gloves, and got digging. "If it's about Griffen Houser, there's not much else to say."

I crept closer, watching as he pulled out what looked like the lower intestines of a carcass. "All I need to know is whether or not he was murdered."

Clive stopped pulling and dropped the intestines, leaving them dangling halfway out of the body. The sudden halt in what he was doing startled me. He turned and glared, his eyes big and wide through the coke-bottle glasses on his face. "That man killed himself. End of story."

I backed off. I didn't want to get on the old man's bad side. Nor did I want him dying from a heart attack in front of me either, all because I'd stressed him out a little. And so I thanked him for his time, left the backroom, and opened the door to the morgue to trick him into thinking I'd left. But in reality, as the door closed, I went behind his desk and searched for a copy of the file on Griffen. And voilà! I found it. I pulled my cell from my pocket and snapped a few pictures, then snuck out the door before he realized I hadn't left.

To: Jeremy Saunders (jsaunders1994@gmail.com)
From: Professor Carter (tulsauniversity.carter@gmail.com)
Date: Thursday, April 14, 2016 5:55:29 EST
Subject: Final Notice

Dear Jeremy,

I'm surprised you worked this hard on your report, only to receive an incomplete grade. Please respond to this email if you'd like a second chance to present. I'll be in the classroom tomorrow until three o'clock. If you decide to stop by, please be prepared to present.

42 · Robert

CONSTANTLY QUESTIONING things and wondering 'what if' was what made me an expert detective. Perhaps that is also the reason why I got the corner office with the view. But now, in light of recent events, I was starting to doubt my abilities as a detective. I knew something was off about this case, and I was determined to find out.

Pulling back into the precinct's parking lot, I swung into a spot, stepped out of my cruiser, and returned to my office. But not before grabbing a cup of water from the commons area to quench my thirst. After I got comfortable in my desk chair, I emailed the photos I'd snapped of the original M.E. report to my work email so I could view them on a bigger screen. Once enlarged on my computer monitor, I skimmed through them and compared them to the M.E. report on my desk.

I ran my finger along the computer screen to decipher Clive's cursive handwriting. It said his lungs were nearly black, parts of the tissue dead. The liver was on its way out too. I continued reading, skipping over Griffen's physical descriptions, such as height, weight, race, and color of hair, because they were the same, and I was searching for something out of the ordinary.

A discrepancy.

Then, suddenly, I found it—in the Medical Examiner's description of how the injury occurred.

DESCRIPTION: Decedent had contact wound to center of forehead. Angle of entry incompatible with intentional infliction.

My eyes widened at what I had read. Then I darted back to the report on my desk. The description had been altered upon sending the report.

I knew he hadn't killed himself. It just didn't make sense.

I skimmed further, looking for anything else that might lean toward suicide. But everything I read proved otherwise. Griffen had been murdered! I reached for my office phone and dialed Mrs. Carter's number, hoping she'd be home. It rang for a moment, then she answered.

"Hello?" she said.

"Hello, Mrs. Carter? This is Detective Stone calling."

"Hopefully, you're calling with news about who killed my husband."

I leaned back in my seat. "Yes, I am. A few hours ago, I received some new information."

"And?"

I took a sip of water. "Well, our forensics team concludes that Griffen kidnapped and murdered your husband with the same weapon he used to kill himself on Thursday." The line went silent. But this time, I heard no sniffling or weeps of joy. And after a long moment of utter silence, it finally broke.

"So, I was right," Eloise said calmly. "The person who killed James killed my husband too."

I was thrown askew. I didn't expect those words to fly out of her mouth. With that, I struggled to think of what to say in response to her statement. There was no way to confirm Griffen had hung James back in eighty-six, especially now that he was dead. However, before I could say that, she cut me off.

"If Griffen was the killer the whole time, then why didn't he kill Kacy and me when he had the chance?"

"I've asked myself the same question, Mrs. Carter." I ran my hand over my face and sat up. "To be honest, I don't think Griffen killed your husband at all. I think it's a frame job."

She gasped. "Like on CSI and Law and Order? Can that even happen?"

"In this day and age, anything is possible."

"Is there anything I can do to help?"

"No. I just called to inform you of the recent findings and to promise you that I will find out who *actually* murdered your husband."

Mrs. Carter began to sniffle, probably from tears of gratitude. "Thank you so much, Detective Stone. You don't know how much this means to me. I know you're a very busy man and could have easily looked the other way. But because of who you are, you're going to make this world a better place."

I smiled as tears bubbled in my eyes from her kind words. Never had I cried or gotten emotional over such a thing as this. I barely cried at funerals. I guess some people believed in the same things as I did—that making the world a better place by working to save lives and stop crime was still possible. Even if it entailed long hours at the office. "Thank you," I said.

Then I ended the call and returned to business, determined to get to the bottom of this case. I took another sip of water and looked through the pictures I'd taken at the Medical Examiner's office. And that was when I found it.

I snapped my chair forward, and water spilled from my cup. A few drops landed on the crotch area of my khakis. *Son of bitch.* Then I shot back to the screen as I set the cup down. *Clive had lied!*

Included in the pictures I'd taken was the cremation certificate. And at the bottom of the page was a signature from Sheriff Wells. The veins on my temples thickened as I clenched my fists. Doubt swirled in my head. There were too many questions and not enough answers. More than ever, I was determined to discover what had happened.

I selected all the files, right-clicked on the mouse, and hit print. Then I jumped from my seat and stormed out of my office, down the hall, toward the printer. A minute later, I stood in front of the sheriff's office, ready to bust down his door. But then I hesitated. I needed to be careful with how I approached this predicament, or else he could lose his shit.

I had nothing on the sheriff besides his signature declaring the body to be cremated—that and the lies Meredith had told me about being friends with the Carters. That was it. There was nothing else to implicate him or his wife. Even if I were to bring it up to anyone else, I believed he'd simply claim it a mistake when filing the paperwork. At least, that was what I would do to cover my tracks. It was the perfect cover-up. In the precinct's eyes, the gun linked Griffen to Charles Carter's murder. Case closed. However, I knew that wasn't true. I had to find a way to get the sheriff to confess to what he'd done. And maybe—just maybe—he'd confess to something worse. Bating him was my only move. I had to take the risk.

I opened his door without a knock and stormed in, leaving it to close behind me with a thud. "You want to tell me why you signed off on Griffen getting cremated before the case was closed?" I tossed the pictures of the autopsy report I'd printed onto his desk.

He was on the phone.

"Honey, I'll call you back," he said. Then returned his phone to the hook.

He sifted through the pages, then looked up at me. "Robert, the guy's dead. Case closed. You really think I need *your* permission to send someone to the burner?" He chuckled.

I crossed my arms. "You do when you plan on botching the report." I leaned in over his desk, my voice quieting a tad. "You and I both know Griffen was murdered. He didn't kill himself. So how about you cut the shit and tell me what's really going on."

He leaned back in his chair and chuckled again. "I don't know what you're talking 'bout, Robert." He patted his belly. "All I see here is a simple mistake. I'll look into fixing it."

"How? The body's gone already."

"Well, I guess you should hurry up and file the report then."

I didn't know what to say. The way the sheriff played it off made me think he'd done nothing wrong. That Griffen hadn't been murdered. But if that were the case, why would the Medical Examiner have written that it wasn't a suicide?

"Great," I said, unsure of what he would fix. "Just to ensure we're on the same page, you *will* edit the report, right?"

His chuckle turned to a full-on menacing laugh. Then it stopped. He leaned forward and looked me dead in the eyes. "Robert, you caught the guy. It just so happens that he killed himself before you could catch him. It's over."

"But he didn't kill—"

"Turn in your gun and badge."

"What? Why?"

"'Cause it seems like you ain't convinced the crime's solved. So I'm relieving you of duty."

I hesitated, not wanting to turn in my service pistol and badge. "But—"

"No buts, Robert. Hand 'em over."

I slammed my badge and Glock on his desk and tucked my hands back in my pockets.

"Now go on, get out of my office," he finished as he waved me off. "Go home and relax."

Never had I ever experienced such disrespect from the sheriff before. In all my years of us working together, of coming over for Sunday dinners, he'd never done such a thing. It was then that I knew he'd covered up Griffen's murder.

43 · Robert

I was outraged.

Felt betrayed.

Was red with anger.

I stormed back to my office and slammed my door. A headache was starting to ensue from all the pressure in my head. I felt I was going to have a nosebleed at any moment. I returned to my desk and sifted through the top drawer for some Advil. I popped the cap, tossed the pill back, and chased it with water. Then I dug around in another drawer for my little black contact book. I knew exactly who to call to handle such a problem. They were the only person to call at a time like this. Once I found the number, I pulled out my cell and dialed Inspector Miller.

Sadly, he didn't answer, so I returned to my little black contact book and found his email. After writing a lengthy paragraph, I attached the photos I'd taken of Griffen's original report along with a picture of the report that had been filed in the system and sent it. Now, all I needed to do was wait to hear back from him.

After sending the email, I decided to pack up all the files from James Edlin's case and head to the basement archives. Despite everything I had uncovered and all the notes I'd taken, I didn't see a reason to hold onto the files anymore. As I packed up the box, I remembered that Rick was the original investigator on the case. I thought to question him, to see why he labeled the case a suicide. It only felt right.

I placed the lid on the box, left my office, and entered the elevator. My fingers repeatedly tapped against the cardboard as I thought of many scenarios—how Rick could have been involved somehow, how he could have been working alongside Blake and possibly Griffen. When the elevator doors opened, my mind calmed.

"Good afternoon, Rick."

"Afternoon, Robert," he said. "I heard you solved the case."

"Oh, did you now? From whom?" I placed the box on the tiny platform and slid it through the slot.

"Eh..." he hesitated, scratching the back of his head.

"Wait, let me guess. Blake told you." Rick went to say something, but I cut him off. "Told you that Griffen murdered James and Charles, and then Griffen killed himself. That sound about right?"

Rick grabbed the box, spun, and walked down the aisle to return it to its designated spot. "I don't remember who told me, but eh...I don't think it was Blake."

"Why wouldn't it be? You and him are friends, right?

Known each other damn near thirty years." I leaned against the fence. "Oh wait, no. I got it wrong. You're good friends with his father, Harry. When was the last you two spoke?"

Rick made his way back down the aisle. "Who, Harry? It's been a while." He shrugged. "Probably a month or two."

"Oh, okay." I spun to leave, then doubled back. "By the way, when I picked up the case, why didn't you mention you were the CI on it?"

Rick shot me a puzzled look as if he was trying to figure out why I would ask such a thing. Sweat began to bead on his forehead.

I crossed my arms. "Tell me the truth, Rick. Why did you label it a suicide when it was clearly a murder?" He was at a loss for words. The silence we shared lasted way too long, which made things awkward. I was beginning to think Rick was having a stroke due to his lack of a response. Then finally, he broke his silence.

"Look, all I could find was—"

"Cut the shit, Rick," I interrupted. "Tell me the truth!"

"I can't!" he shot back. "If I do, I'll lose everything."

"You should have thought of that before you chose to break the law!"

"It's not that easy, Robert. They were only kids. I was told to make it look like a suicide. He wouldn't have it any other way."

"*He*, who? Harry?" I demanded.

Rick stared at me in stunned silence. He wasn't going to say another word. He wouldn't risk losing his pension and the last few years of his quiet life over something that had happened nearly thirty years ago. I understood why, though. He was a cop on top of being old. He wouldn't survive a day in prison. I also understood why he did it. If it was true—if Harry *was* involved, he probably threatened to murder Rick or end his career if he failed to conform.

I punched at the fence in anger, then returned to the elevator. As I felt the slow rumble of the metal box rise, I thought back to our conversation and what Rick had said. "They were only kids. I was told to make it look like a suicide. He wouldn't have it any other way." I assumed Harry Wells, Blake's father, was who Rick was referring to since he had been the sheriff at the time and because Blake himself was too young to have any control over the matter. *Harry* was the one who had covered up James Edlin's death. And if Harry had gone to such great lengths to cover up the murder, then there was a good chance Blake had killed James.

After work, I returned home. As I entered my apartment, the smell of Italian cuisine stormed my nostrils; thyme, basil, zesty cheese, and rich tomato. I spotted baked ziti on the kitchen counter when I closed the door. Kacy had been waiting all day for my return to hear whether Griffen was the killer. Even though I didn't want her getting involved whatsoever, she'd managed to get wrapped up in it anyway.

"So...did Griffen kill Eloise's husband?" she asked as I removed my blazer and hung it up in the hall closet.

I didn't know where to begin. On paper, he'd killed Charles Carter. But in reality, he couldn't have. He had no desire to, and he probably hadn't known of Charles' whereabouts either.

"Eh...yes *and* no," I said with uncertainty.

Her head tilted to the side in bewilderment as she sat on the stool at the kitchen bar. "What? What do you mean yes *and* no?"

I went to the sofa to untie my shoes. "Well, forensics concludes that the gun Griffen used to 'kill himself with'"—I finger quoted as I sat—"was the same gun used to kill Charles Carter. However, I recently came across some evidence that says it's not that simple."

Her eyes lit up with intrigue. "Really? So you're saying Griffen *didn't* kill Charles?"

I kicked off my shoes, stood, and placed them on the storage rack near the front door. Then I joined Kacy in the kitchen, sitting on the stool beside her. "I'm not going to say, Kacy. All you need to know is that the case is practically closed," I lied. The case was far from closed. And the evidence I'd uncovered didn't necessarily prove Griffen *hadn't* murdered Charles Carter. I just didn't feel like explaining my hunch to Kacy. So I didn't.

"C'mon, please?" she begged.

I threw my arm around her shoulder and kissed her on the cheek. "It's all over, darling. There's nothing else to figure out. Honestly, I was thinking about dropping you back off at your father's place after dinner."

"Do I really have to go? I was just getting comfortable here."

She pouted while staring at me with her yellow-brown eyes that resembled a field of sunflowers. However, I needed to finish what I had started—without distractions. Because we all know that business comes before pleasure.

"I've got lots of work to catch up on," I said. "And

thinking about you cooped up in here isn't a part of that. So yes, I'm going to take you home later. Let's eat." After we enjoyed a marvelous dinner, Kacy did as I had asked. Then afterward, she was back in the comforts of her childhood home.

To: Jeremy Saunders (jsaunders1994@gmail.com)

From: Professor Carter (tulsauniversity.carter@gmail.com)

Date: Monday, April 18, 2016 7:02:56 EST

Subject: Last Call

Dear Jeremy,

I'm very disappointed in you for not showing up to class for a third time. I was more than willing to facilitate the process of your report on Camp Mercy, even giving you ample time to present. But it seems like you've taken it for granted. With that being said, I hope all is well. I reached out to Griffen and Blake and they said they hadn't heard from you either. Regardless, I'm still going to do some more research on James Edlin's death since we've talked about it so much here recently. I want to figure out for myself if he really was murdered or not. I hope to hear from you.

44.

THE STROKE of one a.m. marked the arrival of a black Lincoln Town Car outside the Regional Heights apartment complex. The dimly lit parking lot was a stark contrast to the glimmering city lights beyond, and the lack of light from the streetlamps stood as a testament to the complex's negligence and lack of funding.

The old man was wise enough to kill the car's driving lights as he eased into the lot. Then he stopped behind a sedan. With a flashlight, he inspected the paper in his hand before glancing out the windshield to verify the plates on Detective Stone's car. Once verified, he cautiously opened the door and got out. He kept a tight grip on the handle as he eased the door shut in a hushed manner, not wanting to draw attention from any of the residents. Then he searched for any witnesses—drug addicts and homeless people alike —that might be lurking around the premises in search of food or shelter. If he wasn't careful, he might be spotted by someone who could identify him. But luckily, there was no one around.

Before making another move, he took note of the humming of tires against asphalt coming from the freeway a few miles down the road. He had to ensure no one would pull in while he was there. Then he returned to the task at hand. He crept over to Robert's car and dropped to the ground. Then he slid a knife out of his pants pocket and aimed the flashlight at the front driver-side wheel. Lying on his back, the man shimmied under as far as he could and cut the brake line. Then he stood and went for the car. But before he got back in the Lincoln to leave, he pressed the button on his key fob and released the trunk. He opened it and pulled out a tire iron. There was one last thing he needed to do to ensure Detective Stone would perish, and that was to loosen a few lug nuts.

45 · Robert

I woke to my eight a.m. alarm. I was ready for the day and ready to take on the world, starting with finding out who had murdered Griffen and why. I swung my legs over the edge of my bed, got up, and opened the blinds. Dressed only in my boxers, I headed to the kitchen to set a pot of coffee. Then I returned to my room to get ready. Once dressed and with my daily hygiene regimen taken care of, I grabbed my tin thermos and walked out the door.

"Plenty of time to grab a muffin," I muttered, glancing at my Rolex as I trekked down the steps onto the main landing.

I tapped the unlock button on my key fob and got in. The aroma of hazelnut filled the interior as I set my thermos in the cup holder. I drew in a breath. I sure loved the smell of hazelnut in the morning and felt there was no better smell. However, all I could do was inhale the scent. I couldn't drink my coffee just yet. It was way too hot. Plus, it wouldn't be as enjoyable without a cinnamon muffin to accompany it.

I inserted the key in the ignition and set off for the gas station. When I hopped on the highway, I was met with no traffic. That was unheard of on a Tuesday morning. But I didn't mind it. If anything, I was happy that I could go the full speed limit and not have to hover around fifty-five miles per hour to work. All I needed now was a muffin and to meet with Internal Affairs. If I could manage both of those, my already great day would be—

Suddenly, my car started acting up. A sporadic vibration began in the steering wheel, then the whole car. And within seconds, it got worse. The vehicle wobbled uncontrollably. Then suddenly, my car dipped to the right as the passenger wheel shot out from under the wheel well. My thermos went flying out of the cupholder onto the rubber floor mat.

"Son of a bitch!"

I tried muscling the steering wheel to the left and pressing the brake pedal, but the car didn't slow. The pedal lacked resistance. It was then that I realized the brakes had gone out entirely. I jammed on the pedal a second time, but still, nothing happened. Then my focus returned to the road, but it was too late. I was headed straight for the guardrail.

Crash!

The last thing I remember was my car careening across the road, through the guardrail, and into a ruff of trees. However, it didn't just slide down into a measly ditch. No. It flew about twenty feet into the air upon leaving the road, wrapped around a giant Cypress, then plummeted into a murky swamp.

46 · Kacy

When I awoke at ten a.m., I could barely open my eyes. I felt heavily fatigued, as if I had just finished a marathon. It was strange that crust filled the crevices of my eyes even though I felt I hadn't slept a wink that night. It might have been because I had no one to spoon. I had gotten pretty comfortable sleeping in the same bed as Robert by the time he kicked me out of his place. It felt good sleeping beside someone who truly cared about me, even though the mattress itself was backbreaking.

But then I thought my lack of energy probably had something to do with how I kept thinking about the case. How Robert refused to share what conflicting evidence he had found with me. I had been fixated on the case since its conception. I was fiending for the truth, willing to do anything to get to the bottom of what was happening. Not just for Eloise, James, or Griffen's sake but also for my fans. But how would I do it?

I sat up in bed, adjusted my pillows, and recounted everything I'd researched. My only helpful witness was now dead. Granted, he had lied about everything he'd told Eloise and me. But still, his interview was helpful. What made things worse was that Eloise had no more ideas, and Victor didn't remember anything. But then I wondered, *Maybe if Victor saw a picture of his bunkmates when they were younger, he might remember something.*

It was worth a shot. I jumped out of bed and got dressed. Then I grabbed my backpack from the floor and opened it to see if I still had Memorial High's yearbook from 1986. I could only hope that my idea would be a success. I draped the straps of my bag over my shoulders, then walked down the hall toward the kitchen, where my father was nowhere to be found.

"Dad?" I called out.

But I received no response. Then I peered out the window to find the truck missing. For some reason, he was always out doing something when I needed to go somewhere. That was the worst. But then, as I sulked, the F-150 pulled into the driveway.

"Thank God, he's back," I muttered, opening the front door and walking out onto the porch. I waved with a smile as he stepped out of the truck. "Good morning."

"Ah, I'm glad you're up and dressed," he said, closing the truck door. "Now you can help me with these."

I rolled my eyes as I moseyed down the steps and over to the truck to lend him a hand. I had yet to learn what he had purchased. It could have been anything—groceries, decorative pieces, or worse, tools to use around the house and restaurant. When I reached the truck to find him pulling a few window blinds out of the truck bed, I asked, "Blinds? What's wrong with the current ones?"

He laughed. "Nothing. Just wanted to change styles, is all."

I held out my arms, and he dropped two long boxes in them. He grabbed the rest and made his way toward the house, with me following after him. "Hopefully, you don't have any more errands to run because I need the truck," I said.

He remained quiet as he climbed the steps to the porch. With his hands full, my father struggled to open the front door. But after a minute, he turned the knob just enough, managing to nudge the door open with his knee, and we entered. Just in time, too, because my grip was starting to loosen.

"Nope, don't have any more errands," he finally admitted, resting the blinds on the kitchen dinette. I followed suit.

"Cool." He handed me the keys, and I headed back out the door to return to the truck. Then I pulled onto the street and made my way toward Heritage Point.

As I drove, something circled my mind. I never thought my relationship with my father would ever improve beyond what it was. But thinking back to how I had kissed him on the cheek then surely proved otherwise. And to think, the last time I'd kissed him was close to a decade ago. The idea of us rebuilding what had broken brought warmth to my heart—a surreal feeling I cherished until I reached my destination.

The clock on the dash read 11:13 a.m. when I arrived at Heritage Point. I found a parking spot, then headed inside. I quickly signed in and walked down the hall toward Victor's room. I didn't know exactly what it was, but something made me think I'd see his daughter again. However, when I approached his door and knocked, no one answered.

Now, where could he be?

As I turned to leave, one of the facility's staff tapped me on the shoulder, startling me. I spun around to find a heavyset man standing before me.

"Oh, sorry," the man said. "Didn't mean to startle you."

"It's fine." I readjusted my backpack on my shoulder. "If you don't mind me asking, do you know where I can find Victor Pines? This is his room, right?" I pointed to the door.

The man nodded, his double chin continuing to jiggle after his head stopped moving. "You have the right room. He's just out in the commons area, hanging with the others." He leaned in, closer than I preferred. "They're all out there watching a classic on TV." He smiled, and I noticed a spec of something black in between two of his bottom incisors. I was tempted to say something but didn't, not wanting to embarrass him since he seemed a little nervous speaking to me due to him breaking eye contact every few seconds. Nevertheless, I thanked him and walked away.

When I headed back toward the entrance, past the check-in counter, and down the hall toward the main commons area, I found Victor sitting around a relatively large flat-screen TV beside a few others.

I approached Victor and waved. "Hey Victor, do you remember me?" I took a knee and rested my hand on top the armrest of his wheelchair.

He stared at me for a second. His mouth was full of food,

and a look of *who the hell are you* was etched on his face as if I were a total stranger. Then his eyes adjusted, and he reached into the side pocket of his wheelchair and fished out a small whiteboard and dry-erase marker. He jotted down something. When he flipped the board around, it read: YES.

I smiled, as did he. Then I placed my hand on his and looked him in the eyes. "Victor, I need your help with something. With identifying some people. Think you can do that for me?"

He erased his first answer to jot down his second. It read: I'LL TRY with a smiley face under it.

"I'm going to show you a few people from this yearbook. Some people from your past. I'm also going to show you a picture of *yourself*."

He smiled, his teeth gleaming with remnants of food spread about. I took his empty plate and placed it on the coffee table in front of us, then I motioned to his whiteboard, and he handed it over. I slipped it back into the side pocket of his wheelchair, then slid off my backpack, pulled out the yearbook, and set it in his lap. I started by looking him up first so he could see what he looked like at age fifteen. I thought doing so would break the ice for what I was trying to accomplish—something that showed him I meant no harm.

"And this is you, thirty years ago," I said, pointing to his yearbook picture.

Victor let out a noise, a calming grumble similar to a cheerful infant.

Then I turned back a few pages in search of Eloise. When I found her and pointed her out, I said, "This is the woman who came with me the first time we met. Do you remember?"

He looked at me and nodded with a smile. I was elated. Showing him old pictures was working. Despite having three more people to show him, it seemed like we were making some progress. I continued, pulling up Charles next. And that was when I lost him. Victor's memory had forsaken him. He didn't remember Charles. Not the miniature afro, the dorky smile, or the coke-bottle glasses he wore in the picture. Dammit. I feared I wouldn't get any information from him.

I flipped through a couple more pages until I found Griffen. There was not an ounce of recollection from Victor when I pointed him out. Such a disappointment. However, when I pointed out the sheriff, Victor started to groan. His eyes widened, then he looked elsewhere in the room as he tried pushing the book away. His groans got louder every second, as if he were getting quite upset.

I yanked the book from his lap. "What is it, Victor? Do you remember him?" I pointed to the image of the sheriff as I brought the book closer to his face.

Victor shuddered uncontrollably, tears bubbling from his closed eyes. I snatched the whiteboard from his wheelchair's side pouch and dropped it in his lap, then grabbed his hand that held the marker and placed it on the board so he could write.

"Tell me, Victor! Tell me! Do you remember him?" My voice was getting louder. That was when a member of the staff came over and interrupted us.

"Excuse me, miss. What seems to be the problem?" a woman said.

"Oh, nothing," I shot back, standing from my kneeled position. "There's no problem."

With crossed arms, the woman mhmm'd in disbelief. "I'm sorry, but I'm going to have to ask you to leave."

She probably assumed I had abused Victor in some way or another with how her beady eyes glared at me. I couldn't blame her. The way I had come in and interrupted Victor during his lounging time was not only rude but also inconsiderate to the other elderly patients in the facility. It was one thing to do it in the confines of his room but not out in the commons area.

"I'm sorry. I didn't mean to disrupt anybody or cause a scene," I protested. "Just wanted to ask a few questions, that's all." Though my reason for being at the facility was legitimate, the woman didn't buy it for one second. She expected me to leave immediately. I turned back to Victor. "Please, Victor, tell me something."

Victor's eyes opened, and his shuddering ceased. With his eyes still glossy from the tears, he wrote down something before the woman laid her hand on my shoulder.

"It's time to go, miss." She tugged, pulling me away.

"Hold on! Let me grab my things," I said, reaching for the yearbook and stuffing it in my backpack. As I turned to be escorted out of the facility, Victor reached for my hand. "Wait!" I said to the woman trying to haul me out of the place. "Victor's got my hand."

She released her grasp on me, and I turned to find him holding up his whiteboard that showcased what he'd written. In bright red was the word: BAD.

———

After getting kicked out of Heritage Point, I sat in my father's truck and reflected on what I had just witnessed. To my surprise, Victor remembered the sheriff. Had he witnessed Blake hanging James in eighty-six? Did he help him? I didn't know what to think. But upon this discovery, I knew paying the sheriff another visit would benefit the case.

I put the key in the ignition and rolled out of the parking lot. As I did, an idea arose. I could bring some lunch to Robert. Hopefully, it would cheer him up and relieve some of his tension and stress. The food wouldn't be much, but I didn't think he'd mind. Because it was the thought that counted.

I glanced at the dash clock. It read: 12:31 p.m. I stopped at the first fast-food restaurant I spotted and ordered two burger combos to go. And within a minute, I received my order and was back on the road. Fifteen minutes later, I arrived at the police station, pulled into a parking spot, and got out. My heart fluttered with unrest as I walked toward the entrance. I didn't know how Robert would react to me showing up unexpectedly like this with food, let alone be willing to hear my claim that the sheriff was 'bad'.

"Hey, is Detective Stone in his office?" I asked the woman at the counter who was sifting through some paperwork. She was the same woman I'd spoken to a few days prior. I guessed she and the man I'd seen there swapped shifts every other day or so. I was pleased with it being her and not the man, considering she didn't give me nearly as many annoyed looks as he did.

"You must not know," she said, her tone awash with dread.

"Know what?" I asked.

She covered her mouth as I placed the brown paper bag on the counter and leaned in.

"Robert didn't make it to work today. He got in a car accident on his way in."

My eyes exploded in shock. "WHAT?!" In disbelief, my body went numb. I stepped back to regain my balance, but that was when my arm knocked over our food.

It crashed to the floor.

"Where is he?" I demanded.

"Saint Francis Hospital, in intensive care."

"Thank you." With my eyes starting to water, I turned, picked up the bag I'd knocked over, and dashed out the entrance toward the truck. Then I raced out of the parking lot and headed straight for the hospital, the thought of questioning the sheriff again diminishing.

47 · Kacy

When I pulled into the hospital's parking lot, I didn't even try to find a spot. I just brought the truck to a screeching halt at the end of the roundabout near the entrance and jumped out. I sprinted inside. As I ran through the lobby, a moment of clarity hit me. I had no clue where the ICU was. After glancing at every sign above each intersecting hall, I finally found one with 'Intensive Care Unit' written on it with an arrow pointing south. Now that I knew where to go, I dashed down the hall. I took a left, then another left, then a right, almost crashing into a volunteer with a patient who had just come out of the elevator.

"Sorry," I said, not bearing a glance.

All I could think about was Robert as I hurried through the decoratively tiled halls of the hospital. The fear of losing him—losing the only person I'd ever gotten close to— frightened me. And when I reached the ICU, that frightened feeling only grew. I pulled on the handle for the door, but it didn't budge. I pressed the button on the nearest wall, assuming the door would open, but still, it didn't. I grabbed my head in anger. Then suddenly, the door opened, and a nurse emerged. Moving quickly, I snuck in past her as she continued her marching stride.

I stormed up to the circular station in the center of the unit, my body riddled with anxiety. "Where's Robert Stone?" I demanded. But the nurses didn't answer; they just stared at me as if I were a crazed drug addict. I gritted my teeth and looked around the ICU. "Where's Robert Stone?" I repeated, my voice getting louder.

There were a few reasons why the nurses maybe didn't respond when I asked where he was; probably—the way I approached them with demands, the way I looked—flustered and sweaty from all the running, or worse...he wasn't here, and I was at the wrong hospital entirely. It could have been any reason. But then suddenly, someone spoke.

"Ma'am," a nurse said, approaching me from behind. "Please lower your voice."

"What?!" I yelled, spinning around.

"How did you get in here?"

"I asked you a question first. Where's Robert Stone?"

The nurse inched closer. "Ma'am, if you don't calm down, I'll have security escort you—"

"Kacy? Kacy Roe, is that you?" a voice called out, interrupting the nurse.

I spun around just as a woman came up behind me—a woman I hadn't seen since I had left town nine years ago: Robert's mother.

"Mrs. Stone!" I cried out, falling into her arms. I hadn't felt the caress of a mother's love in a long time—the passion, the affection, the warmth. Oh, how I'd missed that feeling. My sense of fear and fright diminished immediately.

"What are you doing here, hon?" she asked.

"I came to see Rob. I just found out about the accident."

She smiled down at me—a smile that was all lips and no teeth. "How sweet of you. Come on, follow me."

I followed Mrs. Stone to a dim room back in the corner of the ICU behind the nurse's station. As I peered in through a set of sliding glass doors, I found Robert lying in bed. I wanted to hold his hands so badly, but I couldn't. He was in rough shape. A winding set of wires and tubes came and went from his body. He wore a neck brace and a cast on his right arm, with a breathing tube down his throat. And also, his face was bruised badly—reddish-pink and swollen as if he'd lost a UFC match. Now wasn't the right time to go in there and hold his hand.

I turned to his mother. "What happened?"

"I'll explain in a second, dear. Follow me." Mrs. Stone grabbed my wrist and led me to the waiting room designated for family and friends so we could speak. As we entered, I found Mr. Stone sitting in a chair, holding a magazine.

His eyes peered up from its pages. "Why, if it ain't the one that got away," he said with a smile.

"Hi," I said, still teary-eyed. I wiped my eyes dry with my collar, then sat beside him.

"I thought you'd left town." Mrs. Stone sat in the chair beside me, sandwiching me in between them.

"I did. Didn't plan on coming back either, but my father had a heart attack, so—"

"Oh dear, is he alright?"

"He's okay. What happened to Rob?"

"Police say he wrapped his car around a tree," Mr. Stone said. "That's all we've been told."

I was in disbelief. Robert wasn't the type to be reckless behind the wheel, at least, from what I could remember. And though I knew the roads could be slick when wet, it hadn't rained in a few days. So, that couldn't be the reason for the crash. Perhaps the same person who called me with a death threat had tried to kill him. That certainly could explain his accident.

Suddenly, a cell phone went off, leading our heads to dart around the room in search of the noise. Then I caught a glimpse of a faint light coming from across the room, protruding from a pair of Robert's dress shoes. I jumped up to answer it, quickly peering inside his shoe to see who was calling. The name on the screen read: INSPECTOR MILLER. I had no clue who Inspector Miller was. Curiosity and temptation struck me, drawing me to answer the call. However, it was too late. I had let it ring through its cycle. As I returned to my seat between Robert's parents, his phone buzzed with a notification. I doubled back to his shoes and fished out the phone. After tapping the screen, I found it was a voicemail that had come in. I swiped to unlock it, clicked on the notification, and pressed the phone to my ear.

"Hey, Robert. I looked at the photos you sent me last night, and I have to say, if what you're saying is true, you might just have something here. Call me back asap so we can meet to discuss it more."

I let out a silent gasp.

"Who was that, Kacy?" Mrs. Stone asked.

"I'm not sure. But it sounded important." I turned to leave the room. "I'll be back later. Call me if he wakes up, okay? Oh, and by the way, I'm going to take his phone in the meantime."

"Will do," Mr. Stone said, his face deep in the magazine.

They didn't have a problem with that. It was probably because they didn't have a problem with me. Robert's mother always used to say, "You're the best girl a boy could have."

I left the ICU and headed back into the main halls of the hospital as I dwelled on what I'd heard over the voicemail. I had so many questions and concerns, not just for Robert's sake but also for his parents. I hoped he wasn't in danger and wished his parents weren't either. I couldn't help but wonder who Inspector Miller was. I was itching to know what was going on. I hated being out of the loop. Always did. And now, with Robert out of commission, I couldn't simply ask him for answers. I knew I had to do something, starting with contacting the person who'd called Robert's phone.

I stepped out of the lobby into the summer heat, crossed the parking lot, and got in my father's truck. Sitting in the driver's seat, I thought to search through Robert's phone first to see if I could find anything that could lead to some insight into the situation before calling Inspector Miller.

I pulled Robert's cell phone from my pocket and unlocked it. I wasn't sure if Robert had emailed the pictures from his computer or texted them to Inspector Miller. However, I figured snooping around his photo library wouldn't hurt. I clicked on the Photos app and stumbled across a few interesting images. They were snaps of

Griffen's autopsy report. Mostly descriptions of his body ailments and such. But as I continued swiping through each picture, reaching the end of the collection, one, in particular, caught my eye. I swiped right, backtracking to an image of the final report, which read:

DESCRIPTION: Decedent had contact wound to center of forehead. Angle of entry incompatible with intentional infliction.

My eyes widened at what I had read. "Griffen was murdered!" I muttered. "Then who killed him?" I trailed further down the image to find the sheriff's signature at the bottom of the page, indicating he'd signed off on Griffen's cremation. It was then that I felt it was the right time to call the Inspector.

48.

The old man's heart warmed as he watched Kacy leave the ICU through the window of another entrance. A slight appreciation developed within him. Visiting Detective Stone after discovering his 'accident' was kindhearted—romantic even. Perhaps the two were intimately involved, or worse, in cahoots. Whatever the reason, he turned and walked off while pulling out his cell phone to call someone.

The man traveled down an empty hallway and exited through one of the many side entrances of the building. Then he trekked down the concrete stairs as the call rang through. After a second passed, someone answered.

"Is it done?" a man asked, his voice stern.

"No. Not yet, Blake. But we've got another problem."

"And that problem is?"

The man scoped his surroundings as he crossed the parking lot before answering, ensuring no one was around to overhear his conversation. "You were right. Robert and the college girl are colluding." He opened the door to the black Lincoln Town Car parked at the end of the lot and got in. "Saw her leaving his room just now."

"Keep an eye on her for now. I don't want to go making anyone else disappear just yet."

The man inserted his key in the ignition and brought the car to life. "The longer we wait, the more risk we take. You already made one mistake leaving Houser alive. We should've taken care of him when we took care of Carter." Blood pumped through the veins on his bald head as he continued. "Remember, this is your fault. If we don't handle this now, things might get worse, and like I told you, I'm not going to prison. I'm too old for that."

"Yeah yeah, I know, Dad," Blake said, annoyed by the situation. "Fine. Take her out."

The old man grunted with a scoff and ended the call as he put the car in drive and pulled out of the parking lot.

49 · Kacy

AFTER BACKING out of the photo library, I tapped Robert's recent calls list and hit redial for Inspector Miller, hoping whoever this man was would be willing to speak with me since Robert was currently incapacitated. With the phone nestled between my shoulder and ear, I started the truck and pulled out of the parking lot.

The line rang, then a voice answered.

"Robert," Inspector Miller said in a cheerful tone.

"This isn't Robert," I said.

"Okay, then, who am I speaking with?"

"His girlfriend, Kacy." I didn't think I'd ever say those words, but I did. It was official now. Sort of. Even though Robert couldn't protest my claim, I believed he'd agree with our relationship status.

"Well, is he available? The matter is urgent."

"Unfortunately not. He was in a car accident this morning. He's in the ICU as we speak." I turned right onto the main road.

Inspector Miller gasped. "Oh, I'm sorry."

"Thank you. I'm just glad he's alive."

"Me too. So, why'd you return the call?"

"Because I believe someone tried to kill Robert. After listening to your voicemail, I think whatever you two discussed is possibly what had gotten him hurt." The traffic light turned red, and I stopped behind a trash truck. "So, what were you two discussing?"

"I'm sorry, but I can't discuss the matter with you."

"Alrighty then, how about you tell me who you are. Can you do that?"

"I'm Inspector Miller, head of Internal Affairs. Robert contacted me regarding a case."

"A case that involves a thirty-year-old suicide conspiracy cover-up?" I suggested. The line went silent. I knew I had hit the nail on the head. "I know you probably think I'm unaware of what's been going on, but I'm sort of involved," I continued. "Have been from the start. And I want to help."

"The risk and legal ramifications of bringing on a civilian wouldn't be worth it. I'm sorry, but—"

The light turned green, and I put pressure on the accelerator. "Look, I know Griffen was murdered, and I also suspect he didn't kill Charles Carter. I believe Sheriff Blake Wells is responsible, and I think Griffen was in on it too. And once Robert and I came around asking questions, the sheriff took Griffen out to cover his tracks. And then went for Robert."

I passed by the post office and noticed gray clouds

forming overhead. A rainstorm was brewing. Hopefully, I'd get home before it started pouring.

"You sure do know quite a lot," Inspector Miller admitted.

"Yes, I do. I suggest you let me wear a wire while I interview—"

"A wire?" he interrupted.

"Yes. A wire. What better way to—"

"Kacy, I don't think you know how serious this matter is. This isn't some TV show. This is real life."

I gritted my teeth, my hands tightening around the steering wheel. I was unwilling to take no for an answer. "Inspector Miller, I know *just* how serious this is. Someone called me, threatening to make me disappear if I didn't stop snooping around. I know you don't know me and all, but I can handle myself. And I mean that with the utmost respect."

Though I knew that someone could be watching me at that very moment, planning to make me their next victim, I remained confident and determined to solve the case. Besides, I'd handled myself for the last nine years with no problems. I felt this wasn't any different.

"Suit yourself," Inspector Miller said. "Come into my office at six today so we can discuss matters further. Depending on how the debriefing goes, I'll consider making you an informant."

"Where's your office located?" I asked.

"In Oklahoma City."

"I'll be there." As soon as I ended the call, I reached another traffic light that had turned red. That was when the heavy downpour began. As I waited, I felt the need to text

Inspector Miller a 'thank you' for allowing me to meet with him. Taking time out of his day for me was surely a blessing. But when I began the text with Robert's phone, the light turned green, and the cars ahead of me took off before I could send it.

I expected an impatient honk from the car behind me since I hadn't moved an inch. However, I didn't hear a thing. I quickly sent the text, then glanced back through the rearview mirror, wondering why the person hadn't tapped their horn. But amid my glance, I discovered it was the same dark-colored Lincoln Town Car that had tailed Robert and me the previous week.

Shit! That's probably the person who threatened me!

I smashed on the accelerator, and the back wheels chirped as I took off. The rear end spun out a little, but I pulled it back. I passed through the light, then hung a left. Unfortunately, the Lincoln did the same. The car was quick, staying on me as I swerved around the minivan ahead of me. The van's horn blared as I returned to the lane, cutting it off. I didn't dare look back to see if the Lincoln had done the same. I was too focused on not hitting what was in front of me.

I shot a glance at the speedometer. I was doing sixty in a forty-five, during a torrential downpour, no less. Racing by schools and daycares was certainly not the place to be. There were too many variables, too many chances to make a mistake. To crash. If I hit someone, I wouldn't be able to live with myself. I couldn't help but think, was this the end? Was this mystery person coming to kill me now? Run me into a ditch to suffer the same fate as Robert?

I shuddered as my hands yanked the steering wheel to

turn onto a narrow street. I glanced at my rearview to find the Lincoln still there. The car was so close it could almost bump me. Immediately, an idea arose. My action would surely infuriate my father, but I didn't care. I wanted to survive. To live. And I knew my father would want that too.

The road ahead of me was coming to an end. I had traveled it many times before, on my bicycle as a kid. I knew it led to a two-lane road that ran adjacent to the freeway. It was at that moment I took my plan into action. I closed my eyes and braced for impact as I slammed on the brakes. The front end of the truck jarringly dipped down.

I heard brakes squeal, followed by a screeching skid, then—

Boom!

The Lincoln smashed into the back of the truck.

I reopened my eyes and looked back at the car through the rearview mirror. From what I could make out, it seemed as though the Lincoln's hood had slid halfway underneath the truck's bed. The person chasing me had to have been hurt. Being in an accident like that was bound to cause a concussion, at the least.

I rubbed my head, recalling how the force from the initial impact shot me forward, and then the seatbelt caught me and whipped me back into place. Talk about whiplash. Luckily, I wasn't hurt. Then I noticed the airbag didn't deploy, thank God. Though I felt a stress headache coming on, I was thankful that I didn't smack my face against the steering wheel, resulting in a broken nose. That only would have made things worse for me because I simply didn't have the time. I was too focused on the case.

I looked to my left to find the bag of burgers I'd gotten

for Robert and me to eat had flown from the passenger seat and smashed against the dashboard, settling on the floor mat. If a slight headache, loss of food, and damaged vehicle were the only result of my daring act, then I'd made out well. After regaining my composure, I realized it was my chance to escape. So I slammed my foot on the accelerator and rocked off the Lincoln, leaving it in a smoking heap at the end of the alleyway.

———

When it came time to pick my father up from work, I desperately wanted to reply with a text saying, *Can't, got a stomach bug.* However, doing so would only delay the inevitable. My father was bound to find out what had happened to his truck, bound to find out someone had tried to run his only daughter off the road. It was impossible to hide that from him. It was time to come clean. So I bit the bullet and replied.

On my way.

The clock on the dash read 3:45 p.m. when I backed out of the driveway. The rain had subsided, but not by much. My nerves were shot. I was afraid to be alone, to leave the safety of my childhood home, fearing the black Lincoln would pop up out of nowhere and start chasing me again. Suddenly, a strike of lightning skirted across the sky. I knew thunder would follow. Yet, I still jumped, jerking the steering wheel a little when its deep rumble finally roared. I needed to calm down. But I couldn't. Every time I slowed to a stop at a traffic light, my gaze shifted to the rearview mirror. My paranoia was at an all-time high.

Ten minutes later, I reached the restaurant and parked near the entrance. I hesitated to pull out my phone and text my father to let him know I had arrived, but then I saw him leave the building. He must have been peering out the window, waiting for me to arrive. I didn't even spare a glance in his direction as he approached the vehicle and opened the passenger door.

"Hey, Kacy," he said, getting in and shutting the door quickly to prevent the rain from rushing in. "How was your day?"

How was my day? Terrible, frightening, and borderline chaotic similar to a Die Hard movie. Nothing could adequately define it. My day had consisted of nothing but disappointments and horrifying events. I turned to my father. "Dad, I need to tell you something. And you need to promise me you won't get angry, okay?"

"Kacy, what's this all about?" His tone was filled with concern.

"I think it'll be better if I show you."

"But it's raining."

"Just c'mon." I stepped out and walked toward the back of the vehicle. The rain pelted my face as I waited for my father to join me at the crumpled tailgate. The tightness in my chest was suffocating, as if an immense pressure was crushing me from all sides. I pressed a hand to my chest, hoping to soothe my frayed nerves. But I believed only hearing my father's assurance would bring me true peace.

When my father finally came from around the passenger side to find what had happened to the rear end of his pickup, he didn't flip out in a fiery rage like I feared he would. Instead, he turned to me and pulled me into his embrace.

"Are you alright, dear?" His hand shielded my head from the pouring rain.

"I'm fine. Just shaken up is all."

"What happened?"

"Someone tried to run me off the road. But I managed to outsmart them. I'm sorry about everything. I'll get it fixed asap." I broke out of his grasp and headed back to the driver's seat.

"There's no rush, Kacy," he said, reaching for my arm. He pulled me back toward him. "I care way more about your well-being than this truck. Don't you forget that."

We returned to our respective seats. Our clothes were drenched from the summer shower. I made a feeble attempt to wring out the excess water from the bottom of my shirt. But before I could, my father grabbed my arm, halting me in my tracks.

"Now, Kacy, I know you haven't told me everything about what you've gotten into or what you do all day while I'm at work. But I want you to know that if anyone ever tries to hurt you, you can use this."

My father pulled a handgun from the glovebox. Witnessing him do so shook me to my core. I had no idea he kept a weapon there. My mind flashed back to the car chase and the time Griffen had fired at me. Had I known about the gun, I could have used it to protect myself. But looking back, using it would have only escalated things.

He held the gun out and waited for me to take it from him. "You do remember how to use one, right?"

I reached out and took the Colt .44 from my father's hand, the weight of the weapon sending a shiver down my spine. Without hesitation, I pressed the button, and the cylinder swung open, revealing the number of loaded rounds. "Yes, Dad," I answered. "I also took a self-defense class after I moved away." I smiled. "I wasn't going to make myself an easy target for anyone."

"Good. Don't hesitate to empty the clip, okay?"

"I won't."

After I returned the gun to the glovebox, we drove home. Then I waited for five o'clock to come around so I could head out to meet with Inspector Miller at his office in Oklahoma City.

50 · Kacy

WHEN I ARRIVED at the Oklahoma City police station, the parking lot appeared empty, with only a handful of cars scattered about. I assumed it was due to the lateness of the day, as most people had already left to go home. I pulled into a spot beside an unmarked sedan similar to Robert's. Before I arrived, I had expected to be greeted by a team of at least three or four people to brief me on what to do in case I were discovered during the interview process. However, as I emerged from my vehicle, I was met by only one person.

"So you must be Kacy," the man said, stepping out of his vehicle. "The one determined to get involved in the case despite the dangers. I'm Inspector Miller...Rodger Miller." He extended a hand.

I shook it. "Nice to meet you."

"Follow me." Inspector Miller led me into the building and up to the front desk. After signing my name on a visitor's form and retrieving a visitor's pass, I followed him down the hall and onto an elevator that led us to his office.

"So you want to wear a wire, eh?" He leaned against his desk and crossed his arms and legs.

I nodded and mhmm'd.

"And you want to do this because..."

"Because I see it as the only way."

"The only way?"

The only way I could get Inspector Miller to truly understand everything was to tell him just that—everything, starting with who I was, then the reason I came back to town, how I stumbled across Charles' body, why I decided to help Eloise, how someone had tried to kill me, and what I thought would happen to me, my father, Eloise, and Robert if I *didn't* help put an end to this charade. And after an hour of explanation, he finally understood.

"I have a plan," I said. "I had scheduled an appointment to meet with the sheriff's wife but canceled it shortly after hearing about Griffen's death. Now, I'm thinking I reschedule the appointment for tomorrow, but with both of them. If I can get them both in a room at the same time, I might be able to get a confession. I might even manage to get his wife to turn against him."

"That's *if* she even knows anything," Inspector Miller added.

"You're right," I agreed. "She might not know a thing. But it's worth a shot, right?"

"More like a shot in the dark, if you ask me." Inspector Miller spun and reached for a manila folder on his desk. He opened it. "Are you sure you want to do this, Kacy? Nobody's making you."

"I know nobody's making me. It's just something I want to do—no, something I *need* to do."

"Okay then. All I need is a signature from you." He handed me the folder, followed by a pen he'd retrieved from his blazer.

"Where do I sign." He pointed at a red X on the page, and I signed my full name. Kacy Adeline Roe. Then I returned the folder to him.

"Text me what time you make the appointment tomorrow, and I'll respond with the address on where to meet to get mic'd up, okay?"

"Got it." He escorted me out of the building, and that was when we went our separate ways, with him returning to his cruiser and me to my father's terribly beat-up Ford.

———

When I awoke the following morning, only one thing was on my mind—scheduling the appointment to meet with the sheriff and his wife at the police station. I strongly believed the sooner I did, the sooner I could let my guard down and forget about everything that had happened, not to mention be with Robert. However, until then, I needed to mentally prepare for what I was about to do. As I got out of bed, the aroma of sizzling bacon and eggs filled the air.

"Kacy? Breakfast's ready!" My father's voice echoed through the house.

I left my room and headed down the hall into the kitchen, blessing my father with another kiss on the cheek. "Good morning," I said with a smile.

"Oh, two times in one week." His tone was filled with

disbelief. "Where's my daughter, and what have you done with her?"

I giggled as I grabbed a plate from the cupboard and loaded up on bacon and French toast. "Oh, stop it, Dad. I'm just glad you've finally changed for the better." When I turned to join him at the dinette, I found him staring at me with a gentle smile on his lips. His eyes showed signs of brewing tears. I was uncertain whether he'd start crying. However, I most certainly didn't want him to. It was too early in the morning for all that release of emotion.

I sat and started eating.

"Got a big day ahead of you?" he asked.

I didn't know what made him think that I did. Perhaps he could sense my eagerness to begin the day, given how I scarfed down my food. Or maybe he was just being fatherly. Regardless, I certainly wasn't going to worry him with the stealth mission I would soon participate in. I felt it wasn't needed since he trusted I'd handle whatever came my way with his gun.

"Eh...not really," I answered. "Just going to visit Robert in the hospital again." Though visiting Robert was one of the many things I planned to do, it certainly wasn't the most newsworthy.

"Okay, well, I'm not going to work today, so if you need anything or want to do anything together, I'm free." He smiled.

"Thanks, Dad. I appreciate it. I'll let you know."

After breakfast, I retreated to my room and called the police station, feeling eager to schedule the interview and get it over with. Thankfully, the person on the other end of the line was accommodating, and we quickly rescheduled for later that day. However, the hard part had yet to come.

I paced back and forth in my room, dwelling on how I'd trick the sheriff and his wife into confessing what they had done. Thinking of every angle and every possible scenario, I was determined to devise a plan that would work. Eventually, I came up with something. I tossed my cell phone aside and got dressed. Then I went to the kitchen, grabbed the F-150 keys, and headed out the front door.

Visiting Robert was next on the list of things I wanted to do for the day. The thought of his car accident plagued me relentlessly, turning my stomach in knots. It was as if the weight of the world was resting squarely on my shoulders. I couldn't help but feel responsible for what had happened to him. Guilt gnawed at me like a hungry animal, my mind racing with self-recriminations. Had I been more careful, more considerate, perhaps he wouldn't be lying in a hospital bed right now. Maybe I would have taken his place. The more I thought about Robert's accident, the more suspicious I became. It was just too much of a coincidence. Perhaps someone had tampered with his car, cut the brake lines, or something equally sinister. It wasn't beyond the realm of possibility that the same person who had tried to run me off the road was also behind Robert's accident. It was a frightening thought, and my mind raced with questions and possibilities as I tried to piece together the puzzle.

When I finally arrived at the hospital, I sat in the parking lot for a few minutes. I did so not because I was afraid to see Robert in such a fragile state but because I'd forgotten to text Inspector Miller immediately after scheduling the interview to inform him of the meeting and its time. I tapped the screen on my cell phone.

KACY:

Appt set for 6 p.m.

Perfect. Meet me out front of the Tulsa Police Station at 5 p.m.

I'll be there.

I felt glad that I'd remembered to text him. The last thing I wanted to do was ruin our chances of catching the killer and putting an end to a thirty-year-old conspiracy.

Immediately after exchanging texts with Inspector Miller, I left the truck and walked inside. As I headed toward the ICU, I spotted Mr. and Mrs. Stone in the hallway, seemingly leaving.

"Hey guys," I said with a smile. I glanced at the digital clock on the wall. "You leaving already?"

"We're heading home to take a break," Mr. Stone said after taking a sip from his paper cup.

Mrs. Stone grabbed my shoulder. "Dear, we've been here all night. Didn't get an ounce of sleep."

The puffy bags under her eyes verified how exhausted she was. If only I could have done something to help ease their stress, worry, and concern, then maybe they wouldn't be so tired. However, the only thing I thought of that might help was what I'd already planned to do later that evening —catch the killer who'd hurt Robert. So I hugged her instead.

"You guys get some sleep, okay? And get home safe."

"Don't worry, we will." Mr. Stone patted me on the shoulder as his wife, and I were still mid-hug.

Once we went our separate ways, I continued down the hall, turning right into the ICU. After being allowed in, I spent several hours by Robert's room, watching through the sliding glass doors as the nurses came and went from his room every other hour—each one swapping out a bag of vitamins, blood, or drugs to ease the pain. Eventually, I nodded off in the chair I'd pulled up outside his room. It wasn't until Robert's cell phone chimed that I woke up. The noise had jolted me from my pleasant dream. I quickly fished the phone out of my jeans pocket and answered it.

"Where are you?" a familiar voice demanded. "You're late!"

I was still half asleep, unable to comprehend what the person meant or said. I pulled the phone away from my ear to glance at the screen. I was speaking with Inspector Miller. Then I glanced at the clock in the upper right-hand corner. It read: 5:03 p.m. It took a couple of seconds for it to register. But when it did, I gasped.

"Shit!" I muttered. I scratched my head. *How could I have slept for so long? Guess I didn't get much sleep last night, either.* I pressed the phone back to my ear.

"I'm sorry. I'm on the way!"

51 · Kacy

I WAS FILLED with dread when I finally arrived at the station. I was late. Really late. And I felt super bad about it. As I scanned the area, looking for a spot to park, I noticed a navy Sprinter van. Beside it stood Inspector Miller. His arms were crossed, and his eyes narrowed in anger as he glared at me.

He flicked away his cigarette and stormed toward me as I emerged from my father's truck. "You better have a good reason for why you're late. We don't have much time to get you ready."

He grabbed my wrist and pulled me over to the van.

"I'm sorry, but I don't have a reason," I admitted. "Just lost track of time."

He smacked the side of the van, and one of its doors flew open, revealing a woman sitting inside.

"Hurry, get in," she said.

Inspector Miller gestured for me to enter the van first. As I stepped inside, my eyes struggled to adjust to the dim lighting. But after a few seconds, everything became clear. The van had been converted into a high-tech command center, with three massive computer monitors mounted above a sleek desk. At the front, a labyrinth of wires and blinking switches lined the wall, creating a barrier between the front and back compartments. I couldn't help but marvel at the level of technology before me.

"Kacy, meet Carissa," Inspector Miller said. "She'll be applying the wire to your body. Undress."

"You've got to take me on a date first," I joked.

Carissa laughed, but Inspector Miller didn't.

"This is no time for fun and games, Kacy." His tone was serious and overly dramatic. "Now, please, your shirt."

I quickly undressed, allowing Carissa to clip the tiny microphone onto the center of my bra. Knowing that every word I spoke would be recorded was uncomfortable, but I tried not to dwell on it. Then Carissa carefully guided two wires down my stomach and around my side, securing them with tape to ensure they wouldn't move as I went about my business. I couldn't help but giggle, knowing I was doing something I never thought I'd get the chance to do. It was all surreal, and I couldn't help but feel like a spy in some covert operation.

"Do you know what you're going to say?" he asked.

I hesitated to answer, catching a glimpse of concern on his face from out of the corner of my eye.

"Kacy?"

I turned to him.

"Do you know what you're going to say?" he repeated, with more emphasis this time.

"Eh..." I sighed. "Yes and no."

"How's that feel?" Carissa asked, plugging the wires into the miniature box taped to my lower back.

I slipped my shirt over my head and pulled it on. "Feel's a little funny, but nothing I won't get used to."

"Good." Then she turned and pressed a button on the far wall and slipped some headphones over her ears. "Speak."

"What?" I asked, unsure of what she was requesting.

Her gaze shot from the computer screen to me. "Speak. I'm running a test to see how clear the audio is."

"Oh, okay. Testing, one, two, three...testing one, two, three. Man, I've always wanted to say that." I giggled.

"We good?" Inspector Miller asked Carissa.

With her eyes still glued to the computer screen in front of her, Carissa gave him a quick nod and thumbs up. As she deftly adjusted various parameters, I wondered what kind of program the police used for such sophisticated operations. It was clear she was a pro at what she did, and I couldn't help but feel a sense of reassurance knowing I was in capable hands.

Inspector Miller grabbed my shoulder, snatching my focus away from the technology. "Kacy, this is very important. Please, tell me you came up with some questions?"

There was no reason to lie at this point. "No. I didn't. But I think quick on my feet, so I'll be fine."

He sighed. "We only have one chance, Kacy. But if you feel you can handle this, then I guess we'll continue. If, at any time, you feel threatened or feel like you've been discovered, just ask to use the restroom. From there, we'll get you out, okay?"

"Get me out?" I repeated. "How?"

Inspector Miller shot a glance at his watch. "By coming in myself and pulling you out, plain and simple. The sheriff isn't dumb enough to hold you hostage in a police station, Kacy." He turned, opened the door, jumped out, and held it open for me. "We'll be parked right outside. Now get going. It's time to make Robert proud."

As I left the van and headed straight toward the entrance to the police station, a shroud of doubts circled my mind. *I hope I don't fail. No, I won't. Oh, God. But what if they notice the wire? Then what?*

My breathing was quick-paced, and my heart sputtered like a machine gun firing off a thousand rounds. I feared we'd never get justice for Charles, Griffen, and James if I was to get caught. I knew that I had to remain calm if I was going to succeed. I also knew that I needed to be smart with my approach, not just for myself but for Robert as well. Despite wanting to run into the station and demand answers, I knew it wasn't that simple. My questions had to be inconspicuous and manipulative. To uncover the sheriff and his wife's nefarious deeds, I needed to teeter between the truth and what I believed. Because I highly doubted excusing myself to the restroom would be a good enough safety net if they somehow managed to catch on to my true intentions.

As I entered the station, I couldn't help but wonder why Inspector Miller believed the sheriff wouldn't hold me hostage. What if the sheriff decided he had nothing to lose? Then what? I shuddered, pushing the thought away. After inhaling deeply to calm my sporadic heart rate, I approached the counter. It was the moment of truth. Either suck it up and prepare to come face to face with the person who might have tried to murder Robert and me, or chicken out and return to the sprinter van outside to discuss another way to trick the sheriff and his wife into confessing.

"Hey." My voice cracked a little. "I've got a meeting with the sheriff."

The man's eyes lingered a little longer than I would have preferred. I tried to avoid his piercing gaze. My nerves were frayed, and my heart was pounding like a jackhammer. I knew I needed to remain outwardly calm. But it was so damn hard to keep up the façade of composure when every inch of me was screaming with panic.

"He's waiting for you," the man replied. "Follow me."

As I followed the man down the hall, a wave of dizziness washed over me, making the walls sway and buckle. My head was spinning. It seemed like the world around me was closing in, suffocating me with its weight. The feeling could have been because of the accident instead of the fear of getting caught. Regardless, I still felt uneasy.

When we finally reached the sheriff's officer, I stumbled to a stop, clutching onto the man's shoulder to steady myself. Everything was dark and hazy for a moment, but then, slowly, the colors began to return. My focus suddenly resharpened. It was as if I'd stepped out of a fog, and my senses were now hyper-aware. They say the anticipation leading up to something scary is often worse than the actual event. The dread, the racing heart rate, even the feeling of ecstasy. I had never personally experienced it before, but maybe it was true. Maybe what I felt had been brought on by the fear of getting caught and failing to solve the case.

Suddenly, the man opened the door and invited me into the sheriff's office, drawing my attention back to the situation at hand. And as soon as I stepped in, all my fears, doubts, and anxieties ceased. I was calm, and my body was still like the sea on a windless day.

$$52 \cdot \textbf{Kacy}$$

"Good evening, Kacy," Sheriff Wells said as I entered the room.

"Thank you again for speaking with me," I said, sitting beside a plump woman.

"You know I'll do anything for a student." Then, motioning to the woman beside me, he added, "I want you to meet my wife, Meredith."

I turned and extended a hand to the woman. Meeting Meredith for the first time was quite the experience. For some reason, I had expected her to be heavier than the sheriff after meeting him—assuming she'd remain home, not working, only cooking and baking the entire station cookies and whatnot. However, she wasn't; quite the opposite, actually. I realized then that I didn't know how she spent her day, but I was determined to find out. With her husband at work, she could easily handle his bidding with a simple phone call. She might have been the one who had run Robert off the road.

"It's a pleasure to meet you," I said, shaking her hand.

"The pleasure's all mine," she replied, her mid-western accent coming out.

I shifted my seat a little toward Meredith so I could see them both equally. "So...did your husband give you the run down on what I wanted to speak with you about?"

She nodded.

"Wonderful! Let's get started. So—"

"I see you didn't bring your bag this time," the sheriff mentioned as I pulled my cell phone from my pocket for note-taking.

"No, I didn't. Since you told me I couldn't use my camera last time, I figured there was no need to lug it around."

He smiled. "Makes sense. Carry on."

I turned to his wife and choked. I had completely forgotten what I was going to ask her. His words had side-tracked me. And in that moment of silence, I glanced back at the sheriff and riffed. "So, sheriff, what are your thoughts on James' case having gone unsolved for thirty years?"

He tilted his head to the side. "What do you mean gone unsolved? The case was solved. James died by suicide."

"Well, there are theories that say otherwise."

"Theories aren't fact," he said.

"Well, I think his death was mighty heartbreaking," Meredith admitted. "Regardless of whether he was murdered or not."

"Honey, please. You're not helping."

Meredith shut her mouth and lowered her head as if she

realized she shouldn't have said anything. "My apologies."

I took note of her reaction and eagerness to correct herself. I had stumped her. The sheriff didn't fall for it, but she did. "If you have nothing to say, it's totally fine, sheriff." Then to Meredith, I added, "How well did you know James?"

Meredith exchanged glances with the sheriff before eyeing me. Then she sank her head again as she started to reminisce. Her thumbs twiddled in her lap. "Well, I sat next to him in algebra." She let out a quick snicker. "He used to always find some excuse to talk to me. Even gave me flowers once." She lifted her head and locked eyes with her husband. Then her gaze averted back to mine. "You could say I sort of knew him."

"You never told me he did that," the sheriff said, leaning forward to rest his arms on the desk.

"I didn't want to tell you," she shot back. "And I threw the flowers away to ensure you didn't find out. You'd already told him once to stop talking to me."

"Sounds like you both knew him fairly well," I suggested, hoping the assumption wouldn't incite an argument between the two of them.

Meredith crossed her legs after readjusting herself in the chair. "We did."

"No, you did," her husband persisted.

"I don't mean to stir up any trouble, guys. I just asked, is all." The sheriff and his wife stood firm in their resolve, acting as an impenetrable fortress of denial and deceit. Yet, as they bickered back and forth, I detected a subtle chink in their armor, presenting a golden opportunity for me to exploit their weakness and extract the truth. It was a risky move, but I was confident I could pull it off. "To be honest, from the sound of it, it looks like that boy really bothered the both of you," I added.

"Something like that," Meredith said.

"No, not at all," the sheriff protested. "He was just jealous of our relationship."

"Oh, really? Sounds like a motive to kill him," I joked. But as I giggled, my joke fell flat, landing heavily in the tense air between us. Their suspicion was palpable, their gazes piercing. I knew then that my plan had failed, and the crack in their armor had sealed shut, leaving me exposed and vulnerable.

The sheriff leaned back into his chair and crossed his arms. "Kacy, you want to tell us what this is *really* 'bout?"

I slid my cell phone back into my pocket. "My apologies for the joke. I took it too far. If you'll excuse me, I'm going to use the restroom real quick, and when I get back, I'll answer your question." I stood and turned for the door.

The sheriff called out to me when my hand was inches from the handle. "Kacy? Why are you wearing a wire?"

How does he know I'm wearing a—I quickly ran my hand around my lower back, grazing over the small box Carissa had taped there. I gritted my teeth. I couldn't help but think my shirt must have gotten crinkled upon sitting down.

I pulled the handle on the door, but as soon as I did, the sheriff said, "Kacy? I asked you a question."

I swallowed the lump in my throat as I slowly turned to face him and Meredith. Even if he and his wife didn't know the truth, they could surely assume it from the wire I was wearing. So I didn't answer him.

"Are you gon' tell us why you're wearing a wire, or just

stand there?" he asked.

My heart thumped rapidly, and my mind was awash with anxiety. Sweat formed on my forehead, and my palms grew clammy as I tried to compose myself. I imagined dashing out of the room and down the hall, successfully escaping into the parking lot. However, as my body failed to act, a more horrifying image appeared—me being tackled by an officer before reaching the door, then getting tased until I pissed myself.

"Grab her," he instructed Meredith.

As she stood from her chair to grab ahold of me, I said, "Don't! They're already on their way in to come get me as we speak. If that wire goes dead, it's all over."

The sheriff stood and fished out a pair of handcuffs from one of the drawers on his desk. "Who's already on their way in?"

"Internal Affairs," I yelled. "Because you murdered James, Charles, and Griffen!"

He motioned for Meredith to continue. "That's quite the claim, Kacy. How'd you come to that?" he asked.

"Because they found your prints on the gun that killed Griffen!" I lied. That was my last line of defense against him and his wife, my last chance to get a confession from them for the murders and death threats.

The sheriff's eyes widened. "Dammit. He didn't wipe it good enough," he muttered.

I couldn't believe my lie had worked. But what did the sheriff mean by "he"? I was on the edge of my seat, my mind racing with questions. Suddenly, Meredith grabbed me by the shirt and yanked the wires from my body. The tape caught a few hairs, and I winced. Then she exchanged the wires and box for the handcuffs from her husband and secured them on my wrists as he ripped the wires from the device.

"Why are you doing this?" I asked.

"'Cause you know too much, Kacy."

"Too much?" I completely lost it and dashed to the door, using my elbow to turn the handle, but instead, I fell to the floor. Something in my head told me to scream, but I feared I'd die on the spot if I did. So I didn't.

"Don't make it harder on yourself, Kacy," Meredith whispered as she pulled me up from the carpet.

My heart raced as I wondered what was taking Inspector Miller and Carissa so long to save me. Had something gone wrong? Were they facing unforeseen obstacles? They might have been trying to devise a strategy to take down the corrupt sheriff without endangering innocent lives, but I highly doubted it. I prayed that they were already here, ready to make a move. I could picture them bursting through the door with guns blazing and freeing me from my restraints after tackling the sheriff and his wife to the ground.

"How do you suppose we get her out of here?" Meredith asked her husband as she sat me in the chair opposite his desk.

Sheriff Wells swept some papers from his desk in a rage. "Gon' have to put her in lockup 'til later this evening. Then have pops come and handle it."

Pops? Who's pops? His father? What are the odds his father is involved in all of this? Could he have been the one to run Robert off the road? Could he have been responsible for killing Griffen and Charles too? I was determined to find out.

"Should we say she tried to stab you?"

The sheriff rubbed his pudgy chin and nodded. "Yes. That'll do just fine." Then, to me, he added, "Okay then, up you go."

He seized my shirt collar with an iron grip and pulled me to my feet. I had no choice but to follow as he escorted me out of the office and down the hall toward the elevator now that my hands were bound. He pushed the call button to the elevator, but the doors didn't budge.

An officer passing by noticed me. "Kacy? Kacy Roe! Oh my God." He glanced at the sheriff and said, "Hey, sheriff. What's going on with—"

The elevator doors opened as he interrupted the man. "She tried to stab me in my office."

The officer's eyes widened in disbelief. "There's no way. *Really?*"

Sheriff Wells nodded.

The officer peered down at me. His eyes were filled with disbelief as the sheriff muscled me onto the elevator. I wanted to speak up, to explain that something wasn't right, but the words caught in my throat. Even if I had managed to say something to the man, I doubted he'd even listen. He seemed too stunned by my earlier attempt to stab the sheriff.

With a heavy heart, I let out a deep sigh and hung my head in defeat as the elevator doors closed. As we began our descent, my hope of being rescued by Inspector Miller and Carissa dwindled. I had failed to get a confession from the sheriff or his wife, but that didn't mean I deserved to be left to my fate. I wasn't upset, though. Well, perhaps a little. Knowing that the end was near, I thought to give up.

However, my sheer tenacity still longed for the truth. So, I asked one last question.

I lifted my head, gazing up at the sheriff. "Since it seems like you're going to kill me and all, can you at least tell me why you did it? Why you murdered those people?" My question was quite audacious. Presumptuous even. However, I had every right to be since my life would soon come to an end if I weren't saved. So, I figured, why not take the risk?

The sheriff peered down at me, his ogreish frame towering over me. "Have you ever been envied? Judged? Well, I have. See, being the son of a sheriff meant I could get away with anything. But power like that had its drawbacks. Meredith was the most popular girl in school. Prettiest one too. And she was all mine. But when James came into the picture, Meredith took a shine to him. His locker was next to hers too, which didn't help. I'd see him slip notes in her locker occasionally." The sheriff looked away from me. "Even with the connections I had, it still didn't prevent Meredith from liking other boys. I gave James three warnings, and he still didn't stop. And when he tried to hold hands with her at camp, that was the last straw."

"Did Meredith know about it?" I asked.

"Told her if she ever thought 'bout leaving me, I'd beat her like I did James."

"And Griffen?"

"He helped me take care of him. Afterward, he and I vowed to keep our mouths shut 'bout the whole thing. But when you and Robert came around asking questions, I had to tie up some loose ends."

"So, you did kill Griffen. I assume you did Charles too?"

"You sure are persistent. Charles and his student got close to finding out the truth like you, so I had to make them disappear too."

It was then that I knew I had everything I needed, the truth I'd spread to the masses via YouTube and the evidence to sentence the sheriff and his wife to prison for life. Seconds later, the elevator doors opened, and I was met with a dimly lit floor that reeked of sweat, fear, and urine. It was a nauseating odor that made me gag. But I didn't puke.

Sheriff Wells guided me out of the elevator and led me down the corridor as a sense of satisfaction surged through me, knowing that justice would soon be served. As we approached the women's cellblock, the officer stationed there unlocked the gate. My heart sank as I realized what was coming next. He approached me and patted me down, his rough hands probing every crevice of my clothing. When he found my phone in my pocket, he pulled it out and handed it to the sheriff. Then, with a rough shove, he pushed me into the cell with a group of terrifying women. They were short and misshapen, with long hair and tattoos that marked them as trouble.

"Hey, you can't take that," I said to the officer as he locked the cell behind me. "That's mine."

"Honey, you'll get it back after you're released," one of the women behind me said.

I turned to face the woman. "I can't let him take it."

"And why's that?" the sheriff asked.

I spun around to find him tapping the screen. My heart fell to the pit of my stomach as he discovered I'd been recording our entire conversation through the voice memos app.

"So you thought you could get your evidence another way, huh?" he asked.

I pressed my face against the steel bars of the cell.

He held it out in front of me. "Delete it."

"Can't." I smiled. "My hands are occupied at the moment."

"Fine. Then I'll just break your phone."

The sheriff's hand shot up. He was ready to crush my phone against the hard concrete floor. However, before he could make his move, the elevator doors slid open with a hiss, and Inspector Miller emerged with his gun already drawn and aimed straight at the back of the sheriff's head.

"I wouldn't do that if I were you," Inspector Miller said.

As I sat on the bench beside one of the women in the cell block, my eyes remained fixed on Inspector Miller, who led Sheriff Wells away in handcuffs. A smile crept across my face, knowing that I had everything I needed to expose the truth. I had anticipated getting caught, so I hit the record button on my phone's voice memos app before I even asked my first question.

An overwhelming sense of satisfaction washed over me, knowing that I'd finally caught the killer. I'd gotten justice for James, his family, Charles, Eloise, and Griffen. And yet, there was a sense of emptiness that I couldn't ignore. The people responsible for so much death and destruction would finally pay for their crimes, but at what cost? So many people have suffered because of them. It was a reminder that justice doesn't always bring closure. Nonetheless, I couldn't deny the satisfaction of knowing I had accomplished what I'd set out to do.

53.

THE BLACK LINCOLN Town Car pulled into the hospital's parking lot and eased into a spot near the front entrance. Harry scoped out the area before exiting the vehicle. He knew he only had two jobs: take out Robert and Kacy. That was what he had discussed with Blake a day earlier.

Harry emerged from the vehicle and headed toward the entrance. The cool evening air nipped at his bald head as he made his way inside. He kept his head down and his hands deep in his pockets as he strode through the bustling hospital corridors. He was just another number to the hospital staff—another person paying a visit to their loved one who was in bad health.

Nothing more.

When Harry finally reached the ICU, he paused outside and surveyed the area with hawk-like intensity. He had to eliminate any chance of getting caught. But as soon as the door opened, he saw his opportunity and slipped past the employee who was leaving. His eyes wandered in search of the security guard, knowing that that was the only determining factor preventing him from finishing the job. However, the guard was nowhere to be found.

After a quick glance to ensure the coast was clear, Harry slipped inside Robert's room and closed the door. He quickly pulled the curtain and plunged the room into darkness. His eyes adjusted quickly to the lack of light, allowing him to approach the bed. When Harry stood over Robert, he found him still and calm. His chest rose and fell with each breath as he was still hooked up to a tangle of wires and tubes.

It was time to end it.

Harry grabbed one of the pillows underneath Robert's head and stood over him. His tall, imposing figure cast a dark shadow on the bed.

"It's time to disappear," he muttered.

54 · Kacy

ONCE THE SHERIFF was cuffed and read his rights, Inspector Miller instructed the other officer to open the cell, freeing me.

"You got the confession, right?" Inspector Miller asked, handing over my cell phone. "Because what we've got on tape isn't enough."

I nodded. "Sure did."

Inspector Miller used a key to unlock my handcuffs, then pocketed them. "Wonderful. I guess your plan did the trick."

I followed him onto the elevator. "You detained his wife, too, right?" I asked, standing in the corner of the metal box as far away as possible from the sheriff.

"Yes. Depending on what information you caught on your phone will determine whether she was involved or not. So she'll most likely get a few years."

The elevator landed on the main floor, and we emerged

into a crowded lobby teeming with officers bustling about the station. I scanned the area for Meredith, but she was nowhere in sight. It was likely she had already been taken to an interrogation room by Carissa or another officer. Regardless, I strongly believed she didn't get away.

The sheriff's belligerent shouting echoed through the lobby as Inspector Miller handed him off to another officer. "This is blasphemy!" he yelled, trying to convince officers of his innocence. "Ridiculousness. I didn't do anything wrong. What are the charges?"

He and I exchanged a glance before being escorted into a room. His beady eyes sent a shiver down my spine, a feeling that unnerved me. And at that moment, I thought back to his father. What kind of twisted upbringing could lead to such a son? Then it sank in. Realizing that his father was also involved in all this almost gave me a heart attack. I gasped.

Oh no! He's the person in the black Lincoln Town Car!

That meant he was still out there. Somewhere. And if Robert was alone, he'd be killed if he wasn't dead already. I sprinted toward the entrance of the police station as Inspector Miller yelled, "Kacy, where are you going?"

"To check on Robert at the hospital because I think he's in danger!" I yelled back, refusing to stop and explain. I plowed through the hoard of officers outside, climbed into my father's truck, threw it in gear, slammed my foot on the accelerator, and raced out of the parking lot. A slew of thoughts circled my mind as I barreled down the road.

Hang in there, Robert. Don't be dead. Don't be dead.

As I raced down the road, I prayed that Robert was still alive. The absence of the Lincoln Town Car behind me only fueled my fear. I weaved through traffic, the blaring horns of angry drivers doing nothing to deter me. All I could think about was getting to the hospital and checking on Robert to ensure he was safe. The thought of losing him caused me to shudder.

A traffic light was coming up ahead, and it was glowing red. However, I didn't have the luxury of stopping. I was too consumed with the thought of Robert and knew that every second I wasted could mean the difference between life and death for him. As my heart raced with fear and adrenaline, I continued barreling toward the intersection. My fingers tightened around the steering wheel, turning my knuckles white. I closed my eyes and braced for impact, hoping my reckless driving wouldn't cause a wreck or harm anyone else. For a second, I felt I was going to crash. A blaring horn pierced through the darkness, but I pressed on, determined to reach Robert. And when I reopened my eyes, I found I had made it through unscathed.

When I came up on the turn I needed to take, I slammed on the brakes and swung left. The rear end slid out and tapped the curb, causing the truck to wobble for a second. But then I was back on it. *Don't be dead. Don't be dead. Dammit. I don't know what I'll do if he—*

I couldn't even finish the thought. I could barely see the hospital doors through the tears in my eyes as I turned onto the property. I jammed on the brakes, and the truck came to a screeching halt under the overhang. By this point, I was bawling. As I kicked open the door, I spotted the black Lincoln across the parking lot, the chrome on its front bumper dented and scratched to hell, and its hood crinkled from when it rear-ended me.

"Oh no! Oh no!" I muttered.

I leaned toward the glovebox and clicked it open to retrieve my father's revolver. The metal of the gun glistened under the truck's interior light. I hesitated for a moment, considering the potential consequences of bringing a weapon into a hospital, but the thought of losing Robert was too much to bear. His life was on the line, and I wasn't about to let him become a casualty in this deadly game. With trembling hands, I slid the gun into my pocket and prayed that I wouldn't have to use it. But knowing the Lincoln was here only assured me that I would.

I dashed inside, leaving the driver-side door wide open, with the keys in the ignition and the truck running. My heart was pounding in my chest as I sprinted down the sterile hallway. My shoes echoed against the linoleum floors, creating a ruckus. I could sense the stares of the few people in the hallway following me as I raced by them. After a few minutes, I finally reached the ICU. I didn't even bother speaking to any of the staff as I brushed past a nurse who was on her way out. There was no time.

When I approached Robert's room, I noticed the sliding glass door was shut, the lights were off, and the curtain was drawn. *Don't be dead. Don't be dead.*

My heart stopped as I gripped the door handle and yanked back the door and curtain in one swift motion. I couldn't wait to see Robert. I couldn't wait to run my hands through his short hair and kiss him on the cheek. However, when I entered the room, I was met with a sight that was nothing short of horrifying. A dark, ominous figure stood over Robert, pressing a pillow tightly against his face. He was suffocating him, killing him in the quietest and slowest way imaginable. However, the real horror was the absence of sound.

The EKG monitor lacked a heartbeat.

It was then that I reached into my pocket, wrapped my fingers around the wooden grip of the revolver, and yanked it from my jeans. The darkness seemed to intensify as I drew in a breath, aimed the weapon at the dark figure, and screamed at the top of my lungs. "ROBERT!"

Bang! Bang! Bang! Bang! Bang!

———

The hard ground was my unwelcome awakening. A security guard's unyielding grasp pressed down on me, constricting my lungs and stifling my gasps for air. My arms were contorted beyond their limits. Any further, and my shoulders would have popped out of their sockets. I strained to lift my head but could barely move it. Then I focused on the nurses surrounding Robert's bed who were attempting to resuscitate him. I couldn't help but think my worst fear had come to fruition.

Robert was gone.

All because I had arrived too late.

Despite my victory in uncovering the truth behind Camp Mercy's hanging and the death of Charles Carter, the cost was far too high; a loved one sacrificed.

"Get off of me!" I screamed, wanting to hold Robert's hand one last time. However, the immense pressure pinning me down refused to yield, crushing any attempt to break free. I was utterly helpless. I cried as I lay there, watching Robert slowly recede into the dark embrace of the afterlife.

I can't believe he's dead.

The fact that Robert had forgiven me for leaving so long ago without knowing why I'd left struck a chord in me. He had been the one. The man I loved more than anything in the world. And now he was gone.

I shifted my gaze to the shadowed figure crouching in the corner, the same one I'd discovered looming over Robert's still form. He was a burly man, his belly larger than Sheriff Wells', and his face bore an uncanny resemblance to the man. Though he was bald and sported a smug expression, he was undoubtedly the sheriff's father. While most of the staff attended to Robert, two nurses tended to the wounded man. I felt no remorse about emptying the entire clip. If I'd had unlimited ammo, I wouldn't have stopped shooting. I would have kept tapping the trigger until the day I died, turning his body into a pile of mush. However, that wasn't possible.

But as I stared at him, I couldn't help but think there was only one reason for him to have been here. And hopefully, with my testimony, the police would have enough evidence to arrest him for murdering Robert. Amid all the chaos, I still remained helpless and unable to move. No matter what I did, I was stuck, left to face my loss head-on. It was then that I gave in and accepted what had happened. That I had lost the love of why life. Afterward, my mind finally calmed. But then, amid the quietness in my mind, a faint sound caught my attention.

"Robert!" I called out, hearing the subtle beat of a heart.

He was alive.

55 · Kacy

AFTER BEING DETAINED, they sat me in a chair across from Robert's room. An officer hovered over me. It was as if they had mistaken me for an idiot who'd try to run with so many cops around. Perhaps many have tried, and almost all have failed, but I certainly wasn't one of them.

For thirty minutes, I tried explaining why I was there, why I'd shot the man, and why I'd brought a weapon into the hospital in the first place. However, they still didn't release me. I couldn't blame them. I had done something illegal, even if it was for a good cause. It wasn't until an officer listened to my request for them to contact Inspector Miller that things began to look up.

A simple call was all it took.

I sighed in relief when the inspector finally set foot in the building.

"Are you okay, Kacy?" Inspector Miller asked, freeing the cuffs from around my wrists for the second time that day.

"I'm better now that the case is solved and Robert is safe," I answered.

He smiled. "And how is Robert?" He averted his gaze toward Robert's room.

I rubbed at the slivered impressions on my wrists. "Alive, thank God. If I hadn't remembered about the sheriff's father, Robert would be dead."

Inspector Miller stopped an officer who was walking by. "What did you get on the suspect?"

"Says he was just visiting. Couldn't get anything else from him. He's getting patched up as we speak."

"Where?" I asked.

"Kacy, relax. He's still in the building."

"As far as you know," I shot back. "We need to find him fast!"

Inspector Miller paused to carefully survey the area before moving along the corridor. My footsteps fell in sync with his as we progressed. Suddenly, we rounded a bend, and I caught sight of the sheriff's father, trying to make a swift exit.

"That's him," I shouted, pointing at him.

The elderly man turned, his limp more pronounced as he started down the hall. I must have got him in the leg. It was a good thing that I did, too, because now I knew for sure he wouldn't get far. We were quick to pursue him. As luck would have it, another officer intercepted him just as we started the chase, effectively blocking his escape route.

After a minute, Inspector Miller drew his service pistol and shouted, "FREEZE!"

The officer at the end of the hall did the same, prompting the elderly man to skid to a halt. His shoes squeaked against the linoleum. Then he spun around in search of an escape route. But we were closing in, and there was nowhere left for him to turn.

It was all over.

Without warning, the old man's hand darted into his pocket and emerged with a deadly weapon. He aimed toward us. In a heartbeat, my life flashed before my eyes. I envisioned my father, mother, Robert, and the decisions I'd made and those I hadn't. I even imagined the life I might have led if I hadn't left home and followed in my father's footsteps. It all played out in slow motion, like a movie unfolding before me. However, there was no popcorn, no soda, only the stark reality of light and darkness. A vivid spectrum of colors enveloped me, and my body felt weightless. Every decision I had made, every moment that led me to this point in time, seemed to have happened by design.

Suddenly, a deafening explosion shattered the stillness, pulling me from the sea of colors. The colors slowly faded back into shapes, revealing the elderly man lying motionless on the ground with his gun cast aside.

Now it was over.

56 · Kacy

"So the case is finally over, and you guys now know the truth of the tragic event that took place in the summer of eighty-six at Camp Mercy," I said to the camera resting on the dresser across from my bed.

It was one week after the incident at the hospital.

"Who would've thought a boy would kill another boy over a girl? I know many of you probably believed it was a hate crime, myself included. However, among the conversations I had with the people in question, none of them came off as racist." I tucked my hair behind my ear and leaned toward the lens, sinking my elbows deep into my knees. "Regardless, it's a shame to think the boy who did it was the son of a sheriff who managed to cover it all up. No wonder it was declared a suicide and remained as such for thirty years." *And scene.*

I slid the camera from the dresser, popped out the SD card, and got the file ready for YouTube. After publishing the video, I glanced over at the clock on my nightstand. It read 7:32 p.m. It was time to see Robert again. I left my room and headed down the hall into the kitchen, where I grabbed the keys to my father's new truck. Then out the door I went.

In my quest for the truth, I had caused significant damage to my father's old vehicle, and I was to blame. To make things right, I decided to buy him a new truck instead of repairing the one I'd wrecked. However, I didn't just get my father any old Ford. Instead, I purchased a new Ford F-250, with the highest tier package available. My father had turned his life around since his struggles with alcoholism and had made a name for himself with his restaurant and bar. He had come a long way, and it seemed he was only moving forward. He deserved the best, and I was determined to give it to him.

Within thirty minutes, I arrived at the hospital. After I entered the building and boarded the elevator, I traveled to the twenty-third floor, where they had moved Robert after he'd woken up from his coma three days ago.

"Knock knock," I said, entering his room.

Robert's gaze averted from the magazine in his hands.

"How're you feeling today?" I asked.

"Better now that you're here," he said with a smile, closing the magazine and setting it aside.

I snuggled up on the bed beside him. "Can you believe it? We finally solved a thirty-year-old conspiracy."

"We?" he repeated, wrapping his good arm around me. "From what I hear, it sounds more like you did it all by yourself, Kacy."

I beamed, then gazed out the window at all the city's

dark beauty. The vibrant lights painted a colorful portrait against the dark sky. "Perhaps, I did."

Robert ran his hand across my face, tucking my hair behind my ear. "I also heard you saved my life."

I blushed. I knew there was no hiding my reaction to Robert's kind words. The butterflies in my stomach danced wildly, and turning away did nothing to calm them. Suddenly, his hand was on my chin, and he pulled me closer. And when we locked eyes, I couldn't fight it. I found myself lost in the depths of his blue eyes. They were so mesmerizing, so calming. I couldn't look away even if I tried.

And as he tightened his grip around me, a confession slipped from his lips. "I love you, Kacy. I always have."

It might have been the pain medication talking, but I didn't care. I couldn't ignore the weight of his words. They left me speechless, and for a moment, I didn't know how to respond. A few years back, I would have run away at the mere thought of hearing those words from anyone. But now, with so much time having passed, the fear had diminished. However, the silence between us was deafening, and I knew that saying nothing would only make things worse.

Finally, I blurted out, "I love you too, Robert."

He pressed his lips to mine, making my emotions burst like a supernova. My insides were on fire. But the feeling wasn't of a burning flame. Instead, it was a tender sense of serenity.

57 · Kacy

ONE MONTH LATER.

Eloise, Robert, and I returned home after a late lunch at a restaurant.

"Thanks for helping us move in," I said to Eloise as I pulled a cardboard box from the back of a Uhaul and dropped it in her hands.

"*Please*, after all the stuff you two have done for me, I have no problem helping," she said.

"And we appreciate that very much," Robert said, returning to the truck to grab another box. "Because I can't really lift much." His arm was now in a sling.

Eloise followed me up the drive, through the garage, and into our home; a one-level rambler Robert and I had recently closed on in Oklahoma City, which was located roughly two hours from Tulsa and my father. Robert had managed to transfer stations with no problem. And with me having a large amount of disposable income, finding a place within our budget hadn't been an issue.

We went inside, and I set the box on the kitchen counter. "How'd court go? I bet it felt nice watching the sheriff, his wife, and his father get chewed up and spit out by the jury."

Eloise placed her box on the dinette as Robert shifted some things about the living area. "It hasn't happened yet. But I'll be relieved once it does. Right now, I still feel I haven't received closure."

"It's okay to feel that way, Eloise. With everything being so recent, give it some time. You'll eventually get your closure."

"Maybe," she muttered as we headed back outside to grab more boxes.

"You ever hear back from the kid? His student?" I grabbed another box and headed inside. Eloise followed me.

She shook her head. "Emailed him yesterday. Still waiting on a reply. They probably murdered him too."

"You might be right."

"But we'll never know until he's found. Maybe we'll never find out what happened to him."

"Maybe. But at least now you know the reason your husband was murdered." I set the box on the floor near the basement staircase as Eloise sat at the dinette and grabbed a bottle of water from the decorative tray in the center of the table.

"Yeah, I guess so." She sighed and took a sip. "For now, that's the only closure I have."

Another hour passed before Eloise finally headed home.

With all the help she'd given us in moving some of the heavier items, Robert and I couldn't have been more thankful. After we finished bringing in the last of our belongings, we sat out on our back porch, on our new wrought iron bench, and watched the sunset. I cozied up next to him and rested my head on his shoulder. As he wrapped his good arm around me and pulled me even closer, I embraced the silence of the evening. It was then that I reflected on everything that had happened; the dreadful call informing me of my father's misfortune, which ultimately led me back home, where I ran into Robert after discovering the body, met Eloise, and solved her husband's murder. It had been quite the summer. Surely, one I'd never forget. But I wasn't upset. If anything, I was elated.

I smiled, knowing everything had happened for a reason. Because in life, nothing happens to you; it happens for you. And though my life wasn't unfulfilling before I came back, I know now that what I thought would turn my life upside down had only made it ten times better. We were beginning a new chapter in our lives, and I couldn't be more excited for what was to come. I gazed at the open fields that stretched beyond our backyard, realizing this place had always been a part of me. Had always been home. And even though I'd tried to forget it and leave it all behind, it had never forgotten me.

So much for moving on.

Love this book?

Tell Esther.

Leave a review on...

www.amazon.com
www.goodreads.com

· Acknowledgements

To my Beta readers: Leila Connell, Katelyn Lavender, Greg Gorton, and Will Nuessle, for trudging through the thick of it.

To my editor: Kate Studer for catching all the plot holes and for sprucing up the verbiage.

To Jenna Moreci, Abbie Emmons, and Alyssa Matesic for providing educational content on YouTube that helped me improve as a writer.

And last but not least, to my family for always pushing me to express myself in every way imaginable.

www.ingramcontent.com/pod-product-compliance
Lightning Source LLC
Chambersburg PA
CBHW010606310726
48969CB00010B/2589